# FREEFALL FACTOR

'Survivors? From that? They'll have trouble finding
enough pieces to make up a decent burial. Come to
that, even a decent sandwich . . . reminds me, I
could use some breakfast. Cummon. Let's go. We'll
call the law from the first phone box we find.'

'Then what?'

'Then we get down to work on Operation
Eldorado.'

'Aye.' Shakespeare spat on the ground. 'Eldorado,
then. There's nowt else going for us, is there?'

'Nothing, Bill, except a bloody fortune and the
good life.'

'Meanwhile, what about ready cash?'

'No sweat. I've got a sort of Post Office account.
They're very good, really. I just walk into any Post
Office and show them my I/D and they give me the
money.'

'Your I/D?'

'Yes, Bill. Unmistakable, it is. A nine-milly
Browning.'

'A well-told story . . . Lovely cameos show Mr
Geraghty to be a talented newcomer to the ranks of
thriller-writers'

*Sunday Telegraph*

# Freefall Factor

---

# Tony Geraghty

CORONET BOOKS
Hodder and Stoughton

Copyright © A. J. V. Geraghty 1985

First published in Great Britain in
1985 by Macmillan London Limited

Coronet edition 1986
*Second impression 1986*



**British Library C.I.P.**

Geraghty, Tony
   Freefall factor.
   I. Title
   823'.914[F]        PR6057.E5/

   ISBN 0-340-39454-4

---

Printed and bound in Great Britain for
Hodder and Stoughton Paperbacks, a
division of Hodder and Stoughton Ltd.,
Mill Road, Dunton Green, Sevenoaks,
Kent (Editorial Office: 47 Bedford
Square, London WC1B 3DP) by
Richard Clay Ltd, Bungay, Suffolk

# Chapter One

'What a bloody awful country! Stewardess, I would like a large gin and a small tonic, if you please.'

'We'll be taking off soon, sir. Then I'll bring you a drink with pleasure.'

'Are you Norwegian?'

'No, sir.'

'Then perhaps we may hope to have an intelligent dialogue about this important matter, after all. I cannot stand a closed mind. I shall be reasonable. I shall not be angry with you. You see, it is only a question of your perception and my perception. It is also a question of logic.'

She watched the hands in fascination. They were huge hands, with fingers like pork sausages, and they carved precise patterns in the air as they revolved on the heavy wrists. He said, 'Officially we started to fly since one hour. So officially, I ask for one drink, *une petite larme de crocodile*. This is logic, yes?'

'Not "since one hour", maestro,' the man's companion interjected. 'In England, we say, "an hour ago".'

'*Merde alors*, Jacobs! When I am asking your banal opinion, which is not frequent and then only to confirm that all men are not equal, I am asking for it. Right now I am asking this intelligent and beautiful lady for a drink. It is her function in her professional life to grant this request and therefore our relations are in elegant balance.'

'But, maestro, you asked me to correct your English from time to time,' Jacobs protested.

'That was yesterday, and anyway we are not in England just now. We are, I regret, still in Norway.'

The girl standing in the aisle alongside them smoothed her skirt over her hips in a quick, nervous gesture. 'I'm terribly sorry, gentlemen, but the skipper – the captain of the aircraft, that is; my boss, you see, really – would never forgive me . . . He is very strict.'

'So was Torquemada. And the Marquis de Sade, for other reasons. It proves nothing. You are not using the power God is giving you to think, young lady. Are you certain you are not Norwegian?'

Sitting behind them, separated by a curtain, other members of the New British Orchestra listened to the exchange with malicious relish and a sense of relief that their conductor had found a target other than themselves. They noted also that the great man, the maestro, Gregor Kazanovitch – nicknamed 'Tempo' when he was absent – had added another item to his encyclopaedia of things hated. Along with twentieth-century English music (with the exception of Arnold Bax), fast food, priests of all denominations and incompetent musicianship was now added Norway. To be sure, the tour had not been the orchestra's greatest success, except for the publicity it had generated, and that had been of the wrong kind.

In the cramped seats of the charter aircraft standing on a limbo of runways which happened to be Fornebu Airport, Oslo, but which could have been anywhere inside the world's temperate zones, the discussion among those who were not yet already asleep circled back over the events of the past ten days like a recurring nightmare. Outside, ignored by the passengers, a dense cloud of smoke drifted over the tarmac from the terminal buildings. What mattered to them was their latest misadventure, the facts of which – in case they doubted them – were confirmed by uncompromising black print lying like tombstones on the morning newspapers scattered about the cabin. For once, the journalist's favourite word, 'story', and the folklore that word conveyed were in accord with the actual event.

With a prominent soloist named Henrietta Fleischer, the orchestra had been performing Grieg's First Piano Concerto. Unfortunately, Fraulein Fleischer was the first German soloist to make an appearance on the Oslo concert platform since the Second World War, and her choice of Grieg, symbol of his country's independence, was misinterpreted by the dour, long memories in her dour, bony audience. Henrietta Fleischer weighed in at sixteen stones

6

in her gown of red and black, and added support to the theory that the piano is a percussion instrument.

She coped admirably with the beginning of the crisis: a piano stool which slowly collapsed under her during the slow movement. When the delicately carved wooden stalk which was Fraulein Fleischer's sole defence against the force of gravity gave way, it did not, as the press reports suggested, snap off with a crack like a pistol shot. It groaned and gave up its useful life rather reluctantly, like a ship's timbers caught on a coral reef. Bob Legrange, the NBO's oboist, who had read English at Oxford and had a pretty turn of phrase, described this opening episode as 'a sort of dramatic re-enactment of McGonagall'.

Miss Fleischer, conscious of what was happening – though not yet aware that she was the possible victim of deliberate sabotage – paused only momentarily in her interpretation of the earnest slow movement, while still contriving to open her legs and grip the recalcitrant stool between her thighs. Then, very slowly, she stood up and, while still playing with her right hand, grasped the top of the broken seat in her left hand with a speed that entranced the diplomatic corps sitting in the front row. A few people smiled irreverently. The Norwegians, when they are not being patriotic, are a fair-minded race, and no one laughed aloud.

Tempo, the conductor, depended upon his left eye to see what was happening around him. His right eye, for reasons never explained, rolled unfocussed and uncon-trolled like a compass in a dense magnetic field. To reduce the distraction this might have caused to his musicians, who depended upon eye contact only slightly less than on their ears and their musical intuition, he wore a patch over the undisciplined organ while at work on the rostrum. Miss Fleischer and her Bechstein were on his blind side. However, when the same solo right-hand phrase recurred for the third time he, too, became aware of what was happening. Miss Fleischer was now standing, still playing the same phrase while holding the top of the broken stool in his direction with the other hand. He leaned down, took it from her, studied first the stool, then the representative of the Ministry of Culture in the front row, and finally laid the thing quietly to rest on the floor. The slow movement gathered momentum again as Miss Fleischer applied both hands to the piano from a standing position. From the wings, a Norwegian official with whom Tempo had quarrelled earlier in the day appeared with another stool, but the conductor angrily, if wordlessly, shooed him away. At this, there was a stifled giggle from the back of the hall.

The movement had proceeded several bars more before Miss Fleischer became aware of a new phenomenon. It seemed to her, very briefly, that her arms were getting shorter. She stretched them, commanding them to obey her, and they complied. Then it happened again. It was now apparent that the grand concert piano, weighing about half a ton, was gradually but inexorably moving away from her in the direction of the second violins, violas and cellos. It would later be revealed that the miniature handbrake attached to each of the instrument's three legs had been discreetly sabotaged.

Even now she did not lose her self-control. The stage was a large one and she calculated that the piano would not collide with the strings before she had completed the movement, at which point everyone could pause while the trouble was rectified. The gamble was brave, but misplaced. Once on the move, the piano accelerated gently, advancing on the strings under a rolling barrage of Grieg. Those instrumentalists who saw it coming reacted with great courage. They remained in their places and braced themselves. But not every one of those at risk noticed the instrument's approach, in spite of the growing volume of sound as it covered the six feet or so between its original position and the strings, still pursued and played by Miss Fleischer. No one was actually knocked down but several people, including the ageing and fragile father of the orchestra, Basil Krivine, were nudged sideways along with their music stands. Mr Krivine, whose temperament had sharpened with advancing years, stood up, shuddered and hurried away through the artists' tunnel to the gentlemen's loo.

The spectacle of his retreating grey head, shaking in disbelief, acted as a catalyst among some people in the audience. They began to laugh aloud. Others turned on them angrily, fingers to lips, shushing dramatically. One objector snarled in Norwegian, 'Don't be so profane. Don't you know this is Grieg?'

'Ya,' snapped a voice several rows behind the objector. 'And played very badly by a fat German.'

'Shut up and listen to the music,' the objector retorted.

'Quisling!' a third voice accused him.

'You call me Quisling? Look at these medals! I was in the Resistance with Knut Hoaglandt when he shot his way out of the hospital here in Oslo. You come over here and repeat that, you accursed little Communist!'

'If that's the way you want it. . .'

Seconds later two men, tall as fir trees, were throwing punches at one another in the aisle. The slow movement ended amid hysterical laughter, shocked screams and the crash of furniture. From her place in front of the piano Miss Fleischer, her nerve at last broken, screamed first in English then in thunderous, rolling German, 'Damn you Norwegians! Damn you all, you dwarfish provincial people!' To ram home the protest she gave the piano a push – leaving several violinists, two violas and one cello prostrate beneath it – and stalked off the stage.

Henrietta Fleischer was dangerous when angry and she was now very angry indeed. Half-way down the artists' tunnel she spotted a large fusebox to which was attached a red handle. She could reach it, just, and pulled it down. Instantly the hall was in darkness. From the rostrum the unmistakable voice of Tempo boomed, 'Gentlemen, the National Anthem. That is, the Norwegian National Anthem.' From the approximate area of the brass the Cork brogue of the orchestra's principal trumpet and Musicians' Union representative, Paddy Moynahan, responded, 'Not without sheet music, maestro. We were sight-reading it at rehearsal. If we made a mess of that. . .'

'Très bien alors,' Tempo roared back. 'The Blue Danube.'

While still musing on these events and pondering the

wisdom of having left his job in Boston to work for a European orchestra, the NBO's American violinist Paul Anders gazed out of the aircraft window at his elbow. Not that there was anything to see, except a fire engine. A fire engine? It moved ponderously into position opposite where he sat and pulled up about fifty yards away. Half-turning in his seat, he called back over his shoulder, 'Hey, Moynahan. You're the guy supposed to know what goes on round here. Why've we got a fire appliance sitting out there?'

From the rear of the aircraft, Moynahan, manoeuvred his considerable bulk round to peer through his own small window. Then he rasped softly, 'I don't know about any fire engine but we've got the police for company and that's a fact.'

These events made no impact whatever on most of the musicians. Apart from Anders and Moynahan only two members of the NBO were now still awake. One of them was Moira Tremlington (harp), the only woman permitted by Kazanovitch to join the orchestra in his pursuit of something he described oracularly as 'a deep masculine sound'. Miss Tremlington, a henna-haired spinster in her forties and a collector of bone china, did not regard it as proper to sleep at this hour, and certainly not in public. She was travelling as usual with her close but forever platonic friend Robert Legrange (oboe). He was wearing his customary flat cap over his balding head, a cap redolent of the hungry thirties. When comments were made about this headgear he described it mockingly as 'a symbol of my tragic under-achievement in life'. Just now the peak was pulled down in a concentrated manner over his beak-nose and bifocal spectacles.

'Do be quiet, you lot,' he said. 'Moira and I are Scrabbling here, and things are getting pretty intense, I can tell you. Moira thinks in all seriousness that "ouzo" is in the *Oxford English Dictionary*.'

On the other side of the aircraft, there was greater interest in what was happening outside. The NBO were sitting, without exception, to starboard. The port-side seats were exclusively occupied by the Margate Ladies'

10

Choir, brought to Oslo to provide the wordless song for one of Holst's Planets. They, too, had had their difficulties during the tour, but as amateurs they were accustomed to catastrophe and did not need to dwell upon it. Now they started to chatter in a shared bubble of excitement.

'I can see three of them, Mavis, three policemen! And they've got guns and things. What a hoot! D'you think they could be making some sort of film?'

The aircraft cabin crew consisted of one male and two female stewards. Until now, the passengers had seen very little of any of them. For information, the passengers depended upon one or two cryptic apologies on the public address system from the captain. The Margate Ladies, who did not fly often, did not remark upon this. The orchestra, cynical and wise in the cost-cutting ways of their general manager, Jacobs, a Scottish Jew known to them as 'the Edinburgh cringe', took it for granted that whatever charter airline this was, it would provide little by way of creature comfort; so they did not comment upon the absence of the cabin crew either. However, when one of them appeared, she was received with profound respect.

'Please, miss . . .' 'I wonder, miss, if you could . . .'

She was a tall, sharp-featured woman with a complexion which Paddy Moynahan recognised as characteristically Irish: black hair, worn with a centre parting and plaited behind into a neat bun, and rich blue eyes. As if undergoing some initiation rite which required her to look neither right nor left, she marched past them down the centre aisle without so much as a flicker of interest, picked up an internal telephone at the tail end of the fuselage and said, 'Right, I'm in position.' Then, 'Very Well. Anything you say, skipper.'

The rear door, through which the orchestra had entered, was opened by a single large green revolving handle. The stairs in their turn were controlled by a black lever on the left side of a dark recess beyond the door. As the steps descended smoothly to the tarmac, sunlight threw her figure into sharp silhouette.

'Hollo, miss!'

The man who called to her was one of three police officers, a man in his forties with more badges than his two younger companions. Of the other two, one was a nondescript youth with pimples on his chin; the other a blond giant who stood sheepishly alongside his senior, apparently unsure what to do with his hands. These by turns he tucked into his armpits and rubbed down the back of his trousers. He was also smiling in an embarrassed sort of way, like a schoolboy found in someone else's apple tree. She had walked almost to the foot of the stairway before the police car came into view. From within the vehicle there came a babble of Norwegian punctuated by radio static.

'I am Captain Nansen,' the older man said stiffly. 'We are having to evacuate your aircraft, please. You are having a bomb somewhere.'

'Are you sure it's us?' she asked.

Another car was approaching them now, a small blue Fiat. Although the driver was in some sort of uniform, it was a civilian car similar to the one she sometimes hired herself for trips to local ski resorts.

'We do not know,' the captain was saying. 'It is perhaps not true information . . .'

'A hoax?' the stewardess suggested.

'Yes, a hoax. But until we are sure, we will have to evacuate your aircraft of all passengers. Then, when the aircraft is blowing up, no one is hurt. You understand?'

The Fiat drew smoothly to a halt close beside the three police officers, then reversed gently, deliberately, until its rear bumper almost touched the aircraft steps.

The stewardess bit her lower lip and frowned. 'If I tell the passengers there is a bomb I cannot be responsible for what they will do. Already they are asking about the fire engines. But I must inform my captain. He takes the decisions.'

The doors of the Fiat opened slowly and two men emerged. One wore an ill-fitting police uniform whose dark blue colour was streaked with grey dust. Combined with his lack of height, a bandit moustache and luxuriant sideburns, the ambience was of Mexico rather than

Scandinavia. Even in this first flickering impression of the man, Naomi Lewis sensed something else which made her want to shudder. Soon she would recognise it as a sort of musky animality which no clean uniform or any number of baths could remove. The man's companion, tall and brooding, broad shouldered and red-haired, wore an anonymous grey business suit that was also a sort of uniform.

The Norwegian police captain, Nansen, glanced at the new arrivals in a surprised way, nodded to them and continued talking. 'We will send buses for the passengers. Be calm, please. Saying nothing about this bomb. Tell them that the aircraft is not working . . . anything . . . no brake fluid, and they must come back to the terminal in the bus.'

The man in the dusty uniform nodded, smiled at them, walked casually to the rear of the Fiat and opened the boot. As the stewardess watched him he winked at her in a confiding way, like a seaside conjuror entertaining an audience of children. The man in the grey suit stayed close to his companion's elbow as if attached to it by some invisible thread. Captain Nansen said something in Norwegian. It was a question of some sort delivered in a tone sharpened by anxiety and it was clearly addressed to the man in the dusty uniform, whom Naomi privately named Moustache. 'Moment,' Moustache replied casually. 'Momento.' He had the boot open now. Frowning with concentration he reached inside. The stewardess heard him saying, in English, 'Help yourself to the other one, Bill. I'll cover this geezer. You watch out for his mates.'

The two lightweight Armalite rifles were fitted with M-203 grenade launchers, loaded and ready for war. As Moustache swung one of these weapons towards the police captain, Nansen stared at the twin barrels pointing at him with the incredulity of someone who is being mugged for the first time. The rifled high-velocity barrel of the Armalite, projected above the wider, unbored snout of the grenade launcher, was less than a yard from his chest. The Armalite, still less the M-203, was not standard equipment for members of his police force. The stewardess, knuckles white as she gripped the stair rail, said softly, 'My God . . .' The man addressed as Bill was now curled into a tight ball behind the Fiat's bonnet, his rifle levelled at the other two officers.

'Stay where you are and raise your hands high,' he shouted. He held the Armalite familiarly, as if it were an extension of himself. He cocked the weapon and turned the safety catch off without altering by a millimetre his steady aim on the man in the centre of the now stationary group of policemen. Moustache threw a quick, snakelike glance at the stewardess. 'You, sweetie. What's your name?'

'Naomi . . . Naomi Lewis.'

'OK, Naomi, come down here . . . Come on, I'm not going to rape you.'

As she slowly and cautiously obeyed the man, Captain Nansen shouted something in Norwegian to his comrades. Even before he had finished, Moustache snapped at him, 'Whatever you just told them, cancel it. Do you know what this grenade launcher will do to you at this range? It'll blow your head clean off just with kinetic energy. The grenade doesn't even have to explode. So watch it.'

The voice was undoubtedly British, with an accent which belonged to the hungry North, Naomi Lewis thought; but like the smell of the man, there was something else in his voice – a sibilance which reverberated and made him seem not quite human. He reminded her of a short period she had spent in an institution for the criminally insane during her training as a nurse. This man, she was certain now, had been in an institution of some kind for a long time, and recently. His companion seemed normal by comparison in spite of his unnerving competence with a gun and calm immobility. As if in a dream she was aware of Nansen replying, 'I am telling my men they must not risk their lives. It is in the book of the instructions when we exercise for these occasions.'

'The wankers can work that out for themselves,' Moustache told him. 'No more talk. Just obey orders. Understand?'

'Yes, I understand.'

With the unwilling help of the stewardess, first Captain Nansen and then one of his companions was disarmed. Naomi Lewis held each pistol at arm's length, as if it were contaminated, and placed it gingerly on the ground. The third officer, the big, blond youth, moved slightly so that the stewardess was between himself and the bandits. Then, as she was about to disarm him, he pushed her towards the gunmen and ran, zig-zagging, to dive behind the police car.

'Stand still!'

The others remained rooted where they were, the police pistols scattered on the tarmac.

'You'd better tell that thick junior of your'n to come out,' Moustache told Nansen. 'And tell him in English.' The captain hesitated, his eyes searching round as if for help from God, or the US Cavalry. 'Get on with it, then,' Moustache added, his dark eyes bright with malice. 'The car's no bloody good to him as cover. In fact, we're just going to use it for some target practice.'

'Thor, can you hear me?' the captain shouted. His voice had a high-pitched, strangulated note as if someone had tied his necktie too tight.

'Ya,' a voice responded from behind the police car.

'You must come out.'

The answer was a long, sing-song stream of Norwegian.

'Right,' Moustache said. 'Let's have the rest of you over here, out of the way. Come on, move! That's better . . . nice, neat line so we can see everybody. Naomi, bring the pistols here, love, and put them in that carrier bag in the boot of our car.'

'Tell him,' the second Englishman called, without shifting his position, 'that this grenade launcher will blow up the car and him with it. I'm giving him ten seconds, then I open fire. Aye, and tell him to throw his weapon out first.'

The order was relayed. The response was total silence. The long seconds dragged by. From within the aircraft, a few voices were singing, 'Oh why are we waiting?' expertly accompanied by a tin whistle. The second gunman began a sonorous countdown. Slowly a blond head, no longer wearing its police cap, bobbed up from behind the police car, then bobbed down again, and finally rose and continued to rise. Its owner was little more than a boy, but a big boy; really a very big boy, Naomi Lewis noted – six foot six at least, and broad with it.

'Let's see your hands, then,' shouted Bill. 'Up!'

The blond giant, head and shoulders above the vehicle, looked earnestly in the direction of the voice. 'I am not in a state of co-operation,' he said in jerky English. 'I will die for the Fatherland.'

'Blow the bastard away, Bill,' Moustache suggested. 'He wants to die for his country, so waste him!'

The man addressed as Bill uncoiled himself, stood up, cradling the weapon easily in both arms, and shrugged. 'No need,' he replied. 'He's no threat. The big prick's an idealist. There's no way he'll open fire first.'

'But the man's armed.'

'Aye, and he's the only one. I'll bet he's never used a weapon in anger in his life. We don't need to waste him. You carry on. I'll keep an eye on him.'

'There are times, wacker, when I think you're going soft,' Moustache said. The blond youth remained standing behind the police vehicle, as his comrades, directed by Moustache, carried a series of zip-sided nylon travel bags from the boot of the Fiat into the aircraft. This job done, Moustache and his companion ushered Naomi Lewis up the steps and prepared to follow her. At the foot of the steps Nansen watched glumly, hands on hips, studying the two Englishmen carefully. Moustache paused just short of the aircraft door, and addressed him.

'That boy,' he said, nodding towards the blond youth, 'is very lucky. Tell your bosses we have now taken control of this aircraft. Tell them we have weapons and explosives. Tell them some of our . . . comrades . . . are already on board among the passengers. Tell them we are not playing games. We detonated the bomb today back at the terminal – to show them we mean business. So tell them. And tell that boy he's very lucky not to be smeared on the runway like strawberry jam.'

They turned away, still on the top step, and studied the

16

aircraft door. Moustache patted it and said, 'We won't close this yet, Bill. Let's sort out the superglue first. Naomi, just stay close to us.'

The stewardess, fingers bunched like a bare-knuckle boxer's, watched as they carefully unpacked a tin of glue from one of the bags and applied it to two slots above the rear door.

'What's that? What are you doing?' she asked. 'You mustn't interfere with the aircraft like that. It's unsafe.'

'Them that asks no questions get telt no lies,' Bill replied. 'We know what we're about.' He was working one-handed, his Armalite still held in the other. 'Right,' he said, dropping the open tin and the applicator into a plastic bag, 'that should do it. Time for a word with the skipper.'

'I'll go forward,' Moustache said. 'You stay here and keep an eye on this lot.' He touched the girl lightly on the elbow, eyes on her breasts in an appraising way, and grinned broadly as she recoiled from him. He paused, the rifle slung confidently and easily under one arm. 'Right, darling, we'll have the steps up and the door closed. Will you do it, or will I?'

'You wouldn't know how,' she said.

'Want to try me? Go on, then, Naomi, you do it.'

The three of them were still within sight of the policemen at the foot of the steps. The taller of the two hijackers, touching his companion's shoulder, nodded towards them and said, 'They've got the message. Let's go inside and get started.' In the second it took him to turn away towards the entrance, Moustache had slid down to a sitting position outside the door on the top step, the Armalite swinging upward like a surprised and angry snake. The young blond giant was fumbling with the holster of his pistol, apparently unnoticed by the two disarmed officers with him, who remained rooted and staring upward as if hypnotised. The youngster finally unlatched the holster's retaining strap but then had trouble with the lanyard leading from the pistol butt to his shoulder. This seemed to have knotted itself, as if to a script by Buster Keaton, round the fingers of both hands. In spite of that, he thrust one hand onto the butt at the moment the first Armalite round smashed into his right thigh and tore a tumbling, destructive path through bone and soft tissue.

The sharp crack of the high-velocity rifle, like the yelp of a wounded terrier, broke some sort of spell. The other two policemen ducked to a squatting position, then moved as if to assist young Thor, who had been thrown backwards several feet, blood from his shattered leg pumping into a spreading pool. Moustache fired again and the stewardess backed rapidly into the aircraft through the open door, hastily pulling it closed. As it began to swivel shut the second hijacker's rifle barrel was thrust into the diminishing gap and, with the energetic support of a boot, it was levered open again. Both armed men now followed the stewardess into the passenger cabin. She stood with her back to the rearmost galley, out of sight of the passengers, as the taller of the two men loomed over her. 'You won't get a second chance,' he said grimly. 'Don't push your luck.'

'But I only . . . the passengers, I –'

'Shut your gob,' Moustache said. He prodded her chest with his rifle. She could feel the heat of the barrel through her tunic and smell the material of the garment scorching. 'You're expendable,' he continued. 'All we need is one pilot. As they say in the Army, you're superfluous to requirements from now on. So you're living on borrowed time.'

If the passengers had not heard the earlier discussion between the hijackers and the police, they had certainly been aware of the gunshots. Near the stern, eyes now peered wonderingly over the rear seats while, further forward, other passengers were standing up to enjoy an uninterrupted view of what was happening. Only Moynahan, the burly Irish trumpeter, sitting near the rear entrance, seemed ready to take matters further.

'Stand up, Fritz, and let me out there,' he told his neighbour. Dumbly, the man did as he was told, folding a newspaper neatly against his chest as he stood to make

18

room. Moynahan's bulk, in its respectable pinstripe suit, filled the aisle. In spite of a slight beer belly he looked like what he had once been, a useful rugby forward whose flat, Nordic face was made flatter by a broken nose. Confronting the larger of the two hijackers, he demanded, 'What's going – ' but the sentence ended in a pained grunt of expelled breath as a rifle butt rammed into his solar plexus. Moynahan jack-knifed under the impact of the blow and was assisted, groaning sonorously, back to his seat.

'You hit him! You beast, you hit him!' shrilled one of the Margate matrons from beneath her cloche hat.

'Better than putting a bullet through him, missus,' replied the man with the gun. His tone was matter-of-fact, like a tradesman announcing that a drain was blocked, but not seriously, and would soon be unblocked. 'Now sit down, all of you,' he added. 'Then we can all relax.'

In an atmosphere of fearful obedience, the passengers scrambled into their seats. Nevertheless as Moustache and the stewardess moved through the aircraft a buzz of muted comment followed in their wake. The second hijacker remained conspicuously on guard near the closed rear entrance.

As they opened the door leading to the flight deck, Moustache blinked. The sunlight was brilliant here and it was already hot. He counted two pilots, one more stewardess, all sipping coffee.

'Michael,' Naomi Lewis said. 'This man is –'

'I'll do the talking,' Moustache interjected. Then, addressing the man in the left-hand seat, 'You the skipper?'

The captain, sandy-haired, white shirted, an array of pens in his top pocket, was dabbing perspiration from the bald patch on top of his skull with a paper napkin. 'That's me,' he said easily. 'You a police officer? What's the situation? Is it true there's been a bomb threat? I only know what Air Traffic have said, and that's not much. Something about an explosion in the terminal building back there, maybe some device on board this aircraft.'

Moustache flicked open the holster of the police pistol at

his waist and cocked the weapon.

'I'm in charge of this aircraft now,' he said. 'Listen carefully, all of you. We have enough explosives to blow us all into very small pieces. That won't happen if you all do exactly as you're told. We know what we're doing and we won't ask the impossible. You'll all have a good yarn to tell your grandchildren when this is over. So just let's do this thing nice and quiet and peaceful, like. What exactly did Air Traffic say?'

'They told us to prepare to evacuate. But we're not flying anywhere, are we? I mean, not if there's a bomb on board?'

Moustache studied him as if examining an exotic insect. Then he said, 'You really haven't got the message, have you, pet? You've just been hijacked. You know what a hijack is, I suppose. Right, I'll be giving you lot a flight plan in a few minutes. First, I want to call the roll. Where's the log?'

'Hijacked? Flight plan? Log . . .?'

'Give me the crew manifest,' Moustache said with slow, careful emphasis. 'I want to know who you are.'

The co-pilot, a young man with large soulful eyes resembling a lemur's and with a freshly shampooed mop of fine brown hair, reached into the briefcase beside him. He paused as the pistol in Moustache's hand followed his movements. 'Here's what you want,' he said, awe in his voice.

Moustache studied the list, then snapped, 'Answer your names. Michael Kilvert?'

'Here,' said the skipper.

'Jon Barnhurst?'

'Here,' said the co-pilot.

'Naomi Lewis?'

'Here.'

'Diana Garrard?'

'Here.'

'Leslie Archer?'

There was a brief, awkward pause. Then the second stewardess, Diana Garrard, said in a tone of polished glass, 'He's hiding in the forward loo, poor boy. You see, we knew there was something odd going on even if the passengers didn't. Leslie's locked himself in there and refuses to budge.' At this admission Kilvert and his co-pilot glared at the girl.

'Right then,' said Moustache. 'We'd better flush him out.'

'That could alarm the passengers,' Kilvert suggested. 'They're somewhat jumpy already, and like most musicians they're a temperamental lot even on a good day.'

'Musicians are they? What sort of musicians?'

'The New British Orchestra,' Diana Garrard interjected. 'They're awfully famous. There was a riot at their concert here. I read it all in the papers.'

'Right then. Keep them happy with some canned music and hand out some drinks. Leave your man Archer where he is for the time being. We don't need him.'

The music was Mantovani, played at irregular speed on a tape of uncertain age, and the drink was warm, blended whisky served without ice. Tempo was attended by the second stewardess, Diana Garrard. He fixed a baleful eye first on the whisky, then the girl. His other eye seemed to have a life of its own. She thought he resembled an angry parrot and she wanted to giggle at the thought. 'Tell me, young woman, are you playing that music in order to soothe our nerves?'

'We thought it might help.'

'And is that because we are in some danger?'

'I won't pretend we haven't a problem, but I'm not allowed to say anything.'

'But it would seem possible, at least, that we are going to die?'

'I wouldn't put it quite as strongly as that. But yes, it could be dangerous, Mr Kazanovitch.'

'In that case, will you kindly turn off that parody of a tune you are playing? If I am about to face my creator, then it has to be Verdi's Requiem, or nothing.'

'I will do my best, sir.' She hovered for a moment. Then she said, 'We've got Ravel's Bolero if you like.'

Kazanovitch studied her carefully. 'Do you know how

Mr Ravel described the Bolero? It was, he said, seventeen minutes of orchestra without music, and I agree with him.'

The knowledge that they had been hijacked rippled through the aircraft from cockpit to tail like a soft, erratic breeze over a cornfield as the ranks of passengers leaned back to relay the news to their immediate neighbours. They had seen it happen, heard the shots outside, had before them the spectacle of Moynahan sitting head down, curled over his pain, but they did not yet believe it. The violence was too simple, too clear, too fast – above all, too arbitrary – to be grasped readily by intelligent people. Its reality required confirmation, discussion, as if the talk could undo the damage, or at least answer the question, Why? Or, more precisely, Why us? As Moustache moved down the fuselage to rejoin his companion, shepherding Naomi Lewis and the co-pilot, Barnhurst, in front of him, the hostages fell silent, their eyes down on newspapers, or shoes, or anywhere which would avoid contact with that reality. From the flight deck, Kilvert talked to the control tower.

'Two, so far as I know. Both British. Very laid-back. I've seen only one man, the one in police uniform. No, no demands yet. We're told we'll be given our flight plan in a few minutes . . . yes, a flight plan. They obviously know what they're doing . . . I don't know. They say they've got explosives. Guns they do have. We've seen them. Yes and we heard that shooting just before they came on board . . . two shots, we heard . . . I can't answer all those questions because I don't know. They've made no demands yet . . . I can only tell you what you know already, that they are well armed. And they're claiming the bomb at the terminal. I think we should go along with what they want for the time being. We could not, I say again, not justify a violent response at this stage. There'd be hell to pay if this orchestra were wiped out. My widow wouldn't be very happy, either. I'll keep you informed, if I can.'

Moustache returned to the flight deck alone, settled himself with apparent familiarity into the right-hand seat and extracted a notebook from his pocket. He studied this for a second or so, then said, 'Now, skip, this is how you're going to fly us. Take us up to seven thousand feet. Do not, repeat not, pressurise the cabin. And keep your hydraulic pressure at three thousand p.s.i.' He tapped a pair of gauges on the console in front of them and added, 'I'll be watching these.'

Ten minutes later, Campbellair's special Oslo charter, Juliet Bravo, started its take-off run. The name of the carrier was picked out in red on a black fuselage, confirming the opinion among aviation professionals that the smaller the operation, the brighter the livery. Campbellair had started life flying antique Super-Constellations from Lisbon to Biafra in the 1960s, overloaded with ordnance and carrying as occasional passengers tough, leather-jacketed Dublin priests of the Holy Ghost Fathers. Now, as then, its fleet – just three medium-range jets – flew charters anywhere. Pistol in one hand, plastic beaker of coffee in the other, Moustache remained in the co-pilot's seat. As they lifted off, he noticed a discreet clutch of small sports aircraft clustered about their own hangar, and a windsock which pointed straight towards him. The cloud base was around two thousand feet.

At the stern, strapped into the cabin crew's jump seat, the second hijacker, Bill, discreetly applied the safety catch to the Armalite resting across his knees, stretched his legs and allowed some of the tension to flow out of his body. Barnhurst and Naomi Lewis were immediately in front of him in two starboard passenger seats. In front of them, separated by a single row of three empty seats, sat the nearest members of the orchestra. No announcement, other than an illuminated sign proclaiming 'Fasten Seat Belt', had been made to the passengers. The aircraft lifted off normally, wheeled out like a black gull over the cold, bourgeois waters of Oslofjord – a waterway lined with private islands, marinas, fishing lodges and rich men's yachts – and sped south towards the Skagerrak and the open sea.

The private, introspective silence settling over them all was interrupted by a squirt of sound from the public address system, a cough, and the words, 'This here?

Right, I've got it.' Another cough, then a chummy Liverpudlian voice announced, 'Good afternoon, ladies and gentlemen. This is not your captain speaking. My name is Major Tom and I've taken control of the aircraft for the time being. So . . . welcome to Major Tom's Magical Mystery Tour. I hope you're sitting comfortably, including you, young Leslie, in the forward loo there. We, my comrade Major Bill and me, we want you to be comfortable, and good. We can't tell you where you're going until we've arrived there.

'First thing I want to say is, don't make trouble for us and we'll all be one big happy family. See, we've got a job to do here and we've got our orders. We're soldiers, see, and we're used to killing people. Now, we don't like it much, but we'll do it if we have to. Just follow the pilot's example and co-operate, and everything will be OK.

'Second thing is a few necessary domestic instructions. For your own safety – and so Major Bill and me know what you're up to – keep your seat belts locked and your hands in sight at all times. Anyone who ignores this instruction will lose some Brownie points, and some of his clothes. Same applies to you, girls. Next thing is trips to the loo. I don't want lots of people milling about. It could cause misunderstandings and things might get out of control. So I'm afraid you'll have to hold up your hands, and Miss – er – Diana, the young lass with red hair and that little silver chain round her left ankle, will tell you when you can go. Anyone who's pregnant, or suffering from a bad heart condition, or piles, or athlete's foot, or something else serious like that, should press the button to call the stewardess. Miss Naomi, the tall, attractive one with the dark hair, will take your names. If necessary, see, we'll have a doctor brought on to the aircraft at the next stop. Smoke if you want. I'll give you further instructions later on. That's all for now, campers. I hope you enjoy your flight with us.'

They were over the Skagerrak now, a slate-grey waterway flecked with vicious white waves. 'I want you to take a 270 degree course from here,' Moustache, now identifiable as 'Major Tom', told the pilot, 'and altitude of seven thousand feet. Got that?'

'Due west, seven thousand feet. Got it.'

Sitting on the forward toilet, the steward Leslie Archer prayed through his tears, 'Please, God, I won't go cottaging ever again, if you only keep me safe.'

Tempo summoned Naomi Lewis and announced, 'My medical condition is a grave alcoholic deprivation but I regret that I have an allergy for this Korean whisky you are giving us. The recommended treatment is a large gin-and-tonic.'

At the other end of the aircraft Moynahan dragged his bulk past his travelling companion and into the aisle. Major Bill, catching Naomi Lewis's eye, nodded in his direction in warning and took a firmer hold of his rifle. When Naomi Lewis reached him, Moynahan muttered, hand over mouth, 'Loo', and walked head-down towards the stern.

'He wants the loo,' the woman explained.

'Right,' said the hijacker. 'He'll have to keep the door open while I keep' – she noticed he pronounced it 'kep' – 'an eye on him.'

'Too late,' Moynahan gasped, and emptied the contents of his stomach over Major Bill's trousers. Then, straightening up, he wiped the back of his hand across his mouth, looked squarely at his captor, and said, 'Jesus, that's better. I had a skinful before I came aboard. That stomach pump of yours finished me off.'

'You stupid bastard,' his victim replied. To the bewilderment of Naomi Lewis, the men were grinning at one another like two schoolboys.

# Chapter Two

Major Tom calculated that he could safely leave the pilot to it for the time being. By now the usual crisis-management operation would have been started by the Noggy authorities: hotline calls to London; Norwegian radar surveillance to guide air intercepts over the Norwegian Sea by RAF Phantoms from Leuchars (who would enjoy a change from shadowing Red Air Force Bears); alarms tweeting and buzzing in hip pockets down at Hereford, and a Pagoda hit team on stand-by there. It was a well-rehearsed machine.

Certainly the skipper, Kilvert, would open up radio contact with the opposition but he could tell them nothing they did not know already and that was very little. So Major Tom decided to take a walk round the aircraft and get acquainted with some of his hostages before the pressure came on. He also wanted to change out of this daft police gear.

'Excuse me,' said Tempo as he emerged from the flight deck. 'Did I understand you correctly in your little homily just now, that you are a soldier and you kill people?' Hand instinctively resting on the pistol butt at his waist, Major Tom replied, 'Like I said, when I have to.'

'Sit down, my friend,' the conductor continued, guesturing to an empty aisle seat. 'I have something important to tell you.'

'What's that, then?' He remained standing and studied the man carefully: an abnormally large head, with one rolling eye and a goatee beard, a cravat, some sort of flower in the buttonhole of a pinstripe suit; big, well-manicured hands which moved like a card player's as he talked. 'We also kill people, but we do it slowly. We are serious musicians: we bore our audiences to death.'

'That meant to be a joke?' asked Major Tom.

'Yes, sir,' the orchestra's general manager, Jacobs,

interjected. 'You mustn't take it amiss. The maestro here has a great sense of humour. But please can you tell us when this will be over? The players have had a hard concert tour, all over Scandinavia, and they need rest before our next engagement.'

'That's like asking the length of a piece of string. Depends how long the operation lasts. If it goes wrong, your next engagement will be busking outside the Pearly Gates.'

'I don't think the Musicians' Union would tolerate that,' said Tempo. 'They are very strict about such things.'

Major Tom grinned, in spite of himself. 'You're a regular little ray of sunshine, aren't you? What instrument do you play?'

'The whole orchestra. I am the principal conductor. My name is Gregor Kazanovitch.'

'You British?'

'No. I am a White Russian. But I have a French passport.'

'The maestro is famous,' Jacobs interjected. 'He is an international star. A legend in his own lifetime.'

'Oh, aye?'

'He is a very important man. His brother-in-law is the French Minister of Culture.'

'I get you. So the Frogs wouldn't mind paying a few coppers to have him back, safe and sound?' Major Tom was studying Tempo with renewed interest.

'Anything, almost anything, within reason,' Jacobs agreed.

Tempo turned his head towards the general manager and fixed him with something between a paternal smile and a glare. 'I think you have said enough, Mr Jacobs.'

'What do you do?' Major Tom asked Jacobs. 'You play something?'

'Only the balance sheets,' Tempo replied. He was anxious now to keep Jacobs muffled. 'He is our general manager. He is a person of no importance. This is a second-rate orchestra which could not earn a living as a military band without a public subsidy. No one here is of much value. The ladies are an amateur choir of middle-aged housewives from Margate who should be confined to singing in the bath. And yes, it is true I am related to René Martin, Minister of Culture, but France is bankrupt these days.'

'So,' said Major Tom, addressing himself to Jacobs, 'everyone's British except for Mr Whatsit here?'

'We have an Irishman, Mr Moynahan. He is first trumpet.'

'The Irish government would not pay to have him back,' said Tempo. 'A popular subscription was raised in Cork to export him as fast as possible.'

'The maestro is joking, of course,' said Jacobs. 'It was a municipal scholarship for him to attend music college in London.'

'Any other nationalities?'

'I don't know about the choir,' said Jacobs. 'We have one German horn player, Fritz Klamp, and an American violinist, Paul Anders.'

'So how much would the orchestra be worth?' Major Tom persisted. 'Say you were to insure them all?'

'We have. After that football team – Manchester United – were killed at Munich I have always insured our musicians when they travel. It is a token insurance, really, for around £10,000 each plus a few extras.'

'They are only worth that dead, not on the hoof,' Tempo snapped. 'And even then they are over-valued.'

'How many players?' asked Major Tom.

'Exactly ninety-nine, plus the harpist, Miss Tremlington.'

'So the orchestra is worth about a million on the insurance market?'

'About that,' said Jacobs. 'Some of the instruments – the ones we use for chamber works by a team of our best string players – are individually far more valuable.'

'You know, Jacobs,' Tempo murmured in a stage whisper, 'there are times when your silence would be very welcome.'

'The instruments . . . how much are the instruments worth?'

'Well,' said Jacobs, 'that violin over there, packaged up

in its own first-class seat, is on loan to us from a collection in Britain. It was built by Guarneri in the eighteenth century. It is worth around £250,000. The cello next to it, again on loan and of great antiquity, would fetch a comfortable £200,000 at auction.'

'Thank you, Mr Jacobs,' said Major Tom. 'That's very interesting.'

'Not at all, major. Some of us are trying to co-operate and I hope you will keep that in mind if . . . if anything drastic happens.'

'So how come the instruments are worth so much?'

'I will tell you why,' said Tempo. 'This I do not mind telling, but I will be surprised if you understand it. Each instrument is unique. It is as uniquely different from other, apparently similar, instruments as one human being is different from another. Each one has its own voice, you know. It has its own peculiar pitch and resonance which, like wine and good conductors, improves with age. Some instruments are mediocre from the beginning. Like some people are mediocre. Are you mediocre, Major Tom, or are you good at what you do?'

'I've survived,' said Major Tom.

'So did primitive man. To survive and procreate and die is to be like an insect on a different timescale, a thinking cockroach. It is to go round in biological circles like a divine sewing machine and finally to be like every other animal in the herd. Most people make that mistake. And then they expect their children to accomplish what they have failed to do. Musicians are always looking for a way out of this vicious circle, which is why they are usually unsatisfied, unhappy creatures. They are trying to find an identity within themselves, which is different, and then they look for ways to announce that identity. But this is very dangerous because the rest of the herd do not like the animal which is different. It is guilty of a biological heresy. So they try to stop it, kill it. To be doing what I think you are doing, Major, is also very dangerous. Are you just trying to survive? Do you have any other aspirations at all? Or do you just have a death wish, which is very boring because there is nothing but silence the other side of the grave? Imagine it . . . total silence! There was once a man called Nietzsche, who found a way round this problem. He believed, you see, that the artist was a superman, able to dominate the beliefs of the people who came after him, through the works he wrote while he was alive.'

'When this job is done, I'm going to open the biggest, lushest brothel in the western world,' Major Tom said, glancing at Tempo's secretary. She, reading *Cosmopolitan*, appeared not to hear a word.

Tempo smiled. 'Ah, you are a farmer at heart. A fatstock farmer. And perhaps an existentialist also. Tell me, will there be any music in the biggest brothel in the world?'

'Reggae.'

'I know the sound. That would make it a very boring house. Such music is repetitive, and perfectly appropriate to the so-called "life-cycle", which is really a machine for getting nowhere.'

Major Tom glanced at his watch. 'I've got things to do,' he said. 'Don't do anything stupid, any of you, and we'll get on just fine.'

As he left, Tempo asked, 'Tell me, Mr Jacobs, why did you help this man?'

'The truth is, maestro,' Jacobs answered smugly, 'that this affair could be good for the orchestra. We've had a mixed press so far, and that's putting it mildly. Who's going to remember *that* when this is over? The PR value of an event like this is incalculable.'

The conductor smiled and murmured in a voice like distant surf, '*Also sprach Zarathustra*, "Behold, I am weighed down with my wisdom, I would have it so that the wise among men are glad of their foolishness, and the poor of their riches. Therefore I must descend into the depths." '

Back on the flight deck, Major Tom settled himself familiarly in the right-hand seat. 'Now then, skipper, where are we?'

'If I'm flying this bird single-handed, I can't handle the nav side as well,' Kilvert replied, eyes on the horizon. 'I thought you were in charge of flight planning. It would

30

help if my second pilot was up here as usual.'

'No need. We'll work it out. Our estimated air speed is around four hundred knots, right? Flying due west. We're about half-way between Oslo and the Scottish coast.'

'Uh-huh.'

'D'you agree with that, or not?'

'I don't disagree. That's about right.'

'Good. Well then, get on your bike, sunshine, and take a left-hand turn onto . . . let's see . . . a course of one-five-five degrees. That should take us over the Dutch coast just south of the border with Denmark. When you've got the coast in sight, either on radar or with the Mark One human eyeball, let me know. If I'm at the back end of the aircraft, ask for me on the public address system . . . Fuel reserves OK, are they?'

'OK for what?'

'For another hour at this speed and altitude and another half-hour in reserve?'

'Yes. But not much more.'

'That should be enough,' said Major Tom. On the bulkhead behind his seat, a black telephone squawked for attention. He lifted the instrument, paused for a second then replied: 'Major Tom.'

'Bill here,' said his companion's voice. 'You'd better have the blinds drawn. We've got company outside.'

'What sort of company?'

'RAF Nimrod, legging it up on the starboard side. They've got the porthole open at the front end. If they've got one of those big recce cameras, then they'll have our I/D sorted out in about an hour and that's not going to help. Those I-twenty-fours will take a picture of you at this range that would pick out the fillings in your teeth.'

'Thanks, mucker. I'll join you in a minute.'

Major Tom sat on the cockpit floor below the window level and addressed his hostages via the handset. 'This is Major Tom. We're changing course as part of a pre-arranged flight plan. Nothing to get alarmed about. I also want everyone sitting in window seats to close the blinds. Repeat, all window blinds to be closed. Naomi, get up front to switch on the internal lights. We still want to see

31

where people's hands are. That's all for now, campers, but get on with it. Otherwise, Brownie points and items of clothing will be lost. Aye, and let's have the second pilot, Mr . . . Barnhurst is it, up here toot-sweet.'

As Barnhurst entered the cockpit, Major Tom gestured with his pistol to the empty seat. The man sat and locked his seat belt. He was reaching for the headphones when Major Tom snapped: 'No need for them. Just prepare to take over flying this crate if I have to kill your mate here. You heard me . . . Now, skipper . . .' Major Tom rose to a kneeling position, thrusting the pistol barrel into Kilvert's ribs. His left hand reached up and eased one headphone away from the pilot's ear. 'Get this once and for all,' he whispered angrily. 'I'm in charge here. Don't say anything, just nod to show you can hear me.'

The man nodded.

'We know about the Nimrod. Get them on the radio. Tell them you're free to talk to them for the time being because we're at the back of the shop. They'll ask how many of us there are. You'll tell them three for sure, perhaps four. Understand?'

Another nod.

'We've treated you all decently so far. Any more trouble and you'll be chopped first. Understand? Good.'

The Nimrod glided alongside Juliet Bravo like a great white shark, camera protruding through its open porthole. As he finished filming, the flight lieutenant pressed the communication button on his intercom set. 'They've twigged us, skipper. The blinds have come down.'

'Pity,' replied his squadron leader. 'Not to worry. We've got some useful voice recordings. Knock off the photography, John. We're going back to Kinloss.'

Mrs Marigold ap-Rhys, ignorant of the Nimrod's presence and much else, had been knitting when the order to close the blinds was announced. She had been knitting when their leader, Mavis Marsh, LRCM, protested at the attack on Moynahan. So long as she concentrated on the garment, she told herself, she would be all right. Now the reduced light forced her reluctantly to lay it aside. The garment – a woollen suit for her first, as yet unborn, grandchild – had been her lifeline to security throughout this, her first trip abroad. She had survived the outward flight, just, not realising that when the doors were closed and the safety belt secured around her, a rising panic would start somewhere in her stomach and rise up through her chest, forcing the air out of her lungs, turning her pink with fear and embarrassment. At fifty-five, with a mezzo-soprano voice whose vibrato was tolerable among amateurs in her church choir, Marigold ap-Rhys was no more fearful of a disaster then any other air traveller. But she was flight-phobic, and therefore threatened by something she couldn't name. The simple fact of sitting inside an aircraft, strapped into a seat, imprisoned by upholstery before and behind her, was like drowning. She had confided in no one about it. Now the blinds had descended.

Alongside her was Florence Mockett, a common sort of woman, originally from London, they said, and brought to Margate by her minicab-driver husband. On the ground, in normal circumstances, Marigold ap-Rhys would have nothing to do with the likes of Florence Mockett. Mrs Mockett's friends called her Florrie. Sometimes she was soprano, sometimes mezzo, but never with any musical sense. She also had a terrible habit of holding a note that fraction of a second too long, after everybody else had let it go. Show-off. Wore cheap scent. Flashy jewellery. And now, well, being locked in this . . . place . . . with the Mockett woman of all people . . .

'I read my tea-cup this morning before we left the hotel,' said Florence Mockett. 'D'you want to know what the tea-leaves told me, Mrs Up-rise?'

Frowning with the concentration required to ignore the dancing beige pattern of upholstery as it threatened to writhe up from the seat in front of her and envelope her like a shroud, Mrs ap-Rhys said, 'I thought we only had tea-bags in the hotel room. Not proper tea, like, at all.'

'Yers. Well, I cut mine open, didn't I? What's the point of a cup of tea, I ask myself, if you can't read the future in

33

the tea-leaves after? So that's what I did. You want to know what the message was?'

'I don't believe in all that superstitious nonsense. I'm a magistrate's wife, you know, and I have to . . .' Her voice trailed off as the pattern shimmered ever more malevolently before her, suggesting sordid, sexual acts, mouths opening, limbs moving, voices moaning as she heard her mother's through the thin plaster of a terraced cottage in the Rhondda Valley all those years ago. She closed her eyes and felt better. Mrs Mockett appeared not to notice.

'Oh, it's not just hempty superstition, mark my words it ain't,' she said. 'I've got the gift, you see, Mrs Up-rise. Been proved right time and again, I have. And the message this morning was that somebody on this aeroplane is going to die before the passing of two sunsets. There was the body, clear as could be, and the two half-circles round it representing the setting sun.'

'Please, Mrs Mockett, no more, no more,' gasped Mrs ap-Rhys, her tiny, veined hands gripping each other.

Opposite Mrs Mockett and Mrs ap-Rhys, at a window seat on the starboard side, the veteran Basil Krivine had found an amusement to satisfy the restlessness of his antique, angular, cellist's fingers. This was the first day for more than twenty years that he had not spent some time playing; his fingers, which became more demanding and hyperactive as he got older, were taking the law into their own hands. He hoped no one noticed as they scrabbled at the vinyl covering on the wall beside him. Tiny pieces they were, at first. The fingers teased and tugged and pulled at each morsel, and then, having removed it from the wall, they rolled it into a tight, neat bundle before dropping the fragment on the floor beneath his seat. He turned to the man alongside him as the fingers got on with their own business. 'Did I ever tell you about performing under Klemperer in Leningrad?'

'More than once, Basil,' the other man replied.

'Yes. 1925 that was. Or was it Moscow? I was still a student, really. Klemperer came to conduct the Philharmonic every year until 1929. We called him "the black devil" because of the way he behaved at rehearsals. He was mad, but a genius.'

'Yes, Basil.'

'Funny thing. I can remember those long-ago things so well now. But I can't remember what happened yesterday. Where are we? Shouldn't we be in rehearsal by now?'

On the flight deck, the menace of the Nimrod withdrawn, Major Tom rose cautiously to his feet. 'Call up Schiphol,' he told the pilot. 'Tell them we're landing there in fifteen minutes. We'll refuel there. Tell their Air Traffic that any attempt to do anything else will be a disaster and any loss of life will be down to the Dutch government, and that's a good way for them to lose the election they're fighting just now. Got that?'

'Maybe they won't give us permission to land,' Kilvert suggested. 'Most of the big airports are closed to hijacks these days as a matter of policy.'

'No question of permission. Tell them we are landing, and if obstacles are put on the runway, then they're responsible for what happens. They've got no choice. Aye, and tell them we're only in transit. All we want is fuel . . .'

Sitting just two rows behind Mrs ap-Rhys and Mrs Mockett, Miss Mavis Marsh LRCM – for that was how she always announced herself – temporarily abandoned her latest letter to her MP. It was the third she had drafted so far on this trip. The others had complained about the absence of toilets in the rehearsal room, which they had reached too late for rehearsal anyway, and the outrageous behaviour of everyone except her own 'gels' at the Grieg concert. This latest turn of events, aboard the aircraft, was by far the most serious. For once the prescience upon which she depended for most things had failed her. She was stunned by the violence used against that musician, even if he was only a coarse Irishman. She could not foresee how it would all end.

'What's the matter, dear? Muse not at its best today?'

Miss Peggy Dunn wrinkled her nose in a smile over spectacles that always seemed about to slip off the end of her tiny, toy shepherdess face. The big blue eyes and well-drilled golden curls suggested lollipops, tap dancing and a vapid Pre-Raphaelite virtue combined with an impressive lack of intelligence. This was deceptive. Her tinkling, trite comments were usually larded with an irony which cut the unwary like concealed razor blades and could even penetrate Miss Marsh's formidable armour. And yet, at the end of every day, just before they went to sleep, all was set to rights when Miss Marsh LRCM, in her nightdress with the yellow butterflies on it, perched on the edge of the bed. Miss Peggy Dunn, in her nightdress decorated with bluebirds, kneeling on the rug before her, was asked, 'Still love me, Peggy?' The ritual never varied. " 'Course I do, you silly old sausage.' 'Then show me.' And then Miss Peggy Dunn would lift the soft, scented folds of the nightdress with the yellow butterflies on it and kiss Miss Marsh gently, and when that was over, she would clean her teeth and each would sleep content on her own side of the bed.

'It's not that, Peggy. I'm worried about the gels. They will be in no fit state for Chichester if this trouble continues. We haven't even started rehearsing the Bach cantata yet. The men's voices will suffer, too.'

'But they are at home, Mavis. How could they be affected? Worried about us, yes, but not in their voices, surely?'

'The first thing they will do when they get their wives back after this, my dear, will be to copulate. One can't blame them. That's exactly as the gels would have it and jolly good luck to them. But we depend on those husbands for at least six tenor voices in a mixed work and you know perfectly well what marital duties do to the tenor voice. By next morning, they've slipped at least half an octave down the register. At rehearsals you can identify those who haven't been celibate within the first three bars . . . Oh, so much uncertainty, Peggy. Shouldn't we chuck the whole thing and go away and breed goats as we promised ourselves years ago?'

Miss Peggy, faithfully observing another ritual, made the traditional response. 'Next year in Jerusalem, Mavis. Music needs you. Goats do not.'

Captain Michael Kilvert, the skipper of Juliet Bravo, was now enjoying a brief moment of optimism. Turning to Major Tom, he reported brightly, 'The Dutch suggest a compromise. They want us to land at a military field near the Hague. They say there's a lot of air traffic around Schiphol.'

They were now running in over the barren, low-lying sand dunes and drab green dykes of coastal Holland. 'Do you know how to get to Schiphol from here?' Major Tom asked.

'Navigation no problem. We fix on the relevant beacon and that's that,' Kilvert replied. 'Trouble is, I don't know which runway approach to use. We have to be set up for that from about five miles out at least.'

'Right then. We'll have to eyeball it and make a low pass over the place,' Major Tom said thoughtfully. 'Tell them we're landing at Schiphol with or without their help.'

After a further exchange with the Dutch authorities, Kilvert turned to his captor and said, 'It's really no good, Major Tom. They insist on Hague Military.' His tone suggested regret, but Kilvert could not suppress a small smile of triumph. They were at six thousand feet and descending gently through cloud.

Major Tom, his woolly eyebrows raised as if he were a schoolmaster dealing with a dense pupil, replied, 'We're landing at Schiphol and that's final. Even if I have to fly this thing in myself. Mr Barnhurst, work out for me a compass bearing to Amsterdam. Skipper, I want one pass over Schiphol Airport from south to north at two thousand feet. You can relay that information to Air Traffic. After that, say nothing else until I clear it.'

'This might be dodgy, Jon,' Kilvert said pointedly. 'Let's have the seat belt indicator going. Flash it on and off so everyone gets the message.'

Naomi Lewis, spotting the sign, slipped her migraine pills

back into her pocket. It hadn't started yet, but the familiar pre-headache symptoms – the vague nausea, the increasing stiffness in the back of the neck, the fine blurring of her usually sharp vision – were familiar warning signs. She had concealed from the various airlines for which she had worked, as well as from her colleagues throughout the ten years she had spent in the business, the fact that under prolonged stress, her nervous system burned off its excess adrenalin in this way. It was like an oil well discharging excessive gas. So now, resigned to one of those rare but frightening occasions when it would happen while she was in the air rather than resting on the ground, she started the routine tour to check that everyone was 'decent'. Only one belt was unlatched, that of a modest little woman, pale, once pretty under a tumble of brown hair, sitting near the stern.

'Fasten seat belts, please,' the stewardess said in her most crisp, impersonal voice.

The woman appeared not to hear her and Naomi Lewis could feel the pain starting to surge upward from her stomach like a hot worm, until it touched the base of her skull. There it settled, throbbing, mocking her. As she pointed to the offending belt, one of the negligent passenger's neighbours shook the pale woman's upper arm and pointed first to Naomi Lewis, then to the belt.

'Your belt,' she said. 'They want you to do it up, Agnes.'

Agnes did so in an abstracted sort of way, then said, as if everyone was privy to her thoughts, 'It's the twins, you see, Roger and Rita. They're only two . . . two years old, that is. I knew God would punish me for leaving them. I just knew it.' The pale face slumped forward into long thin hands and the angular shoulders, sharp as seashells under a cotton dress, heaved and shook as if disturbed by an earthquake of grief. Naomi Lewis resumed her own seat, praying that the pills would work soon. Otherwise, she knew she could not take much more of this.

Amsterdam, a maze of chimneys at the end of a skein of canals beside the Amster, came over the horizon five minutes later. They were now at five thousand feet. 'Take her down to two thousand feet,' Major Tom instructed. Shaking his head, the pilot did so, but he said nothing. 'I want a slow, three-hundred-sixty turn over the city centre.' As they wheeled round, Major Tom saw what he was seeking: distinctive, single-deck trams on the main streets. There was no doubt this was Amsterdam.

Twenty miles to the west lay Schiphol International Airport. By the time they arrived there, all air space in the vicinity had been cleared. Aircraft appeared to be dispersed on all except one runway, across which a fresh wind blew heavy rain at right angles. Even this runway was not entirely clear. A big Pan-Am 747 sat on the end of it, ready to take off.

'Hello, Juliet Bravo. This is Air Traffic, Schiphol. You do not, repeat not, have permission to land. All our runways are occupied at this time.'

Major Tom, squatting awkwardly between the two aircrew, the co-pilot's headphones on his head, reminded Kilvert, 'No reply. Take her round again and put us down on the runway in front of that Pan-Am job.'

'You do realise, I hope,' said Kilvert as they began the turn, 'that if that American jumbo starts taking off as we land in the opposite direction, then there could be a collision?'

'That's just what they want us to think. It's a power play. If the worst happens, well, you've done circuits and bumps I guess?'

'You mean a "go-around". In these conditions? We'd be lucky.'

'I am lucky.'

'Hello, Juliet Bravo. We have you on radar. Please indicate your intentions.'

'Say nothing,' Major Tom told the skipper.

'Hello, Juliet Bravo, please stay clear of Schiphol. We have released a Pan-Am flight for take-off from the runway you just overflew. Please stay in a consistent holding pattern while we get clearance for you to land here. This is not for us to decide. It is government decision that you land at the Hague.'

'Say nothing,' the hijacker repeated. 'You've got your orders. Put her down on that runway.'

The rain grew more intense, and so did the gusting cross-wind as they started an approach from about three miles out. Kilvert and his co-pilot rapidly went through the drills required to drop the undercarriage, open the wing flaps and set themselves up for landing. Barnhurst, peering forward through the windscreen wipers, was giving Kilvert corrections up to the last moment. 'Go five left, down five hundred . . . five left, hold her there, down five hundred . . . good, skipper, you've got it there . . . Oh, Christ!' As they throttled back, flaps down, over the airport boundary fence, they saw, first, the orange tail-light whirling and then the whole monstrous shape of the jumbo as it bounded up the runway towards them.

'Going up!' Kilvert, throttle suddenly full open, hauled back on the control column, hurling Major Tom off balance. Sprawled on the cabin floor, he did not see the jumbo lift off immediately below them, but felt the reaction as each aircraft shuddered in the wake of the other's turbulence. Winded, his mouth bleeding, Major Tom raised himself to a sitting posture, the pistol still in his right hand, safety catch firmly on. 'Make another circuit and try it again,' he shouted.

'No way. We were only inches from a collision,' Kilvert replied grimly. 'You can still hear the passengers screaming back there. It seems we're going to die anyway but you'll have to kill me first. I'll be damned if I kill myself through bad airmanship because of your obstinacy.'

'Hello, Juliet Bravo. This is Air Traffic Schiphol. You have permission to land now on runway two. Continue on your present circuit and we will talk you down.'

'This is Juliet Bravo. Roger. And thanks. Can you tell whether our undercarriage appears undamaged?'

'Wait, out . . . We have you on binoculars and the answer is negative. We see no damage.'

The damage was elsewhere and was non-mechanical. When Juliet Bravo had made its sudden climb the passengers had felt themselves pinned against their seats as if by some powerful poltergeist. Heads were forced back. Mouths opened and released involuntary gasps which in some cases became screams. The shuddering vibration caused by the near-collision convinced some passengers that they had crashed. Several of the choristers were now weeping uncontrollably, praying for the end to be swift, fleetingly haunted by the thought of the families they were leaving behind. In that, they discovered the real pain of death. Like the violence they had witnessed earlier, it was arbitrary and incomprehensible. Miss Mavis Marsh LRCM and Miss Peggy Dunn held hands, calmly prepared to face the end together. The orchestral players sat silent, tense and white-faced. In the centre aisle, a bottle of duty-free whisky, miraculously undamaged, rolled this way and that until, with a pretence that she was still in control of herself, Naomi Lewis retrieved it. It seemed like a long time, though it could not have been more than one minute, before the American violinist, Anders, announced, 'The good news, folks, is we're still alive. The bad news is we're still flying.'

'Flying, are we?' Krivine called back. 'By Jove, so we are. Did I ever tell you about flying to Germany with Klemperer in the twenties? "The black devil" we called him in those days.'

Guided by the ground controller, Juliet Bravo made a smooth if fast approach to the runway. Kilvert, sweating profusely, bit his lower lip as he realised his miscalculation. If the undercarriage was damaged after all it might collapse completely and . . . Instead, the big aircraft bounced ponderously. With full flap and reverse engine thrust, tyres grunting in protest, it rumbled to a halt well short of the end of the runway.

'This is Major Tom back again. Welcome to Schiphol Airport, Amsterdam. I hope everyone's in good order back there and I'm sorry about the bumpy arrival – due entirely to the refusal of the authorities to let us land just to pick up some fuel. Likewise, we're also sorry you have to keep the blinds down. This again is not something we wanted. We don't want to be bloody-minded, but the authorities are trying to take photographs of us and that's a hostile act. We'll be making our reasonable demands known soon; all we want, believe me, is a peaceful end to this little adventure. I'll be coming back there to talk to you soon, campers, after I've arranged for the fuel. Might be necessary for us to stay here overnight as it's getting dark already. I'll keep you informed. In the meantime, you're going to have a five-star dinner. Hope you're still OK in that forward loo, young Leslie Archer. Better come out now, son, or we might get the wrong idea.'

Then, turning to the pilots, he snapped out his next order like a drill corporal dealing with one-day recruits. 'Don't need you here, Barnhurst. Get back to Major Bill's patch and keep out of trouble.' Kilvert, still shaken by the landing, followed his partner's departure with misery in his eyes.

Major Bill, Armalite in hand, stood up as Naomi Lewis approached him, two sick-bags in each hand. 'I need to open the rear door,' she said. 'There are a lot more where these came from, too many for the loo. As you can see, it's like a battlefield.'

Behind her, breaking the rules about unregulated movement, a pink and blue matron with the figure of a blancmange carried more sick-bags. 'Young man,' she said in tones which hinted of Queen Victoria's empire, 'I am Miss Mavis Marsh LRCM, and this is not good enough. My gels, my Margate Ladies, do not deserve to be hurled about the air like playthings in a nursery. Some of them are petrified. What's more, it is bad for the voice.'

'Aye, well, you can open the back door, throw the stuff out. But I want the job done quick,' Major Bill replied.

A chain was formed to dispose of the bags while Major Bill, rifle cocked, sat on his haunches to one side of the door. At the end of the line Naomi Lewis fleetingly wondered whether it would help to push him out, accidentally. As the door closed, reinforcing their imprisonment, the Margate Ladies blew their noses, but in some cases this did not help. Following Mavis Marsh to her seat, Major Bill put a large hairy hand on her shoulder and gave it a friendly squeeze. 'Might help if your ladies cheered us all up with a song,' he said.

42

Instantly she was on her feet, jewelled fingers twitching for attention. 'Sing, gels, sing! Follow me . . . "Land of Hope and Glory, Mother of the Free" . . . One, two, three and –' The women sang without conviction. Some of them did not sing at all, but sat with their faces in their handkerchiefs.

Moynahan, his flat Irish face grimacing as if he were tasting bad stout, tugged at Major Bill's sleeve. 'Listen, Major Bill or whatever your name is, I'll tell you everything you want to know, accede to all your legitimate demands and all that rubbish, anything, if you only stop that noise.'

'Better than having them turn hysterical,' Major Bill replied. 'You Irish?'

'From God's own city of Cork. Long way back. I've been playing in this orchestra for ten years and had a long time on the road as a jazz musician before that. I suppose you fellows are running some sort of revolution?'

'Something like that. I leave it to my oppo, Major Tom, to do the propaganda bit.'

'Well, whatever it is, I'm in favour. The only way to get anything done in this world is through direct action. Even if they meant well, which they don't most of the time, your average government can't get much done. Too many people behind the scenes, pulling strings. The media, the Church, they're all in on it, running the world like it was a private gentlemen's club for their own personal pleasure. They're all power mad. Maybe I should be standing up there with you with a gun in my hand. But then again, you can be as subversive as you like with music and there's not much they can do about you. The difference is, I don't need to risk getting my head blown off. See, it's a weapon of non-violence.'

'Aye, well . . . very interesting. If ever we decide to swop our Armalites for trumpets, I'll let you know.'

'The name's Moynahan, Seamus Moynahan, and there's no hard feelings about what happened earlier,' he said, extending his hand. It was a large, businesslike hand. 'Sorry,' said Major Bill, nodding to his rifle. 'Got my hands full. We'll talk later.'

He returned to his seat, from which he could watch both doors, and eased the blind up from the window. Almost dark out there now and still raining. At intervals on the gleaming tarmac the Dutch had placed armoured vehicles of various kinds: personnel carriers, scout cars and a few light tanks resembling the British Scorpion. There was a lot of firepower out there. Inside the aircraft the stewardesses were serving a meal; for the time being, the Margate Ladies had ceased singing. This sound was replaced, Major Bill noted, with a buzz of animated conversation. The singing had dissipated some of the tension and now the prospect of full bellies had raised morale further. After another half-hour, following precise instructions issued by Major Tom, a single fuel-tanker drove up alongside the aircraft, and just one man, the driver, laboriously replenished the wing tanks.

'Hello, campers. Here's Major Tom with a word of comfort for you. We will stay here tonight and continue our journey tomorrow. When you've been to the loo I want everyone to settle down for a good night's kip. Thank you for your co-operation. Will Major Bill give me a buzz, please?'

Major Bill moved softly aft and picked up the handset.

'It's Bill.'

'I'm sending the skipper back to join you. He's got bolshie and might try something stupid. You'll find some handcuffs in the green bag. When he's fed, put them on him.'

'What about the steward?'

'Ask the two girls to talk to him. Otherwise, we'll have to fetch him out ourselves later.'

Kilvert slumped into a seat alongside his junior, Barnhurst, and stared at the food put in front of him without attempting to touch it.

'Better eat up, skipper,' Barnhurst said at last. 'We don't know how long this is going to take.'

'You're right, I guess, Jon. Never thought anything like this would happen to one of my aircraft. I still can't believe it. How're the girls?'

'Our two? OK, I think. Both reacting as you'd expect.

Naomi's ready to argue with the gunmen on any small point if she gets a chance. Diana's like a schoolgirl enjoying a dorm feast. But then she is young.'

'Too young for this job,' Kilvert grunted, stabbing at his pâté with a plastic fork. 'Not just young, either. Immature and a mite stupid with it. Anyone who comes on her inaugural flight improperly dressed is bad news.'

'Improperly dressed?' asked Barnhurst. 'She's wearing uniform.'

'Plus one gold cross round her neck and a silver chain on her left ankle,' Kilvert replied acidly.

In spite of the fact that it was now dark, Major Tom donned a black balaclava for his conversation with the control tower. In an age of infra-red photography, darkness as such was no guarantee that the security authorities would be unable to obtain an excellent photograph of him.

He called up on the radio and brusquely announced himself as 'Major Tom, in command of Juliet Bravo'.

The voice of Air Traffic replied: 'Wait out, please. We will bring our negotiator to have a word with you.'

The phrase 'have a word' was carefully chosen to convey the chummy normality of such an event. It was chosen by the negotiator, an Army psychologist with long experience of such matters, and written into the hijack brief from which the duty officer was now reading. It struck Major Tom that the Cloggies, as he called the Dutch, were working from a script which was now out of date.

'This is Dick Luytens. What can I do for you, Major Tom?'

'You can convey our demands to the British government. Have you got your recording machine switched on?'

'Well, you obviously know about these things and of course there is a recording made,' Luytens conceded in soothing tones, his English precise and almost accentless. 'At least it means I don't have to write it all down.'

'Right, here goes: We represent the Toxteth Faction of

the People's Liberation Army. Our demands are as follows:

'1. We demand the liberation of our comrades in Walton Prison, Liverpool, without regard to the alleged crimes they have committed. For information, everyone in Walton Prison except the screws and the governor are our comrades.

'2. We demand a restoration of conjugal rights to all prisoners in other British prisons, on demand.

'3.We demand that members of the British armed forces should be allowed to form and join their own trade unions to negotiate working hours and other industrial topics in time of peace.

'4. We demand that future British elections should be decided by proportional representation.

'5. We demand that foreign diplomats in Britain should have no legal immunity from crimes against the British people just because they are members of a ruling clique.

'6. We demand that politicians, Fleet Street journalists and other layabouts who criticise working people should have to spend one month a year doing an honest job in the industry they criticise.

'7 We demand an end to the daft pub hours in Britain. Working men and women should be free to meet their friends in their local pub at any time they choose, not when the ruling class say they can.

'8. We demand that British citizens havethe vote in Irish elections, in the same way that Irish citizens can vote in Britain.

'9. We demand that the American embassy in London negotiates with the British government on our behalf, to see fair play.

'10. We demand that five hundred thousand pounds in used banknotes be made available to us at a time and place to be declared later. The money will consist of British twenty-pound notes worth one hundred thousand pounds, US dollars in one-hundred-dollar bills worth one hundred thousand pounds, German Deutschmarks in fifty-Deutschmark bills worth one hundred thousand pounds, Swiss francs in one-hundred-franc bills worth one hundred thousand pounds. The rest will be made up as follows: Swedish, Norwegian, Danish Kroner, twenty thousand pounds each; French francs, twenty thousand pounds in one-hundred-franc bills; Canadian dollars, the same amount in one-hundred-dollar bills.

'Those are our limited and reasonable demands. As a goodwill gesture, we want to hear them broadcast on the BBC World Service medium wave, European service, at twenty hundred GMT tomorrow, 7 March 1984, and on BBC Radio Four, long wave. And we want the first fifty thousand pounds up front at the same time. When that happens, we shall release all the female hostages except airline crew. Have you got that?'

'Yes, I think so. I cannot speak for the British government, Major, but some of your demands are not possibly going to be fulfilled overnight.'

'We know that,' Major Tom said. 'Proper publicity of the demands, and a solid promise to do something about them, would be a good start. That and payment of the money, of course.'

'Of course. Let me ask for humanitarian purposes, how are your hostages? Do you need any food supplies or medical assistance?'

'We don't need anything except a clear runway tomorrow morning.'

'I'm sorry I cannot guarantee that,' said Luytens. 'That's a matter for the Air Traffic people and you know how difficult they can be. You're a reasonable person, Major Tom, and so is Dick Luytens, so we understand one another. These bureaucrats do not always see things the way we see them.'

'Don't give me that crap,' Major Tom replied. 'You're not dealing with some novice. We landed here today as we said we would. If we decide to go, we go. So be a good lad and just do as you're told. Pass on the demands to the Brit government, and we'll be on our way.'

Colonel Luytens sat back, lit his pipe, and lifted a red scrambler telephone. 'These boys are professionals,' he said when it answered. 'Possibly they have been trained in that new school in Libya. I don't know. I can't even be sure they are political, or just after the money. Their statement doesn't follow the usual heavy propaganda line. But you know, they seem to have no quarrel with the Netherlands. We're just a convenient staging post and a letter-box for their demands to the British. I think, Commissioner, the sooner we get rid of them, the better. But we must keep the British "in the picture", as they would say. Their advisers were very good to us during the Moluccan sieges at Assen and Bovensmilde.'

In the early hours of the following morning, amid an atmosphere blending stale bodies, unshod feet, tobacco smoke and fear, Major Tom walked quietly to the back of the aircraft. The NBO musicians on one side, the Margate Ladies' Choir on the other, were curled into childlike balls of unconsciousness, hands over faces and shoulders, mouths open. He had been filling in the hours since he had declared 'Lights out, campers, and sleep well', working on the door of the forward toilet with his Swiss Army knife. Major Bill was stretched on the floor, back to the rear exit, rifle across his knees, neither awake nor quite asleep.

'Bill,' his partner said softly, squatting on his haunches, 'we've got a waste-disposal problem. That little wanker of a steward is dead. Big bruise on his forehead. By the look of it, he broke his neck when we had that landing problem.'

Bill came smoothly to his feet. 'Aye, he would, wouldn't he? Is there much to him?'

The two men worked in total silence, Major Tom, the smaller man, from inside the toilet, and the other from the companionway. The almost total darkness within the aircraft was relieved only by shafts of light from outside, around the edges of the blinds. The slender corpse travelled light and easily over Major Bill's shoulder until they were almost at their destination. Moynahan, in an aisle seat, had spread his slumbering legs and size-twelve feet across the only path. Delicately as a cat avoiding a puddle, Major Bill stepped over them, but to do so he was obliged to step off the centre line of the aisle towards Naomi Lewis. She, sitting upright and arms folded, head back, mouth open, and dozing only lightly, opened her eyes as the steward's hand gently brushed her cheek. She saw his inverted face as if it were in a spotlight. The face was young, straw-haired like that of a youthful Worzel Gummidge, hair flowing as if under water. The pallid blue eyes were open and alarmed. The delicate, feminine snub-nose wrinkled up, and the rosebud lips, which she so envied, revealed gold teeth in a grimace which might have been real or mock horror. Somewhere nearby she heard a voice reciting the Lord's Prayer. Her conscious mind told her she was dreaming, so she closed her eyes again and at last descended into a deep, opaque sleep where there were no sounds, no images. The face followed her down into the abyss, and then faded from her memory.

There were two vacant seats in a row behind her on the port side of the aircraft. Major Bill eased the corpse into the window seat of this row, fastened its seat belt, put its hands together in its lap, and loosened its tie. The head lolled forward of its own accord.

# Chapter Three

Moira Tremlington was half asleep, dreaming of her cat, Nuisance, at home in Wimbledon, when Moynahan's spatulate fingers prodded her from the row behind where she sat, and passed her a note. It was headed, in capitals, SAMIZDAT ONE and said:

> *What did the terrorist say to the musician?*
> *'Virtuosity killed the cat!'*
> *What did the musician say to the terrorist?*

Miss Tremlington thought hard. Like the rest of the orchestra sitting on the starboard side of Juliet Bravo, she was making a determined effort to ignore the mezzo-soprano howls of anguish from one of the Margate Ladies on the port side. The howls had started as a choked sob in the early hours, risen to a continuous whimper, then a curious keening sound and finally, as they made an uneventful take-off, a roar of grief which her fellow choristers were still trying to stifle. Miss Tremlington knew of no work of literature in which a musician had addressed a terrorist and it was clear to her that this was another exam she was about to fail. If this were a crossword and she were at home with Nuisance, she would consult a dictionary of quotation. Then she remembered Tosca's plaintive plea to the wicked secret police chief, Scarpia, and wrote: *'Visi d'arte; visi d'amore.'* Leaning over her, Moynahan patted her shoulder encouragingly. Miss Tremlington, it seemed to him, certainly lived for her art, but the other bit, living for love, hardly suited the case. 'That's great, Miss Tremlington,' he said. 'All helps pass the time on the road to eternity.' She shuddered. 'Now write your own sample question and answer, and pass it on.'

Beside her, Legrange, flat cap still covering his bald head, suggested: 'What did the harpist say to the terrorist?'

'Oh, thank you, Bob. What a good question! And what did the harpist say to the terrorist?'

Major Bill, striding up the companionway to take over his shift on the flight deck, paused at the word, studied them both, and moved on. Moira Tremlington was surprised that the man's glance made her shudder. She supposed, head bowed over the paper before her, that she was tired. As the loudspeakers crackled into life, she raised her head again.

'Good morning, ladies and gentlemen. This is Major Bill. I hope you didn't have a bad night. Miss Naomi and Miss Diana will bring you coffee and other goodies put aboard just before we left Schiphol, so you won't starve. We have now put our demands to the British government and we are waiting for their reply. We'll keep you in touch with things as they develop. Shouldn't be long now before you're all home, safe and sound. We certainly don't want to prolong the agony. For now, you'll have to keep those blinds closed. Oh yes, and you'll be glad to know that all loos on the aircraft are now working normally.'

Diana Garrard, kiss-curls exactly in place, served passengers from the rear of the aircraft while Naomi Lewis worked from the front. Nearest the stern, occupying a seat alongside the inert steward, Major Tom dozed, rifle across his lap, the sling of the weapon wrapped methodically round his wrist. Alongside them, in the aisle, a crudely handwritten notice asserted: OUT OF BOUNDS TO EVERYONE.

Miss Garrard studied the hijacker carefully. He was now dressed in denim trousers and jacket and a check shirt open at the neck which revealed a tumble of rich brown hair. It seemed to her that he was smaller than the chunky, aggressive man in police uniform she had first seen yesterday. He was now transformed into a cuddly teddy bear, rather vulnerable and, as she would later tell the press, 'a perfect poppet'. Then she glanced at the steward, Archer. He had aged, she thought. Cheeks sunken quite remarkably and a nasty bump on his forehead. 'Major Tom,' she said softly, resting cool, fragrant fingers on his wrist. His eyes were instantly wide

open and alert, like those of a predatory animal. 'Would
you like some coffee?'

'Just boiled water, with nothing added.'

'Is that all? I could bring a lager, if you wanted it.'

'No thanks, sweetheart. Never drink on an operation.'

She glanced at the steward. 'Is he all right?'

'He's not drinking anything, either.'

'No, that's not what I meant. I mean, is there anything
wrong with him? He's very pale. Naomi thinks he should
be doing more to help us out, but I'm sorry for the poor
boy. I think they have a hard time, these gays or whatever
you call them. I mean, they can't help it, can they? They're
just born like that, like some people are left-handed.'

Major Tom grinned affectionately at the waxen face
beside him, as though they shared some secret. 'He'll be
all right. Sleeping it off, whatever it was. P'raps we should
hang a "do not disturb" notice on him.'

'But I don't like his colour,' the young woman persisted.

'Bumped his head a bit when we landed at Schiphol,
that's all. Just needs a little peace and quiet. Talking of
privacy, could you move that curtain from the front end,
back here? The one that separates the first-class sheep
from the second-rate goats? I want to sort out some of our
kit, away from prying eyes.'

'I'll see to it straight away, Major Tom. You know,
you're much nicer than I expected. See, I've just finished
training. This is my first real flight. Well, on our training
course they took us to a place where they had this sort of
pretend hijack thingummy. Naturally we knew it wasn't
the real thing but one of the terrorists kept groping me all
the time. Said it would be worse if it ever happened in real
life and it was useful training. He was a policeman – and a
married man.'

Naomi Lewis appeared at her elbow. 'I need your help,'
she said. 'One of the choir is getting a bit hysterical.'

'Wondered what all that noise was,' Major Tom commented. 'I thought maybe she were rehearsing.'

Hands on hips, Naomi Lewis paused and glared at him.
'That's not very funny. The poor woman had a phobia
about flying before all this. Now, thanks to you, she's a

pawn in some weird game played by a couple of male psychopaths messing with other people's lives according to rules which no one explains to any of us. Can't you imagine what that's doing to her?'

'OK,' Major Tom replied. 'She gets priority when people are released. Meantime, give her some valium.'

'She's had some. She threw it up.'

'OK. D'you know how to give an injection?'

'Yes. I'm a trained nurse.'

'Right. In that green bag you'll find a blue first-aid box. You'll find syringes, pipettes containing measured, safe doses of morphia, surgical spirit and cotton wool. Get on with it, nurse.'

Naomi Lewis clenched her fists, appeared to be about to speak, then did as he had said. Diana Garrard was about to follow her when Nicholls took her wrist. 'She'll manage,' he said. 'Bring that curtain.'

'No. No! No!' A hubbub of female attention and activity surrounded the hysterical Marigold ap-Rhys as Naomi Lewis produced the syringe. The musicians, on the other side of the aircraft, fell into a grim and embarrassed silence.

'Hold her arm for me, someone,' said the stewardess. Then, 'What's your name, dear? Marigold! What a lovely name.'

'I want to go home,' the woman moaned.

Naomi Lewis prayed quietly that this *was* morphia, that it was a safe, measured dosage, and that the patient would not be in some way allergic to it. Efforts to establish whether Marigold was diabetic or had any sort of medical history had been entirely unsuccessful. Naomi punctured the skin and pressed the injection home. Gradually the sobs subsided.

On the starboard side of the aircraft, the conversations quietly began afresh.

'I suppose this situation has one saving grace, Miss Tremlington.'

'What's that, Bob?'

'It concentrates the mind. I mean, about basic things.

What one really believes in. You know, I try not to rattle on about it too much, but for me music isn't just a form of entertaining art, a decoration, a distraction for tired minds. Music defined in that way is nothing more than aural wallpaper. For me, as for Bach and a lot of others, it's a religious thing. One doesn't have to be unduly solemn about it, of course. I think Papa Haydn said he hoped God would not be angry "if I am irrepressibly cheerful in my worship of Him". If this . . . captivity, or whatever it is, ends badly for all of us, I'm glad to have been a musician. Even a mediocre oboist. Do you believe in God, Miss Tremlington?'

'I do when I listen to someone like you.'

At the rear of the aircraft, the curtain had been re-rigged, if clumsily, from one overhead luggage rack to another, and the conductor and his immediate entourage – Jacobs and the secretary – were exposed to public view for the first time since they left Oslo.

'Welcome back, maestro,' someone said. 'When do we start the rehearsal?'

Tempo, breaking the hijack rules, stood briefly and bowed. 'Gentlemen,' he said, 'I knew you were a simply terrible orchestra, but how bad not even I appreciated until the government took the drastic step of hijacking you. So I tried to pretend I had nothing to do with you and hid behind my curtain. Now they have removed it and I have to come clean, as you say, and admit that I am your conductor. So I will have to pretend now that you are not such a bad bunch of fellows after all.'

In the cockpit, Kilvert frowned as a small orange light glowed on the console above the co-pilot's head. He nodded at it and said: 'What d'you make of that, Jon?'

The second pilot, Barnhurst, leaned forward, squinting at the light in disbelief. 'Dunno. Shouldn't be possible. Must be a hiccup in the electrics somewhere.'

Squatting between them, Major Bill asked: 'What's up, then?'

'That little alert light,' Kilvert replied. 'It tells us the back door is open.'

'Well, you're not pressurised, are you? Wouldn't be any

big deal if it were, at this altitude. The worse case is that some of your fat clients back there would be farting more than usual: you'll know that from your own decompression tests.'

'What the skipper means is that it's almost impossible for the door to be opened in flight. So that has to be an electrical fault.'

'Let's hope it's nothing serious,' Major Bill said crisply.

Panting with exertion, Major Tom set the steward's corpse on the floor of the tail compartment. With equal pressure inside and outside the aircraft he had found it comparatively simple to open the two doors which gave access to this dusty lumber room used only rarely for maintenance of the tail section. The first pressure door was part of the aircraft's main hull, yet as he hauled the big handle anti-clockwise the door swung obediently inwards. It was pursued by a draught of air as cold as a Scottish cemetery. A second door, immediately behind the first, opened outwards, leading to a gloomy cavern lined with pipes and cables. Below his feet, tucked into the fuselage, was the main passenger stairway, activated by a black handle Naomi Lewis had used earlier. Straight ahead a catwalk led to the tail cone projecting beyond the tailplane itself.

As his eyes adjusted to the twilight he spotted a red-and-black handle on the far side of the catwalk. By turning this he could jettison the entire tail cone, leaving a large hole through which, in an emergency on the ground, passengers could flee down an escape chute like Christmas parcels in a sorting office. Disposing of the body that way would attract attention. Equally, the roar of two big Pratt & Whitney jet engines would be stunning if he dropped the air stairs. Already there was a noticeable increase in both sound and vibration. He hurriedly closed both doors behind him. 'Think, man, think,' he told himself.

With both doors closed, he reasoned, there should be no particular noise problem within the aircraft if he went ahead now and dropped the stairs. The experiment would be a dangerous one, since he could not be sure whether he would be dragged away from the top of the stairway by the turbulence to which it would be exposed once it descended. Would the hydraulic pressure he had demanded – three thousand p.s.i. – be sufficient to bring the air stairs safely back up into the fuselage again, once the job was done? He could, of course, tuck the steward away in the tail cone for the duration, but that would be bottling out. After Belfast he had no faith in post-mortems. Spare corpses were bad news, however they came to be in that unfortunate condition. So, after sliding the mortal remains of Leslie Archer a few feet away from him over the top of the air stairs recess, he stepped back, held the handle of the cabin door firmly in one hand, got himself very stable with his back hard against the door, and pushed the shiny black lever down vigorously.

The effect was dramatic. A whole section of the floor just below him fell away in a boom of sound, as daylight and a bitingly cold wind swept inward. The steps dropped and then rose again, riding the slipstream like a roller coaster. The body, head away from him, remained where it was. Like the hijacker, it was protected from the worst of the turbulence by the mass of the fuselage near the top of the ladder. It was also trapped by one foot against the passenger's handrail. One arm floated up and down above the body, as though waving to him.

With deliberate care, as though he were tackling a difficult rock face, Major Tom transferred his grip to the handrail, then moved cautiously down one step. As he shifted his weight, the ladder sank below him. Another step, and another, and the boom of the engines was like a drumstick against his inner ear. At last he hooked his shoe around the dead man's foot and dislodged it. In spite of the discomfort and danger of his situation, he watched the steward's body for the first few seconds of its seven-thousand-foot descent into the North Sea. Throughout the whole time he kept it in sight, the body remained in exactly the same sitting posture, though relative to the aircraft it lay on its back, head slightly forward as if studying Juliet Bravo. In freefall terms, he noted, it was a perfect reverse arch position. He thought that very interesting. He murmured, 'Ashes to ashes and all that,' and hauled himself back up the ventral stairway.

With one blue-cold hand he secured his weight to the rear door again, and with the other hauled up the lever controlling the stairs. These snapped shut with remarkable ease, aided not only by the aircraft's hydraulic system but also by the air pressure swooping up under wings and tailplane. As he re-entered the hull Major Tom felt like cheering for the first time since the great caper had begun. Instead he lit a cigarette as he sat shuddering on the jump seat, and called up the flight deck. 'Bill, it's me. Glue works a treat. Things all right your end?'

'Under control.'

'Anyone asks where the steward is, you haven't seen him.'

'I haven't.'

'See, he doesn't seem to be with us any more.'

'You what?'

'Think he must have gone for a swim off the Dogger Bank . . . You still there, mucker?'

'Aye. We'll talk about it later.'

As Major Bill replaced the black telephone, Kilvert eased the headset from his ear. 'Major, we've got a query from the UK Civil Aviation Authority. They want to know our flight plan so they can clear the necessary air space.'

'Go north, straight up the North Sea, then turn left over the Scottish border at Coldstream. Fly over the Cheviots, turn right again over the Irish Sea and then into Prestwick. If they offer you a berth anywhere else, the answer's "no".'

In the Cabinet Office Briefing Room overlooking St James's Park, the crisis managers were just beginning to assemble. Despite its portentous name, the COBRA centre was a modest enough place, like an intimate club cinema, with a lecturer's podium on each side of the screen. On this screen Colonel Timothy Xavier Wainwright – recently recalled to the colours and promoted – was now projecting a familiar organogram. He was not surprised that at this early stage of the operation the great houses of government – Foreign Office, Home Office, Treasury, Ministry of Defence – were represented by the second eleven. The second eleven, in turn, studied him. The man in front of them was deeply tanned, but the tan did not completely conceal the splintered burn-scar that spread along his upper cheek-bone towards the missing lobe of his left ear. One of the myths about him in his regiment was that he spent thirty minutes each day exposing his scarred face to an ultra-violet sunray lamp. But what most people remembered about him were eyes which were deep blue, etched around with lines that suggested laughter but which really derived from continuous service in places where the sun shone mercilessly. A romantically inclined journalist once wrote of him that he had 'the eyes of the desert Englishman, fixed on some far horizon'.

'My name is Colonel Wainwright and I'm the GSO-2 at Recce Commando group HQ. The briefing is classified "Secret". As you see from the screen, we have the usual network of authorities involved, with this office as the co-ordinating centre. Since the last Cobra operation, we've acquired Nesta, a computer already storing a formidable amount of data about known hijackers. Nesta talks to other computers, similarly programmed, in Brussels and Washington. Brussels covers the whole of Western Europe except France, where we have the customary blind spot.

'This slide shows the charter, Juliet Bravo, at Oslo yesterday, and this next one, shot from an RAF Nimrod, on its way to Schiphol. There are a hundred and thirty passengers, ninety-nine male and thirty-one female, plus five crew including first and second pilot. There are certainly two hijackers and possibly more.

'No threats have been made to hostage lives, so far as we know, but other aspects of the hijack lead to the conclusion that the hijackers are trained in the use of weapons and are prepared to use them. The aircraft is now approaching the British coast from the North Sea, on the Scottish border, and apparently intends to put down at Prestwick.

'A list of the hijackers' demands have been circulated with the rest of your written brief. HMG's first decision will have to be whether to agree to the condition that we pay them the first fifty thousand and broadcast their message in exchange for the Margate Ladies' Choir. That course would reduce the risk if we eventually stormed the aircraft. It would also provide us with valuable real-time information about conditions on board. So far we have not broadcast the demands, though there have been some leaks to the press in Holland, picked up by the media here.

'We have, as yet, no solid idea of the identity of the hijackers. They appear to be British. They say they represent something called the Toxteth Liberation Army, which indicates a link with Liverpool. We ran a check through Nesta to look at the profile of this operation so far, and we know of no case where a hijack commenced like this one. By that I mean that the hijacker was always among passengers boarding in the normal way: he did not seize the aircraft by mounting an operation at the airport, after the aircraft had left its stand. However, these people clearly have studied other cases. A team of Free Croats made a declarative use of a bomb in the air terminal at La Guardia a few years ago to give credibility to the plasticine "bomb" they took on board a civil airliner shortly after. In the La Guardia episode, one police officer was killed. In Oslo, a demonstrative bomb at the terminal building injured two officers and one civilian. The significant difference in this case is that the hijackers were not troubled by the need to smuggle material through the normal airport security checks. By mounting a *coup de main* seizure of Juliet Bravo, they were able to load an unspecified amount of equipment on board. At present we have no means of knowing what that is, though according to the Norwegians it certainly includes Armalite rifles fitted with grenade launchers.

'The other significant element here is that the terrorists have been trained in negotiation techniques. They are not just gun carriers. We can only speculate about the source of that training. Libya has been suggested as one possibility. What we can be sure of is that turning these people round peacefully is going to be uniquely difficult.

'A Pagoda team from Hereford is on its way by helicopter to Scotland and the civil police at Strathclyde are manning the perimeter. Radar surveillance of the aircraft is now being beefed up through visual observation by RAF Phantoms. Meanwhile, an identical machine is being made available to our team, for rehearsal purposes, at Strathallan, north of Prestwick. I'll be travelling north today as negotiator, with Dr Rendell the psychologist.

'I'll take questions now. Please preface them with your name and department.'

'Yes. Wilkins from the Tweasuwy. Don't think there's any way we can legally pay this wansome, you know. Even if we could, on HMG's instwuctions, out of the Contingency Fund, it would be half a million pounds of taxpayers' money, and that's sewious. Now, a nine-millimetre bullet costs about twenty pence these days. So Tweasuwy view is that forty pence spent on wemoving the cause of the twouble is better than thwowing away half a million pounds.'

'Mackie, Downing Street PR. We're absolutely certain that to go down the road Mr Wilkins advocates would be more costly than he realises. The terrorists' demands are a very cunning cocktail, a combination of the apparently reasonable and the strongly populist. Look at them – knock the privileged foreign diplomat; straighten out the pub hours, and so on – and you'll see what we mean. I don't think the great unwashed public is going to get much exercised about a few fiddlers from an obscure orchestra but we need to extract the ladies from Margate before the shooting starts. Every one of them is a good suburban woman, with everything that implies on Fleet Street. So on the whole, I'd say we go through the motions of paying the first part of the ransom and broadcast the demands. Those are the only things the terrorists ask us to do immediately. Then sit back and wait for them to make a mistake. We must be seen to be preserving some lives in this. If we just chop everyone on board regardless – or even appear to be willing to do so – then it could cost us a lot politically. It's as simple as that.'

From his seat in the front row, a dishevelled figure in

bow tie and odd socks glared over half-moon spectacles. 'Don't you have voice prints? Reports say these men have accents straight out of *Coronation Street*. Shouldn't we be broadcasting their stuff as a short cut to identification?'

'Your name?' Wainwright asked.

'I'm Angus Howard, Foreign Office.'

'If we broadcast the demands recorded at Schiphol, we accede to one of them, so that's a tactical dilemma. Otherwise, we've picked up a jumble of other auditory material. The only fragment which is half-way clear is an exchange between, we think, one of the orchestra and one of the terrorists. They sound quite matey. I'll play it if you'll wait a second. The amplification in here will distort it slightly.'

At a nod from Wainwright, his assistant ran the tape back to the beginning and pressed the play button.

*'There was once a man called Nietzsche, who found a way round this problem. He believed, you see, that the artist was a superman, able to dominate the beliefs of the people who came after him, through the works he wrote while he was alive.'*

*'When this job is done, I'm going to open the biggest, lushest brothel in the western world.'*

Looking up, Wainwright added, without much conviction, 'The computer suggests one or two names. We are following those up. A voice analyst, some sort of phonetics boffin, is checking the authenticity of the accent. For all we know, it might be someone whose mother tongue is not English.'

'Or a speak-your-weight machine,' the man from the Foreign Office added. 'So whom do you have on your computer?'

'One favourite is the man known as Carlos, "The Jackal",' Wainwright replied. 'It is fair to say that he is an immediate suspect for the more professional terrorist operations wherever they occur, even if they are happening in different parts of the world at the same time. The readiness to use force in Oslo suggests someone of his calibre. His longstanding quarrel with the French government might also explain why he has taken a prominent

French citizen – the conductor Kazanovitch – as a hostage.'

'In that case,' said Howard sharply, 'he surely would have framed his demands differently. As you know, he was almost arrested in Paris, and some of his followers are still in prison there. He has bombed express trains in France and generally made himself disagreeable, and the message is always the same. It is "Let my people go." He would not have associated this operation with scruffy old Toxteth. Who's next on your shopping list?'

'An American criminal hijacker, an old Special Forces hand who called himself D. B. Cooper. But the FBI are convinced that he is dead.'

'And our birds appear to be British,' Howard interjected.

'That's right,' said Wainwright. 'So we're trawling through lists of mercenaries who've been in trouble in recent years. In 1976, you'll recall, a team put together in London went to Angola and created a lot of nausea for us all. They were led by a renegade Parachute Regiment private soldier using the *nom-de-guerre* Callan. Callan was executed by firing squad but some of his lieutenants who were not taken prisoner simply disappeared. A few, we know, went to serve in Ian Smith's army and then moved on to South Africa. We're running a check on the relevant passport numbers.'

'That's not much help if they now have South African passports,' Howard suggested. 'If I may say so, I do not think that a computer is going to be of much help to you. A bit of old-fashioned human "nous" is what's needed.'

The briefing ended. For the time being, only Wainwright and his assistant were left to man the Cobra desk. Wainwright pored over the notes he had made. *'Treasury demanded to know who would put up the funds, even if the PM approved. Legal problems. No contingency fund covers. ECO won't agree to US embassy involvement: UK domestic affair. French embassy's knickers knotted over conductor: want quick settlement, one way or other, for internal, political reasons. Home Office/Strathclyde still want whole thing moved from Prestwick. PR say hijackers getting fairly sympathetic press.'*

'Y'know something boss?'

'What is it, sergeant-major?'

'I reckon I know that voice.'

'What voice?'

'That terrorist on that tape there. I think it's Golly Nicholls. One of the old-and-bold he was, with the regiment before we amalgamated with the Marines and the Paras.'

'I know who you mean all right. I was his troop commander at one time. But this time, sergeant-major, you're way off. Nicholls is dead, isn't he?'

'Is he? I served with Nicholls all over the place. We've thought he was killed-in-action more'n once. Always turned up eventually, he did. Be just like him to set up a thing like this, take the money and open a brothel with it. He used to go on about what he called – what was it? – the Nicholls Nubile Flesh Emporium when we ran out of other things to talk about. Only millionaires were to be allowed in, but he'd make all the lads who'd served with him honorary members. Got to be a sort of standing joke in the troop. Last time it came up was at that wives' party to welcome us back off Op Storm. Nicholls made a speech about the "facts of life". Talked about the lads not missing their wives in Oman because they were quite content wanking, but what really upset them was when he said, "If you think they're thinking of you while they're doing it, ladies, you've got it wrong." That just about wrecked the party. My missus was interrogating me about it for days afterwards.'

Wainwright, mindful of the robust qualities of the sergeant-major's wife, tried not to smile. 'I'll agree with you, sergeant-major, that allowing for the quality of the recording, it could be Nicholls. The subject matter also fits. It could equally well be a lot of other people, and red herrings in a situation like this can be dangerous. Remember how West Yorkshire police got themselves tied into knots over the recording of the guy who called himself "Jack" in the Ripper case? Nicholls is dead. He's certainly dead legally. We've got a coroner's word for it.'

'I'm still certain it's him, sir.'

'Then you're wrong,' Wainwright told him. 'I'm going to Prestwick. I'll call you from there on a secure line. I want some more idents from that computer as soon as I arrive. Understood?'

'SAMIZDAT SIX: *Is Margate the last resort?*'

Paul Anders pondered, then wrote in reply: '*No. W. C. Fields put on his tombstone, "I'd rather be here than Philadelphia."* ' He passed the message back over his shoulder, then turned to his companion, the German horn player Fritz Klampf, and said, 'Doesn't all this remind you of something, Fritz? It's just like being back in school, all this passing notes around and getting permission to use the john. The hijackers become the teachers – parent surrogates – and we're the children. Instead of seeing them as a threat, we start relying on them for our security and curry favour with them. See, there's a symbiotic relationship between hijackers and airlines. The airline treats the passengers just like a child, with all these baby plastic eating trays and all. So, naturally, when the terrorist takes over and assumes authority, we're already softened up. We're a pushover for all the fascist shit that follows.'

Tempo, sitting immediately in front of Anders had already half-turned in his seat. 'That is a very interesting observation, Mr Anders. I think you are right. Mr Jacobs here became dependent on our captors in a regrettable style almost from the moment they appeared. Perhaps we should do something about it all.'

'Like what, maestro?' Anders asked. 'I mean, these guys are professionals. There's no way we're going to do a Wyatt Earp scene here. Someone might get hurt. *I* might get hurt!'

'Something more psychological, I was considering.'

'You mean like chess? Or gin rummy? I seem to remember reading in the *New York Times* a while back that some hostages in South America tried that. The hostage-takers, the terrorists, always lost whatever game they were playing and ended up shooting the hostage who

64

kept beating them. Count me out of the chess game. I ain't no hero. I wouldn't even play snakes-and-ladders with these guys.'

From his position on the flight deck Major Bill summoned Naomi Lewis. 'Major Tom's probably sleeping. Wake him up for me. We're approaching Prestwick.'

'And that's where you let the ladies go,' she said.

'Maybe. If the authorities meet our first conditions.'

'Which are what?'

'No reason why you shouldn't know that, Miss Lewis. It's a broadcast of our demands and some money up front. The first fifty thousand pounds – as a gesture of good will.'

'And if they don't?'

'They will.'

'Well, look, Major, you could at least release the woman who's been yelling her head off for the past twelve hours. She's quiet at the moment but that's only because she's sedated. I think everybody will be less nervous if we get her off the aircraft.'

'I'll think about it. Now go and wake my partner.'

The landing was uneventful, though apprehension gripped the passengers anew. Conversation ended. Eyes closed in silent prayer, and the prayer was mocked by the drumbeat of blood pulsing in the inner ear. Bob Legrange heard it as a rhythmic whisper, 'Be-ware! Be-ware! Be-ware!' To the casual observer on the ground, Juliet Bravo's arrival at Prestwick was no different from any other, except that the aircraft taxied to a remote corner of a disused runway reserved for such emergencies and known as the 'hot spot'.

At Major Bill's insistence Kilvert was obliged to swing the machine round at the last moment so that the nose faced away from the airport buildings and towards the boundary road and the moors. The two aircrew were then removed from the flight deck, Major Bill following them, to sit in isolation near the stern. Unshaven and red-eyed with fatigue, Kilvert and Barnhurst barely glanced at their passengers. To Legrange it seemed that they were broken men, but he did not voice the thought to Moira Tremlington. The pilots were allowed to use the rear toilet, with the door open and Major Bill watching them. The passengers, in turn, watched him furtively as he handcuffed the two men together after they had used the toilet.

Major Tom, completing a shave with a cordless, battery-operated razor, gave them a cheerful wave of welcome with the advice, 'Catch some kip, lads. We'll be here for some time, but your travels aren't over just yet.'

It was Naomi Lewis who noticed the steward's absence. Addressing Major Tom in a louder-than-usual voice, she asked: 'What have you done with Leslie? Leslie Archer, the steward?'

Major Tom, continuing his shave, did not look up. 'Don't ask me, Naomi. I thought he was up front with you.'

'You know damn well that's a lie. He isn't here any more. He isn't on the aircraft . . . I had this sort of feeling, this omen.' She pronounced the word 'omen' as if reading it aloud for the first time; as if it were something not yet understood even when articulated successfully.

Major Tom continued shaving, but in a more circumspect way now. It was impossible to know whether this was because he was trimming the edge of his moustache or pausing, surprised by her attack.

She snatched the razor from him and threw it towards the rear door. 'Listen to me!' She was leaning forward, hands grasping the seat in front of him and her voice shook. 'He wasn't sleeping at all. He was already dead when you had him in that window seat beside you. And then, somehow, you got rid of the poor little bugger.'

Major Tom sighed heavily and folded his arms. 'Cool it, sweetheart,' he said uneasily. 'Did you or anyone else see me kill him? How am I supposed to have got rid of him?'

Kilvert, rousing himself, turned from his seat on the starboard side. 'You're supposed to be in charge, Major. Where is he? He's a member of my crew.'

'I'm telling you, I don't know. The berk stayed in the loo

most of the time and after that he was unconscious in this seat here. Then I went to sleep as well. When he disappeared I thought he was taking his finger out at last to get on with some work. P'raps he just went outside for a breath of fresh air.'

Kilvert and Barnhurst looked sharply at one another, both recollecting, with retrospective horror, the door warning light.

Naomi Lewis leaned closer to Major Tom, placing her nose close to his. Her lips were curled back like those of an angry and frightened animal. 'You bastard,' she snarled. 'You bastard.' Then she spat in his face.

Major Tom stood up. His big hands reached towards her throat. Trying to suppress the hysteria rising within her, she turned her face away. His mood changed disconcertingly now. Grinning like a schoolboy, he patted her cheek and announced, 'That's all we needed. A hysterical air hostess . . . Cool it, Naomi. There's no way I could beat a man to death and ditch the body in this confined space without someone noticing what was going on. Even if we could get the doors open the noise in here would be deafening . . . Silly cow.'

Diana Garrard put a comforting arm round her colleague's shoulder. 'Sit down a minute, Naomi. I'll get you a glass of iced water.' Naomi Lewis, weeping out her frustrated anger, allowed herself to be led forward a row or two. 'I'll get him for this,' she said. 'Chauvinist pig. I'll get him.'

'Relax, Miss Lewis,' said Major Bill. 'He always has that effect on women. Sometimes he even has that effect on men.'

Tempo, at the front of the aircraft, turned to Anders, the violinist. 'What is this noise about back there?'

'I think someone just got bounced from the nursery,' Anders replied. 'As they might say in your country, "*Pour encourager les autres*." '

Major Tom settled himself comfortably into the left-hand seat, picked up the captain's hand microphone and called the control tower. It would be two hours, said Air Traffic, before 'someone authorised to talk to you' would arrive. That figured. They were now entering what the training manuals described as the 'attrition phase' of the hijack, in which every small bit of business negotiated with the outside world took for ever. It was the phase in which, if he and his partner were not careful, they would lose the initiative. He set his alarm watch, eased the balaclava up over his nose, stretched his legs and dozed.

Behind him in the cabin there was now little conversation among the passengers and the flow of 'samizdat' notes had dried up. Unwashed, fed only irregularly, exposed by turns to hope and fear, their world had become an enclosed, unreal cavern in which it was possible neither to move nor to sleep normally. As if to remind them of the danger, everyone suffered from indigestion. So they dozed, suspended somewhere between night and day, consciousness and unconsciousness. Some made the waiting tolerable by playing in their minds Bach and Rachmaninov, Mozart and – in Moynahan's case – a virtuoso trumpet work by Aaron Copland. The only voice was that of Tempo.

'I beg you, Mr Anders, do not become an advocate of the new orthodoxy. I like you. You are an intelligent man. So you know that Schoenberg, Stockhausen and Webern and the rest of them have a lot to answer for – like, in another field, Marcuse and Sartre. This twelve-note scale is a trick, a musical Meccano which anyone can master so long as he can count to twelve. As a method of composition, it is much more easy to teach. It is like a packet of dehydrated garbage food. You simply add the magic ingredient – let us say, a title in Sanskrit – and *voilà*! you are a modern composer. You see, Mr Anders, some of us still believe that music is the voice of the soul of man. This is the link that has been broken by your moderns, the link of sentiment with disciplined structure. It is no coincidence that the symphony orchestra as such is the unique gift of western culture. And now our world is being taken over by barbarians disguised as composers.'

'The whole of civilisation is being taken over, maestro,' said Anders. 'I lived in your city of Paris some while ago, just round the corner from the Palais de Chaillot in the smartest part of town. You know what I heard every summer night through my open window? Tom-toms! That's change. That's the twentieth century. That's movement. This is a very mobile century.'

'Then civilisation must fight back, Mr Anders. This movement is not only backwards. It is downhill, into an abyss.'

'Maestro,' Anders replied in a cool, measured voice, 'for the last several centuries our sort of music's been a closed, pretty world hidden behind a wall like one of your French gardens, full of elegant, obedient white statues, a world for an élite. Now the outsiders are busting down the gate with their moog synthesisers and Armalites wanting a slice of the action. I don't like it either. But that's how it is.'

# Chapter Four

Slumped in the rear of the staff car on the way to Northolt, Wainwright brooded upon his sergeant-major's theory. It was a preposterous notion. Dead men did not hijack orchestras. What was going for it was that, in other respects, it fitted the man. Pity. Might have saved lots of leg work if they had a good I/D at this stage. Against that, Nicholls was – correction, had been – bad news. No bugles, no dead man's auction in his honour after he was killed. Even to think about the origins of the affair, of Nicholls's trial and imprisonment, would be a waste of valuable reconnaissance time. 'Time spent in reconnaissance is never wasted,' as the junior staff college maxim had it, but they said nothing about reconnaissance that took off in the wrong direction. 'Know thine enemy' was another useful maxim, he remembered, collected in the dusty corridors of Winchester. Who was the enemy? In which direction should he be making his reconnaissance anyway? Time to play the inner game, let the eyes close and the radar system inside his head look for plausible targets. It was, after all, that instinct for correct intelligence, rather than the bullet wounds collected on the infected mountains of Oman, which had won him his belated promotion . . . Irrationally, and much to his discomfiture, the radar picked up Nicholls, Nicholls coming out of prison. Somewhere, Wainwright fancied, he still had the letter that had dragged him back into Nicholls's poisonous little world.

> From the Office of:
> Colonel Commandant,
> Reconnaissance Para-Commando
>    Brigade Group HQ,
> Wellesley Barracks,
> London SW3

To:
Lieutenant-Colonel V. R. Butcher DSO,
Commanding Officer,
1st Battalion,
Reconnaissance Para-Commando Regiment,
Wingate Barracks,
Hereford                                    13 January 1983

Dear Victor,
    As you know, Golly Nicholls is due for release on
parole from Bicester Prison next week. He has had a
rough deal. I think the Regiment should have someone
meet him so as to ensure that he doesn't do anything
foolish. John's organisation is willing to offer him
employment on contract, perhaps with his former
partner, S/Sgt Shakespeare, so long as he doesn't carry
too big a chip. Please get someone (perhaps Tim
Wainwright?) to meet him on his release to keep an eye
on him for a few days.
                    Yours aye,
                    Alain Le Mesurier

He had been commissioned to hang about outside the
Bicester Prison in the snow, waiting for a man who
probably would not want to speak to him but who, in the
coded terms of the director's letter, had to be brought
discreetly under control before he did something reckless.

Nicholls, when he emerged, had stepped sideways and
warily through the prison gates like a cautious crab. He
did not hurry away. He remained still in the shadow of the
big prison clock tower, a black shape within black shadow
imprinted on silver snow. He saw two cars sitting
blob-like on each side of the approach road and he did not
like that, for he had expected only one. Since he was the
only prisoner to be discharged that morning, it meant that
both had something to do with him. It occurred to him
that one of them might be his hearse.
    Inside, his day had started like hundreds of others with
reveille and slopping out, but although he knew it was 'F'

– for 'fucking-off-to-freedom' – Day, he felt no particular excitement. The grins, the thumbs raised at him over the long breakfast table, signalled good news which he still did not trust. Then they brought him his civilian clothes in a cardboard box. He faintly remembered the gear. He had worn it towards the end of his trial in defiance of regimental orders, which were to maintain a profile low to the point of invisibility. So here in the box were a T-shirt picked up for two dollars at an American parachute club, bearing the slogan, 'Man does not live on food and sex alone: he's got to have skydiving.' With that, a pair of jeans, light denim jacket, socks and soft-soled track shoes. After prison uniform the clothes felt soft and feminine, reminding him of radiant but painful things he had forced back into the recesses of his memory and which were paraded in prison only for the purposes of mockery, as if they were hostages in some antique war. The prison governor, who held some obscure military decoration, intoned a series of platitudes. 'Model prisoner . . . object here to reform as well as punish . . . parole board greatly impressed . . . new start . . . no backsliding .. back here otherwise . . .'

As he slid obliquely along the darkest corner of all, where the wall in shadow met the ground, the offside doors of the two vehicles opened in unison. One red-haired figure from the vehicle on the right he recognised immediately as his old friend and partner, Bill Shakespeare. The other, in a British Warm and red silk scarf below a tuft of blond hair, was a half-recollected ghost. Both men advanced towards him, slurrying the snow. Shakespeare glanced at the other man, paused momentarily and then trotted up, gathering his partner in a bearhug. At the same time he whispered, 'Watch yourself, Golly. Recovery squad.'

'Ah, Corporal Nicholls,' said the other. 'Good morning.'

'Morning, boss.'

'Welcome back to the world. Got a job for you. Follow me.'

'Thanks, Major Wainwright, but I'm not on the strength, am I? Dishonourable discharge and all that.'

72

Wainwright, hands in side pockets, thumbs flapping outside them, looked down at him through those incredibly blue eyes. 'Past and forgotten, Golly. Sure you had a bad deal but you're not in a wheelchair or a loony bin like Geordie and a few others. We all get shafted one way or the other, eventually. Where's your sense of humour? Why don't you – yes, and you, Bill – join us?'

'Us?'

'Your wife. She got in touch. Guessed we'd see you. She wants to sort out – um – some domestic stuff with you.'

Nicholls stiffened, and Shakespeare noticed, as they moved forward into the light, how old his partner now seemed, even allowing for the grey-flecked beard. Nicholls's golliwog hair was thinning and there were dark patches below his eyes. He seemed thinner, more frail. He paused, blinking, shading his eyes with his hands, seemingly crowded by only two people yet intimidated by the space of fields on each side of the road. 'I dunno,' he said. 'Lawyer handles all that since the divorce.'

'She wants to talk to you about your daughter, Cheryl. And I want to talk to you about a job,' said Wainwright. 'Tell you what, let's all drive down to the Bull for breakfast. You'll join us, Bill?'

'Aye, I'll join you. Golly and me can follow you.'

'Yes,' Nicholls said. 'We'll follow you in Bill's wagon.'

As they swung round behind Wainwright's black Volvo, Shakespeare said: 'You don't have to fall into line with Wainwright. You're a free agent, Golly.'

'I dunno. I dunno. Better see what it's about. Anyway, there's young Cheryl.' They had almost arrived at the inn when Nicholls said, 'Hold on. Drive round the block.' Silently, Shakespeare did as he was told. 'I want time, just a minute or two, to think. Inside you never do or say anything without thinking first. It's become a habit. Got a cigarette?'

'Sorry mate. Kicked the weed six months ago.'

'See, Bill, I've got this idea. Could make us rich. Real rich. But I've got to sus out this other thing Wainwright's offering first.'

Wainwright hated the welfare end of an officer's life. It

was messy, manipulative. Having to explain, sometimes more than once to the same distraught woman, that she had just become a widow was quite the worst job. This one was not much better, in view of what had happened to Nicholls. After driving round the empty streets for ten minutes or so he told himself, 'All part of life's tapestry, Tim Wainwright, so get a grip of yourself and let's get this over with.'

In the coffee lounge of the Bull, Nicholls's former wife Margaret sat and waited, regretting the choice of a split skirt, though it used to be his favourite. It seemed to her that her entire life, all six years of it, had been spent in waiting for him. She was ten years younger than Golly and still an attractive honey blonde. That morning she had replaced the wedding ring she had worn until the day the divorce was finalised and then discarded. Now she sat and waited and turned the heavy, unfamiliar ring restlessly with the fingers of her right hand. When, finally, he entered the room she did not recognise him immediately. It was not so much the beard as the walk which changed him. Once he had been light of foot and graceful as a cat, which was why she had first noticed him one night in a Hereford disco. Now he stooped and walked slowly, almost shuffling, as though he were part of a long and hopeless queue. He was about to walk past her, until Wainwright rose gently and called, 'We're over here, Golly.'

For a second everyone stood awkwardly, then sat again in unison. Shakespeare propelled a chair behind his friend.

Nicholls said, very quietly, 'Thanks, Bill.' Then more loudly, 'Help the Aged Week, is it? You get out of touch in prison.' He nodded to his former wife, a businesslike, noncommital sort of nod, said, 'Hullo, Maggie', and without pausing turned half-round to face Wainwright. 'What's on your mind, sir?'

'One spoonful, or two?' Wainwright asked, hovering over the sugar.

'None, thanks. I'd be glad of a cigarette.'

74

From the suede handbag at her feet, Margaret produced a packet of cigarettes and a gold lighter. Someone, thought Nicholls without bitterness, had been looking after her. 'Thanks . . . nice lighter.'

'Yes,' she said evenly. 'A present from my dad.'

'We've got a proposition for you, Golly,' Wainwright intervened. 'Work you're used to . . . bodyguard jobs and the like. You'd go on the payroll immediately, with six months to get yourself fit.'

'Fit?'

'Just normally fit. Nothing extraordinary. No sickeners. No endurance marches. Just averagely fit. That and a bit of refresher drill with the Browning. Then a six-month posting on contract to somewhere warm.'

'What's the catch?'

'No catch, Golly. You'd be working on a civilian contract, probably with Bill here, at Chevalier. The firm is kosher with HMG and it's run by your old squadron commander, Colonel John. Of course, you'd have to keep your nose clean. No private trips across the water to settle old scores.'

'I think that would be a breach of my parole, wouldn't it, sir?' Nicholls asked. There was the finest edge of mockery in his voice. 'I mean, trying to kill people's illegal, even in Ulster . . . unless you're a member of an approved organisation.'

'Yes, it is,' Wainwright replied sharply. 'And if the team over there got so much as a sniff that you were in the vicinity, they would lift you, or worse.'

For a long second Wainwright and Nicholls stared hard at one another. Then Wainwright said, 'Look, Golly, I'm not leaning on you. All of us, including the people up at Group, know you shouldn't have been convicted. They backed your parole application to the hilt. That's why they sent this reception party, to make sure . . . well, to make sure you got off to a decent start again.'

'No need to worry, boss,' Nicholls answered. 'I've had time to do some thinking and reading since I went inside. Six months, you say? Yeah . . .' He pinched the cigarette out and tucked the dog-end methodically into his trouser pocket. 'Yeah, that should be long enough. I'll take the contract.'

For the first week, Nicholls lived with Margaret and their daughter in a cul-de-sac on a council estate near regimental headquarters. It had been their first and only marital home. After some awkwardness about where he should sleep it was agreed between them, almost tacitly, that he would use a sleeping bag on the sofa in the downstairs living room.

He had retained his beard. Cheryl, a shy five-year-old, hid in the broom cupboard when she saw him approach. By day the child was in a play school while her mother operated a switchboard at a nearby factory, work which suited her quick fingers. Golly avoided former neighbours and friends, as well as the bars and clubs used by his old comrades. Each morning he rose early, before Margaret was awake, packed his rucksack and took a bus to the hills twenty miles away, hills on which he had once broken potential recruits to the regiment. There he started marching. The rucksack contained a spare sweater, a waterproof, a bar of chocolate and several bricks to ensure that the weight he carried was not less than fifty pounds. To harden his feet he wore no socks.

There was reassurance in the familiar sweated labour of the paths he followed, where the wind gusted as if the hand of God were catching flies, and he was one of them. Though his body was free of the confinement of prison at last, he was more aware than ever of being oppressed in every other way: by the need not to upset Wainwright, or Maggie, or the child, or the furniture. Early each evening Wainwright would drop in for a cup of tea and a chat, very casually, noting with approval the dirty boots and the Bergen rucksack stowed in the hall. Wainwright, a bachelor, lived like that himself in a moated house hidden in a dark wood below the brooding remains of a Roman hill-fort.

Towards the end of that week, Margaret said briskly, 'Sorry, Golly, but you'll have to find somewhere else to live, love.' On television, an advertisement for soap powder was extolling the virtues of clean underwear and family life. Nicholls felt the burden on him begin to lighten. 'Why's that, then? You got another bloke?'

'No . . . no, course not. It's Cheryl. She's started wetting her bed at night. I think you're making her nervous. I know you need time to get it all together again but honest, Golly, you've changed. Before you went to prison, you talked. Now, it's well . . . like having a walking statue round the place.'

'Yeah.'

'And that beard. That's what frightens Cheryl, I'm sure of it. Makes you look . . . well, a bit nasty.'

'Yeah. OK, girl. I'll move on. See the lawyer bloke soon and get this maintenance thing sorted out. This firm I'm going to work for, Chevalier Security, is paying me OK.'

'Where will you go?' she asked.

'I dunno. Somewhere quiet; cheap. I'll ask Bill Shakespeare.'

Next morning, during a lull in the activity of the switchboard, her fingers neatly tapped out a familiar telephone number. 'It's me,' she said. 'He's moving out tomorrow . . . No, good as gold about it . . . I felt a bit awful, but we can't go on like this.'

Shakespeare was due to arrive from London the following day. He had been on standby at Chevalier's office in Kensington, yawning over the telex messages and killing time. The only requirement was that he remained within a twenty-minute orbit of the office. The opportunities this provided included three strip clubs, one sleazy cinema known in the firm as the Queer's Delight, a judo club and weight training gymnasium. He used them all. With the arrival of Friday, the Islamic sabbath, it was clear that the VIP whose person he would guard in London was not expected before Monday, so Shakespeare was released for the weekend. In Chevalier's corridors, the rumour was that His Royal Highness No. 566 was last heard of in Marseilles, making an unscheduled cultural visit.

Before he set off for Hereford, Shakespeare routinely

checked his Range Rover even though the car park was exclusively for the use of tenants in the apartment block where he now lived under the name 'Alan Lewis'. There were no strange devices attached to engine or chassis and the petrol cap was still locked.

As he swept westward down the M4 he reflected on the release of his old partner Golly Nicholls and on what had put him inside in the first place. It was the merest chance that Golly had opened fire that day in Belfast and not Bill Shakespeare himself. Even now he was not absolutely sure who had killed the McAlister kid. Around the guys still serving with the regiment there was some sort of buzz that the story had tumbled out of a supergrass. Not that it mattered any more, any more than a lot of other mysteries in the years he had shared with Golly.

When you got down to it, it was funny that their partnership had lasted so long. The thing was a sort of habit. Golly was an OK soldier, but basically a brothel man, a city bloke never satisfied with what he'd got. Aye and what was more, Golly's spare women had got older, dirtier, uglier and smellier during their time together. Shakespeare himself hated the smell of cities and preferred the same woman for all seasons. In that, at least, he was lucky these days. She was a good kid, his woman. No questions asked and a big hug every time he returned, and no hanky-panky while he was away.

Golly . . . mystery man, our Golly . . . there was that time they came under fire on the Indonesian side of the line in Borneo, and when he needed him, Golly wasn't there. Was it, as others on the op suspected, a touch of bottle trouble? Golly reckoned he'd been fixing booby traps and lost the rest of the team in the confusion of withdrawal under fire, but there was no way of proving it. He had an awful lot of blood on his uniform when they found one another on the way home, and that was followed by an Indonesian broadcast about Allied atrocities and two girls being carved up. Another mystery, and Golly could throw no light on it. Never mind, never mind. All water under the bridge.

Just over two hours later, Shakespeare's Rover drew

into the cul-de-sac. It was still light and next door's children were dancing round a small snowman, chanting as they did so. Golly, his rucksack slung over one shoulder, came out to meet the vehicle before it stopped. He noticed that the children waved impishly at Shakespeare before they dived into an entry between the houses, laughter rising above them like bubbles of air over a skin diver.

'Them kids know you or something?' he asked, clambering inside.

'Aye, a bit. Their dad was on the firm when I first joined.'

'Is he regiment?'

'No, police. Special Branch. Left us when they increased police pay and went back on t'force. His missus didn't like London and he got a posting down here.'

In the snug bar of the Plover – known to regulars as 'the Bovver' – the two men played darts before dealing with the serious business of the night, which was to find Golly a place to live. Now, as they sipped reflectively on pints of Abbot, each waited for the other to raise the subject. At last Shakespeare said, 'So you've got to find a new pad?'

'S'right, Bill. Any ideas?'

'Aye. What about that nurses' home you got into in '75?'

'Too much of a good thing, my son. Nearly killed me, three in one night. See, I told the first one it was for Queen and country, but I didn't tell her how I was spelling "country".'

'And she believed you?'

'Sort of. Well, not at first. She thought, naturally, I was a bloody burglar or a professional rapist or something. Well, I offered to leave straight away and gave her my name, number, the works, before I started to go. That puzzled her a bit. Then I explained how Special Forces weren't allowed to fraternise with women for security reasons. I said I hoped to be out soon and I'd be wanting to get married and settle down, with a bloody great gratuity to spend. So, I was sort of window shopping; I'd been watching her on and off for weeks and wanted to talk to her.'

'She swallowed that garbage?'

'That and a lot more, Bill. It was preaching to the converted, like. She *really* wanted to get married, that one. Silly cow.'

'What about the other two?'

'The other two . . . No, it's all a blur. Don't remember much except that they were a couple of high-class scrubbers. Wait a minute, though . . . one did a slow striptease out of her uniform and then wanted to change her mind about it all at the last minute. Real freak, that one. But that first bird, she was great.

'Then the row started. I don't think the hospital would've bothered, really, except for the damage, the ivy and the broken glass. The medical superintendent, or whoever the big noise was, he loved that ivy. Couldn't give a toss about the nurses but it made it easier for him to raise a row. I mean, people wouldn't have taken him serious if he'd complained I was molesting his bloody ivy . . . Happy days.'

'So when do you need this new place?'

'Now. I've left.'

'Aye, well, you wouldn't want a hotel.'

'Too many people.'

'Then what about Acker's caravan? He's doing another Gulf tour and he's asked me to keep an eye on the place.'

'Where is it?'

'Near here, on a small civvy airfield. Acker's got the skydiving bug, same as you used to have, so he keeps his van down at the civvy freefall club we went to one weekend, Air Adventure Sports or something.'

For a moment Golly's eyes glowed with something reminiscent of their old enthusiasm. 'Eh, that sounds all right,' he said. 'As it happens I've been thinking I'd like to get back into parachuting myself. Just for fun, like. It was magic, that spell of cross-training with the freefall troop in America. I've still got my log book somewhere.'

An hour later, with Bill's help, Golly moved into the caravan. It was a creaking, draughty mess of sleeping bags, paperback books, fading pin-ups and parachute gear overlooked by a looming black hangar through whose sliding doors the wind droned like an unquiet spirit. At night, as its metal frame cooled, the hanger cracked with a sound like that of fingers breaking in an interrogation centre. Golly was to spend little time in the caravan. Nearby, after all, there was a comfortable clubhouse containing a colour television, pool table and kitchen, and there he passed the day's idle hours.

It was a month before Nicholls fulfilled his ambition to return to parachuting. Meanwhile, driving winter cloud swept a few feet over the huddle of hangars and packing sheds like an eternal jet exhaust. Nicholls filled the time usefully enough with a basic refresher course, learning to steer an open canopy and to roll safely towards any point in the compass. He packed and repacked the same parachute until he could do it blindfold. For hours at a time he practised exits from the motionless Cessna in its hangar. The aircraft was stripped of all its seats, save for the pilot's, and the starboard door had been removed. As he followed the drill – right foot out to the step, right hand to grasp the wing strut above him, left foot to the step, left hand to the strut – to hunch under the wing, right foot trailing in space only a few inches above the concrete floor, something which had long been stifled stirred within him: a tidal flow of adrenalin that raised his spirits as dramatically as might a sudden, unexpected burst of sound surprise someone who had long been deaf. This pleasure was an intimation of something larger, an approach road to the perfect freedom of freefall. He did not resent being treated as an absolute beginner. It was, after all, more than five years since his last jump and he had forgotten much.

At last the weather cleared and the day came. From three thousand feet the countryside was spread like an iced cake beneath the singing engine of the aircraft. In deep frost the hedge-row shadows took on a strange, subtle complexion blending pink with violet. Under the brittle winter sun, the trees were like miniature cauliflowers. Golly was the first of four novices to be put out of the aircraft, using a military-style static-line parachute secured at one end to the pilot's seat, to pull open the heavy backpack less than two seconds after he fell away. It was as near foolproof as anything in this world. Knowing this, he felt no anxiety. The instructor, kneeling behind him, leaned forward to place an emphatic gloved hand on the pilot's right shoulder. Obediently the aircraft moved five degrees in that direction in a jarring right turn. They were now immediately over the intersection of two concrete runways, black as death against the frozen white grass. The engine note changed to a soft whirr as the pilot throttled back.

'Cut!' snapped the instructor's voice, and the pilot reduced power even further. The engine was barely idling now and the Cessna was rapidly losing momentum. The instructor, an American, favoured the relaxed rather than the dramatic approach to the next part of the business. He tapped Nicholls lightly on the elbow; as Nicholls looked round, the man was grinning at him knowingly through bad teeth. It was, thought Golly, the sort of leer you got from a brothel keeper when he knew that the girl you were taking upstairs had a dose of something even penicillin could not cure.

'OK, sweetheart, get out,' the man said in a leisurely drawl. He seemed to think there was no urgency. A shudder of apprehension, which caught Nicholls by surprise, and then he was standing under the wing, wind dragging him, weight resting on his left foot, looking back at the jump-master as the book said he should. He had not consciously done anything to get here. The repeated ground drills had taken him straight through the nastiness of the exit, just as he had intended they should. The American studied him critically for a second, then lifted a gloved thumb and roared: 'GO!'

As Nicholls pushed away and snapped into a perfectly balanced, symmetrical spreadeagle of arms and legs he looked up at the aircraft from which he could just hear the high-pitched croak of the cockpit stall warning. The instructor was half-leaning out of the door as casually as though it were a garden gate, one thumb still raised and still grinning. Then Nicholls found himself jerked off balance and vertical, feet to earth. The olive green canopy

82

above him burst open like a flower, appeared to collapse upon itself, then opened again. 'All right,' Nicholls told himself. 'It's only "breathing". It's all right.'

His hands, blue with cold, grasped upwards and found the steering toggles. He pulled left and the canopy turned that way, swinging him outwards as it did so; then right. It was calm and silent, save for a whisper of breeze through the rigging lines. The sun reflected from the toecaps of his newly polished boots, and far below him oblivious toytown motorists queued up at a T-junction in their tacky little machines. He felt like God. *Wind direction. Must remember to check wind-drift*. On the airfield, the windsock pointed away from him, if somewhat limply.

At about seven hundred feet he turned upwind to reduce the speed of the canopy and ensure a safe backward landing which would present only the smoothest contours of his body to the approaching earth. For what seemed a long time he held this position, head and elbows tucked in, feet and knees together and slightly bent. Then the ground, remote as a photograph until now, bounded out of its static frame. *Relax, relax. Don't reach for it and . . .* the earth embraced him, bouncing him playfully as if he had been brought down in an elegant rugby tackle. The canopy was still inflated and he was dragged a few feet before he could struggle up and out of the frost, running round the canopy to collapse it before it dragged him further. In spite of the cold, he was sweating and, worse, trembling slightly. 'Adrenalin in this sport,' as the Yank had put it, 'is liquid and brown and it runs down the back of your legs.'

After that day Nicholls's progress was swift. It took just two weeks of fine weather for him to go through the training card of dummy ripcord, real freefall – opening his own parachute after a three-second delay in the same stable posture he had used on the static line – and on through the exacting process of learning 360 degree turns, back loops, front loops, dive exits from the aircraft and – with arms and legs swept back into a delta wing shape – to track across the sky at sixty miles per hour. His exit height had increased from three thousand to twelve thousand feet or more.

He was making progress in other ways. The beard disappeared and, although there was always a wariness about him which marked him as a loner among the small permanent population of jump addicts at the drop zone, some of the old sparkle that had made him a good man in a tight military situation was returning. With the lengthening days he began to learn to fly in earnest, linking up with others in star formations, doughnuts and diamonds in the infinitely variable medium of terminal velocity which younger, more romantically inclined men described as 'sky dancing'. To complete the transformation he replaced his traditional round parachute with a formidable machine oblong in shape, comprising seven individual cells and a total off 220 square feet of ram-air inflatable wing capable of flying into the wind and covering a vast area.

At night, alone in the caravan, he would dream of wealth. He dreamed not in an abstract way as some men dream about Eldorado, or next year in Jerusalem, but in the practical manner of someone who knows he has won a fortune from a football pool and awaits only the confirmatory cheque. Golly, as he had confided to his partner Shakespeare during his first hours out of prison, had a plan.

Towards the end of Nicholls's 'training' period, Shakespeare joined him as he did routinely from time to time, at Air Adventure. In the neat, tidy way of the professional soldier, the Yorkshireman kept all his old skills in good repair and these included basic parachuting. He had long since been overtaken in skill by Nicholls, but this did not concern him. As he put it: 'You go ahead and become a bloody sky-god if you want, Nicholls. All I need is to be able to spot myself out of plane, get out and get stable in freefall and open bloody canopy at right height.'

On a Sunday evening when the club bar was coming to life and a group of first jumpers from Oxford University were excitedly describing their exploits to one another, a pretty, slightly built woman with short, dark, boyish hair began to encourage their boasts until one of the more alert among them asked, 'Have you ever tried it . . . parachuting, I mean?'

'Yes, a bit,' she replied.

'Freefall?'

'Now and again.'

'How many?'

'About eighteen hundred,' she said. 'One day, if I can only apply myself to this sport, I might start to get the hang of it.'

The regulars immersed themselves in electronic games, or snooker, or food, or chatting-up any beginner who was female, young and seducible. For them, the day's jumping was already forgotten. What mattered now, as chronic existentialists, was this hour, this moment, and since it was too dark to parachute, they would turn to some other diversion from the immense boredom of ordinary life.

Away from the crowd at a corner table, beer between them, sat Nicholls and Shakespeare. The girl drifted towards them. Her T-shirt bore the message: 'Three great lies, all told by men!'

'All right then, Bonny, tell us your three great lies,' said Nicholls.

'Well, they're all told by men around any drop zone.' Solemnly, she held up petite fingers and counted them off. 'The first is, *You don't need to worry, I had a vasectomy. The second is, You don't need to worry, I won't come in your mouth.*' Shakespeare frowned into his glass, embarrassed.

Golly grinned appreciatively. 'Someone's been perspiring – I mean gossiping – about me again,' he said. 'So what's the third great lie?'

'Well, before you came here we had George Alpha, a chartered DC-3 Dakota, and they told us you couldn't get hurt jumping the beast. So the third great lie is, *You don't need to worry 'cos you can't get hurt jumping George Alpha.*'

'Who got hurt?'

'My fiancé. He bounced off the tailplane, got knocked unconscious and whistled in all the way from thirteen grand. I followed him out of the aircraft and saw it happen. I flew down right behind him but I couldn't catch him. Stood to attention on my head and tore after him, but

I couldn't damn-well catch him. Then I was down to seven hundred feet with four seconds left before I creamed in myself and I made a mistake. I opened my rig.

'He wasn't a jump bum. He was the only real man I ever knew and this damned sport robbed me of him. She picked up Nicholls's glass and took a long, deep draught. 'Only decent human being I ever met on a DZ,' she murmured, studying Golly carefully. 'The rest of you are the pits.'

Bonny moved on and the two men turned back to their beer. 'Never think she was a schoolteacher would you?' said Nicholls. 'Tell us something, Bill. What are you going to do when you're finished with Chevalier, or when Chevalier's finished with you?'

'Hadn't thought about it, kid.'

'Well, look, you're the wrong side of forty and so am I.'

'So what? I can still use a nine-milly better'n most of the lads still in t'regiment.'

'Yeah, fair enough,' Nicholls agreed. It was true, too. After training with an American anti-terrorist team, Shakespeare had returned as an ambidextrous gunman capable of a seventy-five per cent hit probability while firing from the left hand. It was a useful technique, particularly when the room being hit was equipped with doors hinged on the right. 'What I mean is,' Golly persisted, 'you'll want to do something else, sometime; something that makes you independent. You can't guard wankers all your life. We've both been on other people's payrolls too long.'

'I'm not complaining, sunshine. The money's great. The only hardship about BG work is the boredom. These prats we look after don't need a bloody bodyguard most of the time. They want a minder like they want a Rolls-Royce and an Afghan hound and an under-age blonde. You'll find out.'

'Yeah well, that's what I mean . . . What would you do if you were *really* rich – all the money you wanted?'

'I dunno. Here, yes I do, though. I'd keep pigeons.'

'Pigeons? Bloody pigeons?'

'Aye, racing birds, homing birds. I'd have the biggest

loft in the country. My dad used to breed them back of our cottage. He were a gamekeeper. Any bird lost three races, one after t'other, he strangled. Survival of the fittest, he called it. He was a hard old rascal. Once followed a squirrel so he could rob it of its nut hoard just before winter . . . Actually, I'd prefer falcons but that can be a bit dodgy in this country. There's laws against knocking off other people's game with falcons.'

'Why falcons?'

'Not just falcons,' Shakespeare replied, fingertips linked in concentration. 'Any decent hunting bird. A buzzard, eagle, anything. You can train any bird of prey to hunt with you. Turn them loose into the sky, flush out the game with dogs and then your hawk, or whatever, dives on it at about eighty miles an hour. I really got the bug in the Gulf. Wrote to you about it, didn't I? See, a bird of prey flies like an avenging angel. Get one trained properly, your own bird, see, and you practically read its mind. Aye and it reads your mind, too. You can march and fly all day, hunting. There's little kestrels in this country and they hover over their prey like the last judgement. Then there's your eagle. When it pounces on a rabbit it grabs it by the skull with its talons, spreads its wings over it so no other swine can see what it's caught. They call that "mantling". Then it crushes the skull like you or I could crush an egg in our hands. Unless you knew what was going on, you'd think your eagle was making love to the poor little bastard underneath it.'

'Bit like women,' said Nicholls.

'Hawks are much more reliable. Trouble is, you need hundreds of acres somewhere like Caithness to do it properly in this country. It's a millionaire's game.'

'What's the best hunting bird, then? I mean, the very best?' Nicholls was studying Shakespeare with intense interest.

'Oh, your Gyr Falcon. Dukes of Atholl, when they owned the Isle of Man, had to pay the King of England an annual rent of two of them. Outflies anything, even from a standing start on the ground, and most hunting birds can't do that. Most birds have to be already aloft, in pride of place as they say, before they catch owt. But not your Gyr. You only find it in Arctic Canada and Norway. They're protected. Even Arab princes can't get them these days, not at any price.'

'So a nice estate somewhere, and a cage full of Gyr Falcons, is something you wouldn't turn down . . . I mean,' said Nicholls, casually, 'it'd be better than doing BG jobs all your life?'

'Aye, a damn sight better. Best thing since the old times in the regiment. It's the boredom that's so killing these days. But I'll never have that sort of money.'

'You never know. That might be no problem. Get us another beer, Bill, and I'll tell you.'

When Shakespeare returned with the beer, Golly was leaning forward intently, as if at an operational briefing. 'Now, listen carefully, Bill. This is classified "top secret", "cosmic" and, furthermore, it's just between us. Not a word to anyone else, right?'

'Right.'

'Remember that politician bloke who left his clothes piled up on a beach and tried to disappear?'

'He got nabbed.'

'He got nabbed because a lot of people wanted his number. He was a big political wheel. If you or I disappeared, nobody would be particularly worked up over it. I mean, your old mum might wonder what had happened, but it wouldn't be the same as a Prime Minister going *awol*, would it?'

'I don't want to disappear. Why should I want to disappear?'

'Not you, mucker. Me. I disappear. But first, I take out a soddin' great life insurance policy, and when they decide I'm dead, you collect. Then we split the take, or use it to make more money, till we've got enough.'

'Eh up, Golly. Let's get this clear. You do a disappearing act and an insurance firm pays out? You're off your head, kid. It's like getting money out of the taxman, getting money from the insurance. When my old man died . . . Oh, forget it . . . they'd want to see the body, or a death certificate at least.'

'What they get,' Nicholls insisted, smiling, 'is a death certificate but not a body.'

'That means using a bent doctor,' Shakespeare objected.

'No way. It means getting a genuine death certificate. Listen, if someone disappears down a coal mine and they can't recover the body, there's an inquest, right? Everyone says, "We saw him go down in the cage and then creep along this gallery, and then there was this accident and half a ton of shit fell on him and we know he's dead." So a verdict of death by accident or something like that —'

'Misadventure,' said Shakespeare.

'Yeah, misadventure, and the guy's next of kin collects and cries all the way to the bank and they live happily ever after.'

Bill took a long and thoughtful draught of his ale, wiped his mouth with the back of his hand, and drank again.

'Where'd you get all this stuff about miners getting malleted, then?'

'In stir, prison,' Nicholls replied. 'From a law book. Halsbury's *Laws of England*, page one-o-five-six. It was practically compulsory reading in there and I was on the library waiting list for a year before I got it. What it says is,' Nicholls closed his eyes in concentration, '"Inquest without a body: Where a coroner has reason to believe that death has occurred in or near the area within which he has jurisdiction in such circumstances that an inquest ought to be held and that owing to the destruction of the body by fire or otherwise, or to the fact that the body is lying in a place from which it cannot be recovered, an inquest cannot be held in the ordinary way, he may report the facts to the Secretary of State, and the Secretary of State may, if he thinks it desirable, direct an inquest to be held touching the death. In preparing such a report the coroner should take all circumstances into account. If the body has been disrupted, valuable evidence would be the discovery of some vital organ. Discovering a limb, for example, is no proof of death." ' Nicholls opened his eyes and grinned triumphantly at this feat of memory. 'I like that last bit,' he said.

'How are you going to do it?' Shakespeare asked. 'I

mean, there's no coal mine round here. And which of your vital organs are you leaving around?'

Nicholls grinned again and pointed an index finger towards the ceiling. 'I disappear up there, at about twelve grand,' he said. 'I go to heaven without passing "Go". It can't fail. All you need to do, Bill, is pick up the money for us after the fuss is over.'

Shakespeare stifled the temptation to press his partner for details of exactly how the disappearing trick would be achieved, if only because he sensed that Nicholls would not reveal it. Instead, he said quietly, 'You get five years if it goes wrong. P'raps more. You're only on parole.'

'No way, mate. First, it won't go wrong because it can't go wrong. Like I say, I had years inside to think about this. I used to look at the sky through a few inches of window, wondering how it could be done. Then one day I latched onto the secret and it's dead simple. And as for you . . . well, they might have their suspicions but they wouldn't be able to prove a thing. And then they'd forget.'

'And you'd be dead? Legally dead, that is?'

'Yeah, as dead as that McAlister kid in Belfast or anyone else you know that's dead.'

'It means you've screwed yourself where Chevalier's concerned . . . everything else. . . . you'd be out on a limb. The regiment wouldn't touch you again. You'd be dead.'

'Wouldn't need to worry, would I?' Nicholls was still smiling. 'I mean, I'd be dead and rich . . . dead rich. As for the regiment, where were they when those bastard lawyers threw me to the wolves?'

'Look, Golly, this thing is a con, isn't it? I mean, a real, professional con. It's not just a giggle. And . – well, it sounds a bit daft, maybe – but I never thought of myself as a professional criminal. Nor you, neither.'

Nicholls leaned forward, the grin changing to an expression of profound hatred. 'Nor did I and nor did most of the guys in Bicester Prison,' he said with quiet venom. 'You don't need brain surgery at birth to go to prison, you know. Most of the blokes in there are the unlucky ones. That was the big lesson I learned inside.

Criminals are just people. The clever ones never go back. They've lost their virginity, that's all; after you've done time and come out again, that's all it adds up to. Killing somebody the first time's the hardest. I still remember the face of the first man I despatched . . . and I don't mean no student jumper from a Cessna, neither.'

By now the bar was becoming crowded with the well-modulated accents of the gliding and amateur flying fraternity and their slim, bitchy women. The parachutists were drifting away to the Bovver and fried scampi. Shakespeare still sat, lost in thought.

'So what do you think, then, old mucker?' his partner asked. 'Are you in or aren't you?'

'I want to have a think about it,' Shakespeare replied slowly. 'I'll be back here next weekend. We can chew the fat then.'

'Yeah, all right. But no word to anyone, right?'

'Right,' replied Shakespeare. 'I'd better hit the road. Got to be up early in London tomorrow.'

As he climbed into bed that night, she asked him, 'How's Golly?'

They had steered clear of the subject throughout a leisurely dinner and an even more languorous love-making on the deep carpet of the lounge, so as not to disturb the child. Then they had bathed together, whispering their shared laughter, and tiptoed to the bedroom, she conscious of her wet nakedness, to set the alarm clock to rouse Shakespeare at five a.m.

'Golly's fine, love. Happy as a pig in clover.'

'I'm glad. I've still got a soft spot for him, Bill, but it's no good looking back, is it?' In an abstracted way her forefinger, its long, elegant nail red against the brown skin of his chest, traced patterns on him which slowly faded as if written in invisible ink.

'You've got lovely skin,' she said. 'You know, I don't mean this in any nasty way – I don't mean Golly any harm – but sometimes I wish he'd just disappear. It sort of gives me the creeps sometimes, knowing he's wandering around just a few miles up the road. So like I say, I wish he'd disappear.'

Shakespeare stretched over her to extinguish the bedside lamp. As he did so he murmured, 'Happen he will, Maggie. Happen he will, one way or t'other.'

Back in London later that day, Shakespeare knocked respectfully on an open mahogany door. 'Can I have a word, boss?' he said. 'It's about Golly. I think we might have a bit of a problem.'

# Chapter Five

It was the last lift of the day and, in truth, they should not have gone so high. At fourteen thousand feet the setting sun stretched a long finger of admonition at them through a letter-box-shaped hole in a slab of black cumulus as it rolled in from the west. Through this hole, the dying sun's beams focussed like a pantomime spotlight, transmuting the aircraft wings to gold and reflecting specks of copper off every particle of moisture vapour between the aircraft and the ground. It was as if what awaited them outside was not empty space but some other medium – neither fire nor water nor air but something less tangible than all these – through which they might disappear from the world into another dimension as a result of their impertinence.

As the plane banked round to begin the run-in the same magical colour suffused its interior, burnishing their helmets, faces and jumpsuits. The earth, by now, was as dark as a sepulchre. Only the lights of the motorway and the orange glow of a city over the horizon offered some clue to their position. Even these, like the random dots of light from individual farms, were becoming obscured by the first insidious hints of encroaching cloud between the aircraft and the ground. Nicholls, on his knees at the open doorway, head arching out into space, estimated that they would whistle into the cloud at about six thousand feet. Assuming that the cloud was still quite thin, they should be well clear of the danger it presented of freefall collision by the time they had reached three thousand feet and break-off height. Meanwhile Nicholls, as jump-master, had to find the release point at which they would leave the aircraft.

Over his shoulders the others peered down with silent concentration. At his right was Bonny Richmond; immediately behind him was Bert Ingram, a police small-arms expert; on his left, Joe Chieu, the American. Up front the pilot eased back the throttle, the tension in his face unnaturally magnified by the instrument lights shining below his chin. They were all now convinced that Nicholls's scheme was an even greater miscalculation than it had seemed before they took off into the gathering dusk. Equally they knew it was too late to bottle out of the jump.

In the aircraft door, Nicholls's small, tense frame relaxed almost imperceptibly. 'Give me ten right!' he shouted. The pilot obediently swung the aircraft round to its new course, ten degrees to starboard.

On the ground, others were gathering round Marchmont, the chief instructor, and they were talking in subdued tones. 'Shut up! Shut up all of you!' Marchmont growled. Then, as he heard the drone of an engine far above, he turned upon the group and said, 'Get over to the control tower, one of you, and tell them to switch on the runway lights . . . Don't bloody walk, then. Run!'

Nicholls, content that the pattern of defective and partly extinguished motorway lights he had noticed from the ground – three were out on one side of the road, two on the other – were indeed the reference point he had been seeking, shouted, 'Cut!' As they prepared to get out of the aircraft he saw the runway lights come on immediately below them. From this altitude they resembled a sprinkle of glistening dew. Ivan Marchmont doing his thing. Well, a row had been coming anyway . . .

Nicholls clambered out of the plane, foot perched on a small step above the starboard wheel, hands grasping the wing spar. He hung out as far as he could and nodded to the others. Joe Chieu, who was to close fourth on the formation, slid round the outside door, left arm and leg spread against the fuselage, only his right hand and foot both still inside the aircraft to support his weight. For both men, exposed to the wind blasting them at almost one hundred miles per hour, the next seconds were a test of strength as well as nerve. Quickly and with great neatness, Bert Ingram joined Nicholls on the spar. As the heaviest man, he would fly base for the formation. Bonny Richmond, feline and alert, leaned forward from the door as if she were Ingram's shadow. All their bodies were now compressed into one tense, sweating mass, half in and half out of the tiny machine. Nicholls kept them poised like that for no more than a second before he shouted, 'Ready! Set! Go!' The pilot felt the aircraft rock as they disappeared into the golden mist below him: Ingram first, to clear the way for Bonny, who would have to pin him, followed by Chieu and finally Nicholls.

They did not fall. A fall, by definition, is an uncontrolled affair. Rather, they swept down as a peregrine falcon might fall upon its prey. Ingram's baggy jumpsuit, which looked like a clown's outfit on the ground, now flared on each side of him like huge wings stretched from elbow to waist as if he were a flying fox. With arms and legs fully extended to reduce his descent rate, he hung stable and solid on the same heading as the aircraft, reliable as a compass. Above him Bonny closed up her arms and legs into a compact, foetal package to fall fast. Then, with only a few feet between them, she slowly stretched her legs and dived to close the gap, her hands grasping Ingram's big wrists.

Both now flew face to face, rolling gently. Ten seconds had passed since they had left the Cessna and they were still accelerating towards terminal velocity, the wind already tearing at goggles and drawing flesh back from their cheek-bones as they smiled through the golden light. Nicholls and Chieu, legs tucked in, arms hanging behind their shoulders, rode down towards them like bats, Nicholls breaking into the formation from one side and Chieu from the other. The formation creaked and rocked, but held together. Twelve seconds gone. The four-man group encountered terminal velocity – one hundred and twenty miles per hour in the starfish, slow fall position – and all the jumpers felt its mysterious power taking hold of their bodies as if to remould them into more efficient flying machines. This was the speed at which the merest dip of a shoulder, foot or head could produce dramatic aerodynamic results, not all of them intended. The difference between this affair with the elements and the slow, ponderous sub-terminal jumping of the first twelve seconds out of the plane was what a grand prix racing car is to a family saloon, and they knew it as they grinned at one another in shared rejoicing. Whatever awaited them afterwards did not matter in this moment of ecstasy. They were vividly alive and uniquely free; the knowledge of it made them a little mad with happiness. Twenty seconds gone and the gold suddenly disappeared as they fell out of its reach and into a half-light which was neither night nor day.

Nicholls, looking round the formation, nodded slowly, deliberately, as a conductor might to his first violins. The team broke, wheeling round Ingram, the baseman, like seagulls, to build a diamond with Ingram at the front, Chieu and Nicholls on each of his legs and Bonny Richmond closing the formation by linking her arms to the two men's inner legs. They flashed through the murk of cloud, broke again and reformed the star, riding down the pitiless darkness to three thousand five hundred feet. Sixty seconds gone and Ingram, eyes fixed on his chest-mounted altimeter, broke free and waved his arms across his body. The others also broke from the formation now, turned instantly and dived away, arms and legs streaming behind them, to seek the sanctuary of clear sky in which to open their parachutes without entangling anyone else.

Under two hundred square feet of oblong, ram-air canopy each turned downwind, across the hangar, in single file and then upwind again, the canopies biting onto the stiff breeze that heralded the cloud, the cold front and the approaching storm. At about fifteen feet each jumper sank the steering toggles to hip level, increasing the canopy's angle of attack to stall point. The result was impressive. A bone-breaking rush towards the ground diminished to the walking speed of a geriatric ward. First Ingram, then Nicholls, Chieu and Bonny made comfortable, matter-of-fact, stand-up landings on the patch of illumination beside the bar.

Ivan Marchmont was a small, powerful man whose nervous eyes never rested anywhere for long. It was as if he knew that the whole world were one huge banana skin about to undermine the tenuous stability of the skydiving

96

centre he had patiently built up over ten years and long, colourful bank overdrafts. He awaited the nocturnal relative workers with the air of a man who has a duty to perform.

'You're all grounded, all of you, indefinitely,' he snapped.

Bonny, canopy clutched in front of her like a huge bath towel, ran to him and kissed him. 'Oh cummon, Ivan. That was a mind-blowing four-man. Don't be such a bear.'

'Grounded, I said. This isn't a Micky Mouse jump centre and I'm not standing for it. And where's that so-called pilot? I want a word with him.'

'But no one got hurt, Ivan! Golly Nicholls gave us a super spot.'

'Might have known he was at the bottom of this. Well, he's grounded along with the rest of you.'

Nicholls, playing his man with great delicacy, said, 'Fair enough, Ivan. I was pushing it, mate. It's down to me and I'm sorry.'

No one had heard Nicholls even hint of apologising to anyone on the drop zone before. Marchmont, aware of the interested audience growing round them, paused in his anger.

'Tell you what,' Nicholls added, as if he had just thought of the idea, 'when you let us out of the doghouse, why don't we set up a real night relly jump, near midnight, with you in charge of it?'

There was an excited murmur of collective interest from the group, loudest from those who were still only learning the basics of freefall flight.

Marchmont, struggling to conceal his relief at the absence of any casualties from Nicholls's escapade, also sensed that Nicholls's instant and respectful tribute to the chief instructor's authority was blended, very finely, with a challenge to his own parachuting nerve. He replied, 'This isn't the time or place to discuss it . . . In any case, it would be hell's delight getting Civil Aviation clearance . . . we've got enough trouble with the neighbours already about daylight jumping. After this epic of yours tonight, God knows what the hangover will be.'

Over the next few days the scheme developed its own momentum, particularly among the four who were grounded. In the bar, others clustered about them as they drew diagrams on pieces of paper and argued about where identification lights should be worn. Marchmont, who combined painstaking casualty-avoidance with careful, deliberate innovation, found it unexpectedly easy to obtain official clearance for a single pass over the airfield with the biggest jump ship available, a twin-engined DC-3, at twelve thousand feet. The jump was to take place at ten-thirty, half an hour after dusk.

A week after Nicholls and his team had made their unauthorised descent, the chartered Dakota rumbled away into the dusk with a dozen of the club's most experienced skydivers. This time Marchmont himself was jump-master; the aircraft would be guided to the release point by ground control and the pilot would decide when they were over the spot. There were limitations. The formation was to be a simple star with no attempts at more elaborate manoeuvres. Anyone who had not broken into the formation by five thousand feet could forget it.

At the pre-jump briefing Marchmont, his worried eyes more restless than ever, repeated, 'Remember, you won't be able to see the ground until you are almost on it, and if you're still in freefall that will be too late. The ground shall rise up and smite thee! The problem is disorientation. So we stick rigidly to a break-off at four thousand five hundred feet, lots of separation, and canopy opening at three thousand five hundred feet. That gives you ample time – over eight seconds – to track away and still be under canopy about one thousand five hundred feet higher than usual. If you have even a suspicion that your main canopy has malfunctioned, don't try to work out what has gone wrong. Don't try to repack it on the way down. You will – I repeat, will – chop it away instantly and deploy your reserve. Is that understood?'

Everyone nodded solemnly. The adrenalin was flowing. For these people, all experienced parachutists, the energy it generated was deliberately concentrated upon the job in hand. Such control was at the heart of their sport. Each of them had learned it through repeated exposure to a lot of fear. Just one of the group announced he was going for his nervous pee. It provoked no particular comment. They had all reacted that way at some time, and would do so again.

There was reason to be nervous. For most of them this was the first night descent. After the light aircraft they had used until now, the Dakota, with its twin engines, seemed enormous and noisy. They heaved themselves up through the starboard door and into the echoing hull, emptied of its seats, to squat awkwardly on the floor. Marchmont counted them, then shouted to the pilot, 'Take it away!'

If there was a bad moment, it was this, as the engines revved to something like their maximum power in the last of the pre-flight checks. Then the machine ground forward, faster with every second, bumping and lurching and stirring stomachs. Marchmont controlled his own reaction by breathing deeply. Those nearest the door caught a last glimpse of the hangar, silhouetted by the lights of the bar beyond it, and then they lifted off into thin air. There could be no going back now. Nor would any of them wish to. As Joe Chieu told his freefall novices, 'My last instruction is, when you get into that star, you *smile*.'

During the twenty-minute climb to jump height, as they sat on the carpeted floor of the plane, no one spoke. Inside the fuselage only one faint red light was on, to preserve their night vision. Some of the group, eyes closed, worked over in their minds the flight manoeuvres this jump would require, hands and heads making small, birdlike movements as if they heard soundless music. Compared with the buoyant, jokey atmosphere of a collective effort on this scale by daylight, the atmosphere in the plane was quietly tense.

Furthest from the door, his back resting against the pilot's compartment, Nicholls gently touched his chest strap, his eyes peering at his nearest neighbour's altimeter . . . yes, his altimeter *was* working and it agreed with its neighbour that they were at twelve thousand feet. The Dakota banked sluggishly, pressing him against the side of the fuselage as it turned on the heading for the run-in over the drop zone. Between his legs rested the body of another jumper. Nicholls read the slogan painted on the back of the man's helmet and grinned. It said: *'Please do not wake for in-flight meals.'*

Slowly, like sleepwalkers, they rose to their feet, checking helmet straps, slipping goggles down, pulling on lightweight gloves. Moments later, at the first word of warning from the cockpit, 'Stand by!' Ingram and Chieu leaned towards the open door. As the first two 'floaters' they would have to cling to the outside of the fuselage on each side of the door while the rest of the formation crammed in and around it from within the aircraft. Marchmont, flying as base, had walked backwards into the door, holding Bonny Richmond's forearms for a linked exit which would leave no chance of muddle or wasted time at the beginning of the descent. Base was the least glamorous position but it gave him the best chance of keeping an eye on what was happening as everyone would fly to him, and he preferred things that way. The others pressed close around them like a rugby scrum.

'Ready!' shouted Marchmont, leaning imperceptibly backward, towards the open sky. Bonny and the others responded, leaning forward to his time. The sky dance began here.

'Set!' All leaned the opposite way, Marchmont pushing them back into the plane. 'Go-o-o!'

They flared out of the door into the darkness like one unbroken stream of light. Nicholls, at the back of the group, watched them go and then sat down again. The seconds passed painfully. He was alone in the darkened passenger section of the plane now, rejoicing at his isolation and terrified by it. The pilot, satisfied that the jump was successfully under way, opened up the throttle once more.

Marchmont counted the jumpers as they entered the formation. Just before they reached the agreed break-off height, there were ten in the star with at least one floating some yards away to his left about twenty feet below them. Even if the detached spare man de-arched now there was no hope of his closing the gap. But a ten-man at night was

100

good. Very good. Ten green shoulder lights, shaped like pencils, bobbed together like Christmas tree illuminations. Marchmont glanced at his altimeter, broke Bonny's grip on his sleeve and waved off the formation with a flamboyant sweep of forearms. He waited four seconds as everyone fled from him, then reached under the bottom right-hand corner of his container, tweaking out the small pilot parachute concealed there, held it away from him and released it. His main canopy unrolled smoothly out of the backpack. Around him the other canopies were cracking open and their triumphant owners whooped happily to one another.

'Skydive!' shouted the American. 'Skydive!'

The canopies banked against a full, yellow harvest moon like birds out of a science fiction story and swung down towards a circular pea-gravel landing pit illuminated by car headlights. In almost windless conditions the jumpers flared down to stand-up landings, and as they did so, champagne corks exploded about them from the edge of the pit.

Everyone talked and no one listened. Already intoxicated by freefall, they drank from the bottles as they passed among them. It was as if the parachutists were newly released victims of a long and dangerous siege.

'Right, kiddies, back to the hangar to debrief. And remember to give your names to Bonny as you go in. She's calling the roll.' In response to Marchmont's sonorous order they moved reluctantly in little groups up the grass track leading from the drop zone.

The debrief was a sobering affair. It turned obsessively on what had happened to Nicholls. His disappearance was so incredible that some of them glanced expectantly towards the door even as the obvious questions were being asked.

'Right,' said Marchmont after twenty minutes had passed. 'He's in trouble and we have to find him. Bert Ingram: will you telephone your mates on the local force and tell them we're working over an appropriate search area now? We'll keep them informed. Joe Chieu: bring us the photo of the DZ, mate, the big aerial photo.'

The photograph was set up on a stool and Marchmont went to work on it with a chinagraph pencil. 'We assume he left the aircraft at the same time as the rest of us and that he opened, or tried to open, his rig at three thousand feet and it malfunctioned. If it was a total "mal" and he didn't get his reserve out, then allowing for freefall drift, he should be on the DZ about here, say a hundred yards from the pit. If he got the reserve out and still had trouble . . . well, he might have gone downwind somewhat, say as far as the chicken farm five hundred yards north, over here. So this shaded area is what we are looking at.'

Chieu and the others, with torches, left to start a box search of the area while Ingram was explaining the problem to the local force, whom he described fondly as 'the Noddies'. 'Squad car and blood wagon on the way, Ivan,' he called across the hangar to Marchmont. 'They say that on a Saturday night it'll make a change from breath-testing us.'

Ingram was a large, sad man with a sad, walrus moustache and drooping eyes which belied his legendary ability with any sort of pistol. Marchmont, still studying the air photograph, asked him, 'Bert, have you ever picked up anyone from a DZ after something like this?'

'Can't say I have, Ivan . . . Bits and pieces of flesh after an IRA bomb in London and one or two suicides on the old Underground, when I was a young PC.'

'Yeah, probably similar. Very messy. I once had to test-jump a canopy belonging to an old friend who'd died wearing it. First thing I had to do was wash the blood out. I put the rig in the bath at home and trod it out, like grapes . . .' He shrugged on a lightweight jacket. 'I'm off to the search area. Keep an eye on the phone till I get back. Then we'll rethink it all if Nicholls doesn't turn up.'

At midnight a second conference took place, this time with the local police present. The search team had combed the impact area exhaustively. All they had found in the wheat stubble was a ripcord handle dropped by an excited student making his first freefall jump the previous day. By now Marchmont, with characteristic thoroughness, was working on the next most rational hypothesis. This was that Nicholls had been the victim of a premature canopy deployment and had opened high. But in that case, why had he not simply turned in tight circles, down to the drop zone?

'Maybe,' Ingram suggested, 'he was injured and couldn't steer his canopy.'

'He might just have hit the tail on the way out,' Bonny said, deadpan. 'It's happened before.'

Ignoring this, Marchmont continued, 'If he opened high and travelled under canopy downwind from around twelve thousand feet the search area grows a bit. Anyone got an Ordnance Survey map?'

The local police sergeant brought one from the squad car, and Marchmont resumed his calculations. 'Wind, say, ten miles an hour plus maximum forward speed of canopy, that's another twenty-five miles an hour, descending at fifteen feet per second . . . eight hundred seconds, which is thirteen minutes under canopy or about a quarter of an hour at thirty-five miles an hour . . . say, almost nine miles. Could be more. Yeah, anywhere between the DZ and Hereford.'

'Nine miles, did you say?' the police sergeant asked. 'He could be in Hereford? Well, that's off our patch for a start. You've come to the wrong division.'

'Nine miles,' Marchmont repeated as if to himself. 'Or anywhere between. There are gravel pits, roads, high tension wires, the River Wye . . . He could have gone in anywhere.'

The police sergeant relaxed visibly. 'You haven't found a body, right? This is a missing person, no more'n that. Even then we'd want a report from his next of kin.' Turning to his driver he said briskly, 'Cummon, lad. We'll have some trade on the motorway by now. Them Rotarians have been wining and dining.' He paused at the hangar door and half-turned towards the parachutists. 'If we find him, we'll send him back.'

As he left the hangar he added, in a stage whisper, 'Daft buggers. It'll be flying saucers next.'

The ambulance crew more politely accepted a pint of beer apiece before departing. 'If anyone turns up in Casualty, we'll telephone you,' they promised.

Nicholls made a demi-flèche exit into the full blast of the slipstream, standing upright with his hands a few inches from his hips, and watched the aircraft stream away from him against the brilliant night sky. On the port wing, one red light glowed steadily, and on the tail another flashed orange. 'Just like Hereford disco in the old days,' he thought. Five seconds later he opened the rig, an all-black Pegasus canopy discreetly imported from the United States and packed into a container identical to the one he usually carried. It was a necessary precaution. Parachutists are obsessed not only by their own equipment but also that of their fellow jumpers. New gear would have prompted unwelcome questions. Satisfied that the new canopy was flying normally, he extracted a compass from the knee pocket of his jumpsuit and slipped it round his chest strap, alongside the altimeter. At eleven thousand feet he turned south, into the wind. In still air, the Pegasus would give a forward speed, in full glide, of twenty-five miles per hour . . . but against a wind strength of about ten miles per hour, descending at fifteen feet per second for seven hundred and thirty-three seconds – say, twelve minutes . . . three miles from the DZ, maybe four, allowing for the spot at which he guessed he left the plane. It was less than ideal, but by now Marchmont would be looking for him on a downwind route.

There was a further problem about the upwind route that night. It drove straight towards a densely wooded ridge about five hundred feet above the surrounding countryside. A tree landing was something he must avoid at all costs. The Malayan campaign had demonstrated that you didn't break trees on tree jumps: you broke your legs or your back. So it seemed that the target DZ would have to be the castle on top of the ridge or rather the parkland around the castle.

To gain as much forward speed as possible he let the

steering toggles up as high as they would go and lifted his feet to reduce drag. The canopy bucked forward and he was suddenly aware of the wind cracking noisily against the stabilisers as they flew vertically, like bunting, from each side of the canopy. Sure as hell, he thought, that will be audible on the ground.

At two thousand feet he saw the ridge ahead of him. The castle stood out in bold silhouette off to his left. He turned towards it, cutting at an angle across the wind. There could be turbulence down there . . . nasty. Lights! Lots of lights in the castle. And the sound of music. Bagpipes? They were playing bloody bagpipes down there. Either it was Scottish dancing or another Jacobite rebellion. Well, if it was a rebellion they couldn't leave that one to the regiment. Most of them were Scotsmen anyway. A few hundred yards short of the castle he made a series of spiral turns and then, at about five hundred feet above a dense wood, set himself up for a landing up the slope and into the wind. So far, so good, Golly lad; toggles down to shoulders on half-brakes and nicely lined up for a sufficient space between two oak trees.

There was something odd about the tree on the right. It was changing shape. Something very large, as big as a tree yet not a tree, it seemed to be waving at him. Only in the final seconds of the descent did he recognise the creature for what it was. The elephant turned to face him, its trunk raised in alarm, ears moving back and forth like radar antennae.

'Fucking hell!' he whispered. 'All I needed. A fucking wildlife park.' Instinctively he pulled down violently on the left toggle to steer away from the creature. The canopy lashed round like a bolting horse, swinging him outwards. In the next second he had crashed sideways into the tree, simultaneously aware that he had been winded and that there was a searing pain somewhere in his ribs. Then he was hanging motionless, his feet suspended above the ground, his canopy a shredded mess in the branches above him, helmet pushed over his eyes, his mind trying to fend off a remorseless unconsciousness that settled over him like night itself. He did not know how long he remained like that. When he started to come round he was aware of being touched from head to toe with great gentleness by something soft, cool and hairy. The probe explored his helmet, cheeks, neck, armpits, crotch and finally his feet. It exuded an odour of fresh grass.

Nicholls opened one eye, wondering if this was Malaya or Borneo. The elephant, whose trunk was fingering him, was apparently well disposed as well as inquisitive. 'Piss off,' Nicholls growled. The animal backed off a pace or two, ears flapping, then leaned forward again, extending its trunk towards him. From the castle a few hundred yards away the sound of the Gay Gordons clattered across the park. In front of the building, on a terrace of remarkable white stone, a couple in evening dress embraced. 'Piss off,' Nicholls said again, more vigorously. Jesus, the pain! The elephant, he now noticed, loomed over him. He peered down to discover that his feet were no more than six inches above the ground.

Gingerly he unhitched the velcro tabs securing his legs. One effect of this was to tighten the harness across his chest. The pain became even more intense, but at least he could touch the ground now with his toes. With slow, deliberate care and in spite of the pain, he unhitched the chest strap, then stumbled and finally rolled into a ball of hurt on the grass, where he lay for several seconds. His mind was simultaneously grappling with two basic problems. The first was whether his back was broken. The second was how to recover the rig from the tree. He also glimpsed the grotesqueness of his situation. It was no more ridiculous than most of his experience as a Special Forces soldier, but this time he was out on his own, beyond the law, with no radio, no helicopter waiting to casevac him to hospital. He was not even carrying morphia. The sense of isolation was suddenly threatening and he thrust it away. Instead, he concentrated first on wriggling his toes. He could. That should mean that his spine was still approximately where it was supposed to be. Next he swivelled his head from side to side. Nothing wrong with the old traverse. It was when he slid a cautious hand round to his left armpit that he found the pain. There was a bit of damage there. He breathed deeply, carefully. Lungs apparently undamaged. OK, Golly, he told himself, worst case is that you have a cracked or broken rib which hasn't punctured anything inside, mate, so you can stop whingeing. Maybe, at best, just badly bruised. So on your feet.

He struggled upright and walked a few cautious steps back and forth, raised his arms slowly up and down, and then turned his attention to the rig. The harness, reserve container and chest strap with its altimeter and compass were within easy reach, below head height, but the risers and rigging lines looped upward into the dark foliage above him. From the gloom of an adjoining paddock he heard the deep-throated growl of a lion, as if the devil himself were snoring. On the terrace beside the castle, the woman's evening dress had slipped off her shoulders and her escort was kissing her naked breasts. The elephant, standing a few yards from Nicholls, whisked its ears uneasily, turned about, and moved off. The creature's ponderous bulk and silence in movement were an eerie combination. It was like some big ship slipping away from a quay.

Ignoring these distractions, Nicholls reasoned that the canopy, since it had supported his weight, was well snagged on the branches and that he was not going to recover all of it. The most important thing was to make it as inconspicuous as possible. From a pocket in the left sleeve of his jumpsuit he extracted the knife he always carried as a last resort for dealing with canopy entanglements in the air with other jumpers. It was the work of seconds to razor through the lines on one side of the harness. Then he teased and hauled the gear away from the tree. The shredded remains of the canopy followed. None of the seven cells was undamaged, yet the block nylon construction of the material ensured that it hung doggedly together, if only by a whisker here and there, so that no clue to his arrival was left. It was a bonus he had not counted on, and it stifled the doubts he had felt only fifteen minutes earlier as he lay on the ground. He now set to work methodically to roll the canopy into a small, tight bundle which he repacked roughly into the container, lashed together with spare rigging line. Having checked the ground to ensure he had forgotten nothing, he walked away towards the perimeter fence. The lugubrious shape of the elephant padded after him. The couple on the terrace were now horizontal, and out of sight.

The fence, when Nicholls found it, proved to be of chain metal and about fifteen feet high, curved outward at the top. A six-inch gap below the fence would permit him to slide the parachute gear through, but it was insufficient for Nicholls himself. There was nothing for it but to climb over. As he attacked the fence, fingers clawing though the chain link, rib-soled track shoes braced against it, the elephant fondled him again. Cursing the animal, he had reached the top of the fence when its trunk curled about his body, gently but firmly plucked him off and set him back on the ground again.

Nicholls paused, sweating from the pain in his side as much from the effect of the climb, and took stock of the situation on the other side of the fence. What he had taken to be a road between the fence and some trees a few yards away he now perceived for what it really was, a deep cutting. To drop from the top of the fence, as he had intended, could have been fatal or – even worse – a short route to the paraplegic ward. He recalled the map and immediately remembered the railway. The cutting followed the line of the ridge. It was one of the many potential hazards of this drop. If he could find a way into it, this would be a good route out of the place.

It was some time before he discovered the way. He found a route over the fence with the help of a sapling growing from the embankment above the cutting. Cautiously, he slid down the silver birch, holding it almost exclusively with his right arm. The left arm, by now, was almost immobilised by the pain from his injured ribs. He sat on the ground, suddenly weak and tired. Through the mesh behind him, a familiar trunk pressed gently towards him; it struck Nicholls that the animal had been trying to save him from his own stupidity. Well, he wasn't the first. Nicholls unzipped his jumpsuit, reached into the pocket

108

of the denim jacket he wore beneath it, found a large bar of chocolate and broke it into two equal portions. 'Thanks, Jumbo,' he murmured. The end of the trunk closed round the offering like a sea anemone, and the creature went away, content at last.

From the trees across the cutting, an owl hooted. Nicholls could just see the shadow of the tunnel entrance, about two hundred yards to his right, with one green light glowing alongside it. He retrieved the parachute. The rig was light, less than twenty pounds, but the compressed nylon against his back made him sweat profusely. He tucked goggles and gloves inside his jumpsuit. As a precaution against accident during the climb down to the cutting, he wore the helmet. It was essential to get away before daylight. Already the nocturnal sounds of the countryside were growing as small animals awoke and scurried about their business. If they were not yet awake, then at the very least the fields and hedge-rows were turning in their sleep.

The brown sandstone slabs at the entrance to the tunnel were dry and rich in handholds. As he dropped the last six inches onto the gravel beside the track he heard a woman laughing, or perhaps crying, from the direction of the castle. He sympathised with the bloke. You could never be sure how they would react afterwards. Ten yards into the tunnel he felt secure enough to check the map. In the light of a pencil torch he noted that Westingholt Station was about three miles away. With luck he would be there before the staff arrived. He could use the station gents to clean up and shave off his moustache, then take the first train to anywhere. Impatient to be gone, he hastily stripped off the baggy jumpsuit and extracted the plastic fertiliser bag concealed within it. The parachute gear, lumped shapelessly inside the sack, was only slightly incongruous. The denim jacket and jeans he wore beneath the jumpsuit were nondescript garments now, stripped of the souvenir patches which had made him instantly recognisable at any distance on the DZ.

He started walking. He wished Bill were with him to share the big moment. He'd done it. He'd bloody well done it! Bill would have said, as he always said, 'Listen, sunshine, you may think there's a light at the end of the tunnel, but watch out, 'cos its probably a train coming the other way.' Grinning into the darkness, Nicholls humped the sack onto his good right shoulder and began walking. The walls, slick with damp and fungus, reminded him briefly of the Belfast sewer. But this time he was the train coming the other way. Or as an American Special Forces buddy once put it, 'Yeah, though I walk through the valley of the shadow of death, will I fear no evil, for I am the meanest motherfucker in the goddamn valley.'

If he had any lingering doubt, it was about how Maggie, young Cheryl and maybe even Bonny might receive the news of his disappearance. He also knew that when the job was done, he would be able to make it up to them. He'd be rich and they'd have to take notice of that. Already he was within arm's reach of another sort of freedom, the freedom of a new identity.

Later that morning, at Paddington Station, he extracted a package from an automatic luggage locker. Everything – new clothes, passport, national insurance card and driving licence in the name of James Duncan of Liverpool – was intact. Duncan, as Nicholls has been careful to establish, was in an old people's ward and had been happy to sell his identity for a bottle of Scotch. Soon afterwards, hair restyled in a crew cut and dressed in an anonymous suit, he left Victoria Station on the lunchtime train to Brighton.

By now two alert schoolboys, whose rear garden spread its toes into the River Wye, had noticed something snagged on the stones beneath a bridge fifty yards away. They found a blue and white parachute canopy and a white helmet bearing the name 'Nicholls'. They told their mother, who did nothing until next morning, when she heard a local radio news bulletin. Immediately she telephoned the police, who recovered the items and took them for identification to Ivan Marchmont at Air Adventure Sports. Then, when an extensive search had failed to find Nicholls, they notified the local coroner.

# Chapter Six

Somewhere in front of him, shrouded in the gloom that held the half-slumbering bodies of the orchestra on the right and the Margate Ladies on the left, Shakespeare became aware of an unmelodious but rhythmic whistle, a sort of half-snore. It was late afternoon in the world outside but in here, with the blinds down, the atmosphere was that of night. He also noted that waiting in these circumstances was beginning to corrode even his wakefulness. It had been seven hours now since Air Traffic had curtly informed them that they must wait for someone authorised to talk to them. In spite of Shakespeare's efforts to stay alert, his mind turned back to images of Margaret: Maggie in her split skirt and Maggie naked after their shared baths, Maggie pirouetting with the only bunch of flowers which he, or probably any man, had ever sent her. There was one particularly sharp image. She sat before an oval mirror, a towel about her slender waist, otherwise naked. A blue ribbon held her long blonde hair in place. In one hand, a small bottle of perfume, while the fingers of the other caressed the neck just below her jaw. There was something about the movement of her fingers just then, a slow, circular movement, which acted on him like an aphrodisiac. And afterwards, betrayal. . . He suppressed the rest, reminding himself that such dreams were notorious in his guerrilla warfare days. Evans-the-Hunch, who got his in Belfast in spite of his university education, called this state of mind – what was it? – 'the auto-obituary'. As he stifled that fading family album, it was instantly replaced by the image of a white buzzard he had trained, the Snowbird, which he had launched on fine mornings over moorland. He attributed such unwanted memories to simple dehydration; calling Diana Garrard, he ordered drinking water for himself and his partner on the flight deck.

111

When she appeared at Major Tom's elbow, she carried a handwritten note as well as a plastic beaker. The note said:

*Dear Major Tom,*

*All this waiting around is somewhat boring for us all, even if it is inevitable. The musicians would like a chance to understand what you are trying to do. How would you like to meet some of us for a discussion? It could be a profound education for everyone. At least it would help us to pass the time.*

*Yours, Gregor Kazanovitch*

'Tell him I'll think it over,' Major Tom instructed the stewardess. 'Now, how do I pick up Radio Four?'

'Not on any of this equipment, Major. Why don't you use my tranny?'

She was standing close, her thigh just touching his shoulder. He raised an arm, slipped it round her waist, and she relaxed her body further against his. 'And where do you keep your tranny?' he asked.

His hand drew slow, confident lines across her buttocks. She giggled, excited by the anarchy that this man had introduced into the regular, disciplined world of Captain Kilvert, for whom the aircraft merited the reverence others bestowed upon their church. 'Not there, Major Tom. There isn't room.'

His hand was inside her skirt now and her thighs flexed with the excitement of it. 'In my position, Miss Diana,' he said quietly, 'I can't be too careful, can I? I shouldn't leave any stone unturned.'

Encouraged by his hand, her legs opened. She was wearing no underwear. His fingers found the hairline and made fine scratches along it with surgical precision. Then, very gently, he stroked her clitoris until her thighs shuddered uncontrollably.

She, still trembling but suddenly sober, said, 'I'll get that radio.'

As she left, Major Tom inhaled appreciatively the odour still clinging to his fingers. When this operation was over, if not before. . .

\* \* \*

The BBC News at six p.m. led on the hijack. On a Saturday such a story was a godsend to hard-up news editors seeking an alternative to sport and the usual round of political speeches. Major Tom noted that the report included the line: *'The hijackers' aims are not yet clear, though reports from Holland, their last stopping place before their arrival at Prestwick earlier today, speak of demands made by a hitherto unknown body calling itself the Toxteth Liberation Army.'*

Another hour passed, and the flight-phobic member of the Margate Ladies' Choir surfaced from her drugged state in a sporadic bubble of sniffles. At last the hiss of static on the aircraft VHF link to the control tower was broken by a voice which said from the cockpit loudspeaker: 'Hello, Juliet Bravo. Do you read me? Over.'

'Juliet Bravo. We read you. Over.'

'My name is Colonel Wainwright. What is your name?'

'You can call me Major Tom.'

'We'd like to clarify a few things, Major Tom. Our first concern, as yours must be, is for the safety of the passengers. And the crew, of course. So long as they suffer no misfortune, we can guarantee that your lives will not be at risk either. Do you understand that?'

'There's no danger to the passengers or crew if they, and you, do as you are told,' Major Tom replied.

His mind was racing over several possibilities. Could it be Tim Wainwright? If they had recalled Wainwright, was it as a one-off for this operation? Did they already have his I/D? That should be impossible. His cover, starting with a valid death certificate and the doctored passport of Jim Duncan of Liverpool, plus an American passport for the trip to Oslo and the existing 'Major Tom', was as deep as the Maginot Line.

While they had been fighting in Oman, Wainwright was not a bad sort as ruperts – officers – went. Then he remembered coming down from the dock in Belfast, and Wainwright waiting to hand him over to the Ulster screws with a 'Sorry, Golly. We must look at the possibility of an appeal. Meanwhile, don't worry. You're to be flown to England today.'

He remembered his answer then and he didn't regret it

113

now. 'You can piss off, Wainwright. You and the rest of the regiment's thrown me to the wolves. This wouldn't have happened before we were amalgamated. You can stuff your appeal, your Army, your law-and-order and your regiment right up your rotten little jacksie.'

Now, in very different circumstances, here was Wainwright again, 'Next thing I want to discuss –'

'Listen, Wainwright,' Major Tom interjected, 'we aren't working to your agenda. We're working to mine. Why haven't you broadcast our demands? Why is there no money up front? If you're acting in good faith, you should have had that lot jacked up by now and we could release the female passengers. As it is, I already have a bird here needing medical attention. So what's the problem then, Colonel? Having trouble getting our act together back at Cobra, are we? Take your soddin' finger out, lad.'

'One thing at a time,' Wainwright replied.

'No. There's no point in you talking to us until we get some results. Don't call us. We'll call you in two hours.'

'The bastard,' murmured Wainwright as the link with the aircraft was cut. 'He's stolen one of my best lines.'

The taunting voice of Major Tom, heard for the first time undistorted by airborne recording equipment, confirmed his sergeant-major's intuition. Wainwright was convinced now that one of the hijackers was that insubordinate little fucker Nicholls . . . Nicholls, ready to crow the moment he thought he had you by the short and curlies. Dead or not, it had to be Nicholls. Frowning, he lifted a second telephone.

' 'Scuse me, sir. Urgent telephone call for you.'

'I'll take it in the secretary's office.'

Armed with a tonic water fortified with a slice of lemon, Brigadier Vincent Butcher, Director of Special Forces, loomed over the nodding heads in the club bar. The heads, as usual on this first Saturday of the month – the president's night – were fighting over old battles, re-igniting old quarrels, selling one another anything from life insurance to time-shares, and collecting the gossip from those who were still serving. The pink list, with its recommendations for promotion to half-colonel, was overdue. As a result, Butcher was obliged to demolish three rumours about members of his team at Group HQ before he could slip out of the bar, past the specially commissioned portrait of the Queen Mother, and down the creaking stairs to the private telephone.

'Butcher.'

'Wainwright. I'm on an open line, as you know. I need to talk to you on a secure line, sir. We've got a very tricky PR problem up here.'

'It's your operation, Tim.'

'I know that. I also think you should know the backwash which could result from this one. It's an in-house problem.'

'What's that supposed to mean?'

'Sorry to be cryptic, sir. Let me put it this way. Some of *them* might have been – probably were – some of us a short time ago.'

'So?'

'Means they know the drill, for a start. Also means the media could have a field day at our expense, whatever the outcome.'

'Who's involved?'

'D'you remember our man in Bicester? Another might be his former partner, the Bard.'

'Yes, I think I'm with you.'

'I'd suggest when we get the I/D confirmed we don't release that to the Cobra briefing. You know what Whitehall is. Some of the hatchet men would use it to chop us for good.'

'That must be your decision. I repeat, it's your operation.'

'But this has a domestic dimension. That's why I thought you should know.' Wainwright spoke with slow, deliberate emphasis. His chief was one of the Army's self-loading rifle generation, using a weapon whose sonics were not measured before it was issued. He was therefore notoriously deaf in one ear. This time Wainwright wanted to be sure the deafness was not political.

'Yes, I see that. So how are you going to play it?'

'Very soft. We go along with them.'

'Give in, just like that?'

'They can have their party political. The guts of it have been leaked by the Dutch anyway, so they score no new points if the stuff is confirmed and broadcast. The money's the only other firm demand. There's no way they can escape with that quantity of paper. It's simply too much to shift. They're trapped in that aircraft, or any other they take.'

'Parachutes?'

'No point. They still can't shift such a weight of paper, wherever they go. So my strategy is to play it their way, get the other people to safety as quickly as possible and then bore them into surrendering, however long it takes. The psychologist believes it will work and I agree with him. Any other course, in my view, could be fatal to our image with HMG. Arguably, it could result in the end of the organisation. Amalgamation hasn't helped, but this-'

'Right. But on no account must the media know we're buying them off, even as a temporary expedient.'

'I'd like your support at the next Cobra briefing, sir.'

'I wasn't intending to be there at this early stage. No one's dead yet, so far as we know.'

'The next briefing, sir, is in about two hours, at twenty-two hundred.'

'How're you getting there?'

'RAF to Northolt, then staff car.'

'I'll see you there.'

Next, Wainwright telephoned Downing Street's chief press officer, Harold Mackie. Mackie was more than an official mouthpiece. His robust way with eminent lobby correspondents and ministers alike had earned him informal policy-making powers of the sort normally discovered among non-elected officials in an American rather than a British administration. After a lifetime in political journalism, his appointment to a senior position in the Civil Service administrative grade had caused much grief among the regular mandarins. They did not admire his habit of smoking Woodbine cigarettes while sitting with his scuffed shoes on his desk, occasionally picking his nose. He had the Prime Minister's confidence, not least because he worked compulsively. Thus he was to be found this Saturday evening, a lean, saturnine, bespectacled figure, alone in his office. He was busy analysing the early editions of the serious Sunday newspapers. All were leading on the hijack, a fact which had driven a major speech by the PM on Common Market farm prices round the corner onto page two. That alone would not please the Leader, Mackie reflected. So when the scrambler telephone rang, he assumed that the call was from Chequers.

'It's Colonel Wainwright, Mr Mackie. I called in the hope I would see you at tonight's Cobra committee.'

'Yes, I'll be there. Where are you just now?'

'At the scene of operations. I've been thinking about your remarks at the earlier briefing today and I endorse the strategy you proposed. I think the FCO might swing our way if we let them know why the French are so wound up over this conductor chap, Kazanovitch. Seems he's the brother-in-law of the French Culture Minister, a Monsieur René Martin. The Martin family, I'm told, are part of the wallpaper of French politics. They're very powerful. But to shift the Treasury we'll need the backing of the PM and, possibly, the Inner Cabinet.'

Mackie was pleasantly surprised by Wainwright's dedication to his own, non-violent approach. As he put it, 'You boys don't win any medals for low-profile solutions as close to home as this. Fleet Street don't like it much, either. Like Nero watching his gladiators, they like a bit of blood, you know.'

Wainwright then telephoned the Cobra centre itself.

'Sergeant-major, it's Colonel Wainwright. Your suspicions about the opposition up here might be correct. I want you to rouse the Ops Officer at Hereford and arrange for mug-shots of Nicholls and his old partner, Staff Shakespeare, to be brought up here.'

'Shakespeare's picture? Bill wouldn't touch a caper like this with a dung fork, boss.'

'Well, someone's riding shotgun with Nicholls. If one of them is Nicholls, the other half has to be Shakespeare. No harm in checking. . . Oh yes, and while you're on to Wingate, ask them to bring Mrs Nicholls up here.'

'I don't think much of that idea, boss.'

'Why not?'

'You obviously didn't hear that Golly's wife remarried. Her new husband's Sergeant Collison, and he's training with the team on the other kite up at Strathallan at this moment. Since he's adopted Golly's nippers –'

'Damn . . . Wait one, though. Collison doesn't need to know we've brought Mrs Nicholls into play.'

'Sorry, sir,' said the sergeant-major in a tone of reproof reserved especially by senior NCOs for errant officers. 'It's more complicated than that.'

'How's that, then?'

'See, sir, if it is Bill Shakespeare in there wi' Golly, then its double trouble for the ex-Mrs Nicholls. See, while Golly was inside, Bill was sniffing round Margaret and doing all right out of it. Rumour was that Bill was the father of her second, the one who was born after Golly died.'

'I didn't hear any of this.'

'You wouldn't, but it was all round the sergeants' mess.'

'Very interesting,' Wainwright said. 'Very interesting indeed. Thanks, sergeant-major.'

To Wainwright's considerable relief the Cobra conference went 'very much in the right direction'. With the Treasury isolated he got backing for the broadcast and payment of the first fifty thousand pounds – also tentative approval, once the hostages were released, for payment of the remaining ransom. Wilkins, the Treasury spokesman, angrily demanded and got an official minute instructing him to draw the cash that night from the Bank of England duty officer. Still grumbling, he disappeared into the night in search of a taxi, and a suitcase large enough to accommodate the banknotes. Mackie also hurried away to summon his favourite lobby man to an unattributable briefing. The demands of the Toxteth Liberation Army would be quoted in full, with a little official garnish that 'it is understood in Whitehall that the Government rejects any mediation by any foreign power, however friendly'. As a new lead to the only big running story, it was certain to capture the late night headlines.

Wainwright was locking his briefcase when his chief, Brigadier Butcher, appeared at his elbow.

'Well played, Tim. Now we've got a bit of tapestry to add to your excellent scenario.'

'What's that, sir?'

'This is to be treated as top secret. I've spoken to the PM in the light of our earlier chat on the telephone. It seems to us that once all the hostages are released, after payment of the full ransom, the chances of random casualties are greatly reduced if the aircraft has to be stormed. After all, you have only five airline crew and the two targets left on board. We then have two dead terrorists who might or might not be Nicholls and Shakespeare. Nicholls is legally dead already, of course, and Shakespeare has no next of kin. I think we find, at that stage, that it is impossible to identify the bodies. That wraps the whole thing up quite neatly and relieves us of the political embarrassment you mentioned earlier.'

'Sir, we're on thin ice, legally, if they don't resist arrest.'

'Oh, they'll resist all right, if they are who we think they are. But I'd suggest you make damn certain that none of your point men have served with either Nicholls or Shakespeare. We want a contact, but not one of the social kind.'

'And what happens when we get a positive I/D by showing the photographs to the released hostages? We've got to have that before we hit the aircraft. Afterwards, how do we square it away with a failure to identify the guys in question?'

'As I keep telling you, Tim, it's your operation.' The brigadier smiled down at him, nodded as if to say, 'Get on with it', and added: 'Good luck.'

Nicholls sprawled half-in, half-out of the captain's seat of Juliet Bravo, turned to his partner with a characteristic twisted grin and sang, very softly,

*The working class can kiss my arse,*
*I've got the foreman's job at last.*

Shakespeare recognised the signal as Golly's crow of triumph over an opponent. He had known that something special was afoot when Golly had asked him to come forward, breaking their own operational procedure specifying that one of them had to be with the hostages at all times. As a compromise, he had left the door linking the flight deck with the cabin open. Now they conducted their conversation in a near whisper.

'What's on, then, Golly?' he asked.

'Negotiations have begun and you know who they've put up for the job? That friend of every loyal serving soldier, Major Wainwright, though he's Colonel Wainwright these days.'

'*Tim* Wainwright?'

'Him for sure. I'd know his voice anywhere.'

Shakespeare's face darkened. 'Aye, lad, and he'd know your voice anywhere as well. All right, so we knew it was a pound to a pinch of shit that we'd end up negotiating with someone who might know us. But this isn't exactly good news. I don't know why you're so happy.'

'I'm happy, Bill, because if I'm going to screw anyone, I would rather screw that bastard Wainwright. He and the legal eagles rubber-dicked me into thinking I had nothing to worry about when I went into that court room in Belfast. I'd had months of bail, waiting around when I could have gone walkabout. Then when he's proved wrong and the case goes against me, Wainwright hands me over to the civvy prison authorities.'

'I know all that, Golly,' Shakespeare said wearily.

'Right. The musicians' collective out there wants to have a palava with us. Should be good for a giggle and might keep them out of mischief. Cummon.'

Shakespeare followed him into the cabin and loomed in the background as Nicholls, arms folded defensively, shoulders hunched in concentration, declined the conductor's offer of a seat. He was not really in a mood to chop words with some bloody-minded musician so he said simply, 'Right. We're here. State your case.'

'*Alors – comme on dit?* The bottom line of your demands is the broadcast and the money?' Tempo asked.

'Yeah. You could put it that way,' Nicholls said warily.

'How much money, may I ask?'

'Half a million.'

'Dollars? Pounds? Potatoes?'

'Pounds. Sterling.'

A quiet sigh of surprise, almost a whistle, rippled through the group of musicians to whom Major Tom had agreed to talk. 'I don't think it's too much. The orchestra's insured for a million. Throw in the market value of your instruments and the Margate Ladies over there and it's a nice, reasonable figure.'

'Let us not beat about the bushes, Major. You are really in this for the money. The other material, the political campaign, is just . . . *coup de théâtre* . . . for show?'

'No. Not entirely. I do get very pissed off about the things in that manifesto. Particularly the English pub hours. The broadcast will get people thinking about that. Real issues, things that affect people, day to day.'

'With half a million in the bank, you could afford to buy your own pub,' Bob Legrange suggested with a wan smile.

'It is clear, Major Tom, you do not understand musicians. Here are our lives in danger and for what? For reform of the English pub? The brass section, who are all alcoholics, might support you in this, but the rest of us' – and Tempo waved an arm about him – 'we would rather die for something a little more dignified.'

'Like what?'

'Oh, I don't know.' Tempo shrugged. 'My wallet, perhaps. Not because of the money inside it, but as a symbol of my right to be myself. Certainly if the government wants to stop me making music, or insists I make only one kind of music – their kind – this I would die for. Otherwise it is like running a restaurant where you pretend manure rissoles are best beefsteaks.'

'What we really want to know,' said Anders, 'is the real reason you guys are doing this. Personally I don't believe all this crap about parking tickets for diplomats, longer pub hours and sex for prisoners. Sure those things matter, but they ain't life or death issues. I wonder if you know yourselves why you're taking such a risk.'

Shakespeare, standing behind Nicholls, Armalite pointing vertically over his shoulder, leaned forward slightly. 'The reason we're doing it, sunshine, is that we're doing it. To prove it can be done.'

'Ah, now we are going somewhere,' Tempo said. 'It is beginning to make sense. You are trying to beat the system, yes?'

'No,' said Nicholls. 'We are beating the system. We both got screwed by the system. Now it's our turn.'

'You could have made a mistake,' suggested Legrange. 'There was a writer and moralist called Matthew Arnold who wrote, "Walk according to the best light you have, but be sure that light is not darkness."'

'Aye,' Shakespeare retorted, 'and there was an Italian called Mussolini who said it was better to live one day as a lion than a lifetime as a sheep.'

'Didn't he wind up dead, dangling from a lamp-post on the sidewalk?' Anders asked.

'Happen he did. We all die, one way or another, sometime.'

'Oh, but I understand,' Moira Tremlington interjected:

> 'My candle burns at both ends;
> It will not last the night;
> But ah, my foes, and oh my friends –
> It gives a lovely light!

That was Byron.'

'Not Byron,' said Legrange. 'Edna St Vincent Millay, circa 1920.'

'Whoever wrote it, I couldn't've put it better myself, lady,' said Nicholls. 'Don't you people ever feel like breaking away?'

'All the time,' said Moynahan. 'See, we're a bunch of individualists ourselves, just like you fellows. We're obliged to work together in a band for economic reasons. The band's a lifeboat. We take our turn on the oars and we don't rock the boat . . . not too much, anyway.'

'Mr Moynahan is talking his usual Irish nonsense,'

Tempo said. 'In their private lives most musicians are entirely unsuccessful. They get divorced, they go bankrupt, they get drunk. They are only at peace when they make music, because that they are good at doing. In order to be so good they have no time, no energy, for anything else. You can say they only come alive when they perform. When they make a good performance, it compensates them for all the things they are not good at. No one applauds them for being good husbands, or fathers, or for staying sober between concerts, you see. Outside music they are nobodies. Only the discipline of an elite group makes them somebodies.'

'What do you guys do when you ain't hijackers?' Anders asked, deadpan.

Nicholls and Shakespeare looked at one another, each waiting for the other to answer. Finally Nicholls said, 'We hang around outside police stations late at night and mug young policemen on their way home.'

From a groundswell of mirth, Legrange's voice cut in: 'That's not good enough. We create beauty. What are you creating? You've got to justify what you're doing. Morality isn't something abstract. It's about living with other people, recognising their right to live.'

'That,' Nicholls snapped back, 'is for the punters. That's the way the bigwigs who run things keep you under their thumb. Listen, if we're willing to take our chances on a caper like this and we don't get it right, we pay for our mistake with our lives. Your lives too, perhaps. Ours for sure. OK, that's our choice. But we also reckon that if we get it right, we've earned what we pick up. We've earned the right to lift two fingers to the establishment and go our own way.'

'That's fair enough,' Moynahan asserted. 'I agree with you. The best western music came out of the late eighteenth century when every composer from Mozart to Beethoven was backing the people who lifted two fingers to the establishment. Look at John Gay's *Beggars' Opera* and the way that turned up in Nazi Germany as *The Threepenny Opera* to show people Hitler was a criminal. The slave music of America had the same effect: the lyrics

123

were codes to describe escape routes. Music's a revolutionary force and we're part of the revolution just by being musicians.'

'You overlook something very basic,' Tempo corrected him. 'Mozart and the others wrote at a time when they thought men could *grow* with freedom. Beethoven was stone deaf when he set the "Ode to Joy" to the music of his Ninth Symphony. Because he could triumph over adversity, he made the mistake of thinking every human being was as strong as Beethoven. Instead of a race of giants, to match the vision of the artist, the world has been taken over by a race of pygmies. That is why Beethoven and Mozart got it wrong and Nietzsche got it right. The only true supermen, who take fate by – how do you say? – the scruff of the neck and control their own destiny, are the artists, the creatives.'

'I didn't understand a bloody word of that,' Nicholls said serenely, 'but it all sounds like bullshit to me.'

'Then I will explain it to you slowly in words of one syllable,' Tempo replied. 'People have a reason for living, or they die of boredom. The early Christians believed in something called Original Sin. All they meant was a fuel in the human system called "boredom". You say you are soldiers. Why be a soldier?'

'Because we like fighting,' Shakespeare told him. 'It's something you civilians never latch onto. You think we have to fight for a cause, or hate the opposition, or something. Boxers box because they enjoy it. They don't always expect to win. We're the same.'

'As you fellows see it,' Moynahan interjected, 'You're working your passage to some sort of freedom?'

'The hard way, my friend,' Nicholls replied. 'And we don't know if we'll ever get there . . . Right then. Any further questions? Conference over, campers. In ten minutes' time I'm due to talk to the authorities again. I want to arrange a casevac for the lady in the choir who's been so noisy. If anyone has to come aboard to help her, I want you all to stay in your seats and say nothing to nobody. Just total silence. Understood? OK.'

'Same applies if any attempt is made to storm the

aircraft,' Shakespeare added. 'Get your heads down and stay still. That's your best chance of survival.'

In the event, elaborate arrangements to evacuate the choir – arrangements painfully welded together between Nicholls and Wainwright by radio – did not require a stretcher party to board the plane. In the early hours of Sunday morning an airport bus and an ambulance halted twenty-five yards from the rear door of Juliet Bravo. The vehicles faced away from the aircraft; none of the ambulance crew was permitted to dismount.

Marigold ap-Rhys was the first person to leave. With the help of two of her colleagues, she walked slowly down the companionway to the open rear door. She was a dumpy, maternal figure with a turned-up, piglike nose and several chins. She moved like a somnambulist, her dress unbuttoned almost to the waist. Naomi Lewis, ignoring an order from Nicholls to remain seated, stood to fasten the buttons.

'Don't do anything daft, Naomi,' he said. 'At this stage of the game, everybody's expendable.'

She addressed her answer to the skipper, still sitting handcuffed near the stern. 'Captain Kilvert, I'm going to help this passenger down the steps. I'm going in front of her and I will walk backwards, facing her. Otherwise, the chances are that she'll simply lose her footing and break her neck. Then I'm going to walk her to the ambulance. I'll be back, though. You're one crew short already.'

Balaclava down, Nicholls moved to the top of the steps behind the two women. Across the darkness the sanctuary of the ambulance beckoned, its lights on, doors open, clean blankets in a neat, reassuring composition of grey and red domesticity. Step by step, the two women moved out of the aircraft and down towards the concrete. Impatiently, the rest of the choir thronged the doorway behind Nicholls. In these conditions, he was uncomfortably aware that his silhouette against the lights of the aircraft interior made him a perfect target for any sharpshooter out there in the darkness. But a high-velocity round could also strike one of the hostages behind him, a

125

fact from which he drew some comfort. At the foot of the steps, Marigold sank down slowly, settling like a bag of flour, her body shivering uncontrollably.

'She can't do it,' Naomi Lewis called. 'We'll have to have the ambulance closer.'

'No way,' Nicholls replied. 'One man from the ambulance crew, and only one, can help you shift her.'

The man who appeared in answer to Naomi Lewis's shouted appeal was, Nicholls noted with satisfaction, middle-aged and apparently harmless. He and the stewardess had to pull, push and lift the heavy and feebly protesting woman into the vehicle. Just before it drew away, Nicholls heard Naomi say, 'Acute claustrophobia, shock and exhaustion. She needs oxygen.'

'Please, please, can we go now, Major Tom?' pleaded Miss Marsh.

'Just one thing, missus. You and the other ladies will keep your word? When the people over there ask you questions, or show you photographs, you don't help them.'

'Of course, Major Tom, of course.' Inside her creased pink-and-blue dress, the blancmange bosom was heaving like a camper's inflatable bed. 'You heard that, gels? We keep faith with Major Tom and Major Bill. No tales out of school, remember. They've behaved like perfect gentlemen. None of us has been molested, and for that we should be grateful.'

Naomi Lewis remained at the foot of the stairs like a one-woman guard of honour as they left. They walked at first, but then the walk became a trot, then a run and finally a stampede which left shoes scattered as they fled. From within the bus, as it filled with their relief, a great buzz of excited voices flowed across the lonely, glistening tarmac. As she made her entrance into the vehicle, Mavis Marsh proclaimed, 'Now for a bath and some clean knickers.'

The bus had not started moving yet; in spite of that the distance between the vehicle and the aircraft grew as the space emptied of their scurrying figures. Naomi Lewis turned her back on the scene and walked resolutely back up the steps. On the runway behind her, delivered by the ambulance, was the suitcase.

The bus drove towards a battery of press flashguns and the road to a school converted into a reception centre. Miss Marsh dismounted first and swept like a galleon into the building, to be met by one of Wainwright's assistants, who showed her two photographs.

'Oh yes,' she declared. 'No doubt of it. That's him. That one there is the man who calls himself Major Tom, and the other one is Major Bill. We got no sleep, you know. We were in fear of rape every moment. It was the way those two awful men looked at one. . .' In the many colourful accounts which followed, no one immediately recollected that a steward had disappeared from the aircraft somewhere between Oslo and Prestwick.

After the choir's departure, Nicholls selected Miss Tremlington as his courier. He reasoned that every kind of camera would be trained on the suitcase and the approaches to it. As Wainwright's presence as negotiator meant that his own cover was probably blown, efforts to photograph him were no longer of such importance. Therefore it would be no bad thing to remind Wainwright that there were still some females on board Juliet Bravo. Female casualties, as Wainwright well knew, created a bad image. Furthermore, Miss Tremlington was less likely than anyone else he could think of to try to leg it to safety. It was for this reason, when he asked for volunteers to collect the suitcase, that he had politely deflected offers from Jacobs and from Moynahan.

Miss Tremlington had not volunteered, but after some reasoned discussion she had seen his point that she was the most reliable person to do the job. 'See, miss,' he had explained, 'it's just possible that if I do it myself, or send Major Bill, someone might take a pot-shot at us. Then, well, anything could happen. There's no hurry. We'll all get some sleep now and think about it in the morning.' So the steps were retracted, the rear door closed and the suitcase left where it was. Observing the scene through a nocturnal telescope, Wainwright's assistant commented,

'They're in no hurry. Just think of it. Fifty grand lying there, waiting to be picked up.'

'That and the rest,' Wainwright replied enigmatically.

With more space in the aircraft, the tension diminished. Each musician now spread himself across several seats, under a blanket, and collapsed into a profound sleep. So, too, did the aircrew; behind his curtain at the stern, it seemed, so did Nicholls himself.

Shakespeare, on stag, rifle across his lap, sat quietly in a first-class seat near the front, apparently slumbering, his ears stretched for any sound from outside the aircraft. He had attached a string to Nicholls's wrist, to be tugged vigorously as a crude but effective method of alerting him silently to any sign of trouble. It was an old trick they had used many times before in covert observation posts around the world. At around five a.m. he noticed that the cord shuddered slightly, then went slack. He wound it in a little and observed that there was no weight on the line. He presumed it had either unknotted itself or been cut. He eased the safety catch of his rifle forward, slid out of the seat and down to the floor to peer along the aisle. Inert feet and tousled scalps hung over the ends of the seats but there was no movement otherwise, except on the part of Golly's curtain. Shakespeare crouched quite still, rifle cradled across his left forearm. After twenty minutes or so the curtain was pulled briefly to one side and Diana Goddard emerged. She paused, tugging at the side of her blue uniform, then moved with light grace into her aisle seat on the port side. Once there, she tucked a blanket demurely round her legs, folded her arms, closed her eyes and went to sleep. The cord now travelled away from Shakespeare, under the curtain. Shakespeare waited for a few moments, then tested the line again. This time it was weighted. There were times when he wished Golly would give his balls a rest.

The case, when they went for it, proved too heavy for Miss Tremlington to lift, as Nicholls had guessed it might be. So he walked down the steps with her, aware that her presence would inhibit any attempts to shoot at him. After

128

more than two days it was good to breathe fresh air.

'Do I have to wear this balaclava, Major Tom?' she asked as they walked slowly down the stairs. 'It's awfully itchy.'

'It's only for a couple of minutes, and for your own protection,' Nicholls replied. She did not understand this, but there was much in life she did not understand, and she had learned to accept that. So she did not argue. She was dressed in her Norwegian outfit – green topcoat over a green woollen apron dress, red blouse, red long-johns and scarlet gloves. This ensemble, combined with the black headgear and her tall, beanstalk shape, lent her an appearance of grim, androgynous unreality.

It was her image which dominated the television screens that afternoon, accompanied by speculation that one of the terrorists was 'thought to be a woman, or even a man dressed as a woman'. In Liverpool particularly, viewers passed cheerful, unemployed hours trying to identify her and plaguing the police with telephone calls about their guesses. Wainwright's team, studying the video recording, concluded that it was not Shakespeare, though the opinion was not unanimous. By comparison, the compact, denim-clad figure alongside the mystery person went comparatively unremarked.

As the two re-entered Juliet Bravo they penetrated an invisible wall created by the odour of stale bodies but, within, the atmosphere was sweetened by the sound of a violin. Shakespeare was armed and alert on the jump seat, the curtain temporarily thrust to one side. Beyond him, leaning forward in their seats, the musicians' attention was fixed on Anders. He was playing a melody which Miss Tremlington identified in a whisper as 'Slow movement, Beethoven Violin Concerto in D.'

'What's going on?' Nicholls asked. Moynahan turned his head and placed a forefinger to his lips.

Shakespeare replied softly, 'Wanted to try out his violin. No harm in keeping the lads happy. Means they're not chattering. With luck, it'll also screw up any parabolic mikes they train on us.'

Miss Tremlington moved stealthily to her seat alongside Legrange. Rosary in one hand, he was weeping silently.

She was surprised by her own calm and boldness as she took the other hand in hers, gripped it protectively and whispered, 'Your pills, Bob. Take your pills.'

The musicians were still playing two hours later, with such instruments as were not in the hold, when the cabin crew began to serve lunch. Nicholls moved to the cockpit for the next round of negotiation with Wainwright. The lunch was the same dish they had had for lunch, breakfast and dinner since leaving Schiphol: an olive, a slice of processed meat, a fatigued lettuce leaf, increasingly stale bread, and coffee. As a favour to some of the more fastidious players, Moynahan was offering to eat any unwanted food; soon he had three additional trays of it alongside his own. .

'How are your food supplies?' Wainwright asked.

'Eating like kings and plenty of scoff in the larder,' Nicholls replied.

'Right. I've got some good news for you. I think we're going to be able to meet the rest of your demands, but it'll take time.'

'It always does,' Nicholls replied. 'But we're not going to sit on our fannies indefinitely, waiting for someone to hit us. If the government wants this over quickly, if it wants to cool the publicity, then it's in your interests to come across. We'd like the cash in two tea-chests, by the way.'

'Will two tea-chests be sufficient? I'd think you'd need a lot more than that,' Wainwright suggested.

'Two tea-chests,' repeated Nicholls. 'Just two. They can be delivered to the rear cabin door of the aircraft with a type Forty-C Goliath fork-lift truck. One driver/operator, two journeys and at least thirty minutes' notice to us of each delivery. Any fancy business during the operation and we start shooting one musician every minute.'

The next twenty-four hours, in the memory of the New British Orchestra, were memorable only for Jacobs's remarkable publicity *coup*. He had said virtually nothing since they had been on the ground, so when that Sunday afternoon he turned to the conductor and said, 'I've been thinking, maestro', Tempo focussed his good eye upon him with an expression of benign surprise.

'Why, Mr Jacobs. It is Mr Jacobs, isn't it?'

'You will have your little joke, maestro.'

'But, my dear fellow, I thought you had died. Indeed I was about to ask Miss Tremlington back there to write an obituary for you. You know, something along the lines of "Mediocrity became him like greatness in other men." '

'Maestro, as you know, I have seen this affair from the beginning as an opportunity for this orchestra, in the way of public exposure. I think we should give a recital on the runway. We would have to give our word not to try to escape, of course. Naturally, the acoustics are not all they might be and we could not put the whole orchestra with yourself on show. But the inner group, the string quartet, could certainly do something. It is a fine afternoon out there.'

Tempo looked thoughtfully at his general manager. 'Something from Mozart, perhaps,' he murmured. 'Something familiar. This is not an occasion to proselytise your English Birtwistle.'

'The music is immaterial,' Jacobs said. 'At this distance no one will hear it anyway. Certainly not the critics.'

'Just as well, Mr Jacobs.'

'We will be seen, you understand. There must be many television cameras out there just aching to photograph something. We must be seen to be committed to our art even when our lives are in imminent peril. It's just a matter of persuading Major Tom.'

Tempo looked at his general manager carefully and said slowly, 'That is a truly original idea, Jacobs. I congratulate you.' Then he summoned Major Tom, his normally fluent English breaking down as he tried to communicate the relevance of 'our latest idea to help everyone from this impasse'.

Nicholls was at first unmoved. It wasn't in his operational plot and he wanted to calculate the implications. It was Jacobs who finally converted him.

'From your point of view, Major, ' said the general

manager, salivating with excitement, 'you win some excellent publicity. We are seen to be free to continue to practise our art, while you are given good publicity for your cause.'

It was a quirky, almost whimsical scheme which appealed to Nicholls's sense of mischief. It was another way to roast Wainwright and the rest of them. He gave a quick nod and said, 'OK, you're on. Full marks, Mr Jacobs. You can have up to five musicians just outside the rear door there for thirty minutes. If even one of them tries to leg it, you'll be five musicians under strength. Let's give it a whirl.'

Anders was the leading advocate of a tarmac recital among the musicians. 'We do it with a bit of style,' he declared loudly. 'Can we dig out our formal evening gear?' Then, teasing the conductor, he suggested, 'Why don't we play one of these moderns, say, Tchaikovsky?'

'Tchaikovsky wrote in clichés,' Tempo replied loftily.

'That's what his critics always say, maestro,' Legrange said. 'He's the musical equivalent of Emily Brontë. Everyone sneers at their work until they actually study it.'

The programme finally chosen comprised Mozart's Quartet for Oboe and Strings, K. 370, and a Haydn Quartet in E nicknamed 'The Joke'. Legrange, apparently recovered, gave a sparkling performance. At first he had not wanted to take part. He had admitted to Moira Tremlington 'an intense foreboding'. He had spent the first night of the hijack awake, his eyes closed, reciting the Lord's Prayer as he waited for death to take him. So intense was this foreboding that even music ceased to signify anything. His prayer had gone unanswered. All his life until now music had been the cement that had held his personality together. The years of painful rehearsal, a sort of entombment from normal human company, he had accepted gladly as the price of enlightenment. Now, faced with a vocabulary which was alien to that experience – the monosyllabic vocabulary of violence and death – he found no comfort in his hard-won art. It had all been a con trick performed by himself upon himself; a gigantic displacement activity to relieve him of the grubby burden of growing up in the real world. In this situation, he told Moira Tremlington, music was the key to the door of an empty room. 'I know now,' he said, 'the meaning of the words "Why hast Thou forsaken me?" '

Surprisingly, it was the rational, humanist American, Anders, who talked him round.

'Bob, you're religious, right?'

'Right.'

'Did it ever occur to you that in this century serious music has taken over from the Church in spreading something – well, I guess in your terminology, something spiritual – in this pigstye of a world? It's the last hope of humanising human beings. It's the only universal language. If ever there was a situation where music could make a point about the human spirit, this is it. . . And furthermore, buddy, we haven't gotten enough instruments in the cabin to be able to play a decent tune without your oboe.'

'Something cooking out there, sir,' said the sergeant-major, binoculars steady as a sniper's rifle on the aircraft. Simultaneously, the radio on Wainwright's desk in the Air Traffic Control room barked at them.

'Tango-One to Sunray: five men carrying possible weapons exiting aircraft by rear door.'

Wainwright joined his assistant at the window, watched incredulously as cases opened to reveal string instruments, plus one oboe, murmured, 'Weapons my arse', and then added, more audibly, 'Sergeant-major, contact the police command post. Tell them some sort of concert's being performed on the runway by a group of hostages. I want the superintendent to tighten up perimeter security. While we're all watching the musicians someone might be breaking through to the aircraft from outside.'

On the desk behind them a telephone was ringing insistently. Wainwright's signaller answered it.

'It's who? Wait one.' Then to Wainwright he said, 'The *Daily Mirror*, boss. Can we confirm the orchestra's playing "Colonel Bogey" on the runway?'

'Tell them to ring the police information room, then

hang up,' snapped Wainwright. 'Answer no questions, not even about the weather.'

By now a red telephone – the direct, secure link to Cobra – was also ringing. Wainwright responded to this himself.

'Sunray Prestwick,' he said.

'That you, Tim?'

'It is.'

'This is your brigadier. What's happening?'

'Looks like five of the hostages putting on some sort of concert.'

'Yes, I know. We've got them on vision but not sound. What're they playing?'

'Music, sir,' said Wainwright, replacing the receiver.

From various vantage points around the airport, hungry, inquisitive microphones picked up enough of the lilting dance rhythms, broken by gusts of wind, to dramatise the pathos of the musicians – standing, as one television commentator put it, 'like street buskers in a windswept circle without so much as a single sheet of music among them, rather than the distinguished professionals they really are' – and above all to mock the security authorities with a cheerful blandness. What the cameras captured was an image of intense rapport between one instrumentalist and another, a dense, tangible and luminous flow of energy and love as well as a singing, soaring melody which even moved Nicholls to comment, 'If they could parachute, they'd make hot relly workers.'

By the time the police had discovered the television cameras and moved them on, the musicians had reached the end of their programme. They paused as the last chord sighed into inaudibility, instruments still tucked under their chins, as if they were cocooned from reality by the sounds they had created, which still resonated in their minds. From the aircraft door above them Jacobs applauded clumsily, the clattering of his hands echoing off the tailplane like huge drops of rain. Then they slowly broke rank and methodically repacked the instruments in their cases. Only Legrange did not move. He stood, holding his oboe, looking with bewilderment at the green hills around them until Anders gently touched his shoulder.

'That was superb, Bob,' he said. 'It was a privilege to play with you.' Then, signalling with his eyes to another of the quartet, he added, 'Cummon. Let's get you back inside before the cold gets to you.'

That night, after the item had led the main television news, the scrambler telephone on Mackie's Downing Street press desk burred angrily. An all-too-familiar voice said, 'Mackie, enough is enough. I want this hijack nonsense brought to a conclusion within twenty-four hours at the latest. Please relay that to the Cobra committee immediately.'

Mackie sighed. Although the end had been willed and the means were not specified, the PM was the right as usual; or as the PM would put it 'Absolutely right'. Short of having a cuddly dog with a begging bowl at its feet, the hijackers could not have produced a better commercial if they had employed the Saatchi brothers. Wearily he lifted the telephone and said, 'Treasury please.'

# Chapter Seven

Bonny Richmond washed the chalk from her fingers into the tiny sink of St Cecilia's staff room, reflecting again that some education committees never recognised that adults as well as children worked in schools. They had gone now, the children, in a clap of sound like a summer storm, but still she lingered, putting off the errand which Ivan and the others had imposed upon her following Golly Nicholls's disappearance a few days before, days which already seemed like a lifetime.

She had once asked Golly if he had ever been married. Come to think of it, it was the last time in his caravan and he had glanced at her quickly from the corner where he sat, pulling on his socks, the big toes making holes in them, the dark eyes laughing and the sly Scouse voice telling her, 'Oh, many times, Bonny, many times. But never for long. Will you marry me? You're a great fuck, you know. One of the greatest.'

The way he said it, it sounded like a sincere compliment; but the eyes, like those of some of the little boys in her care, spoke volumes of mischief.

'You? A bloody parachute bum? Your sort wants a woman both pregnant and out at work earning the price of your next relly jump. No way.' They had both laughed. Then she had said, 'You know the difference between men – men like you – and women, Golly? You just want a fuck; you just want to empty yourself as if you were dumping some rubbish in a garbage can, and hurry away to play some other game. Women want more than that.'

'That's right!' he'd retorted without a second's pause. 'That's why you're never satisfied.'

She had not asked any of their mutual acquaintances. All of them were jumpers and it was not the sort of question they asked about one another. As Golly himself had once said, in a rare moment of introspection, sport parachuting was like the Foreign Legion, something they joined to forget about what existed outside. Then, ten days ago, Golly was dead and gone, leaving nothing anyone could bury or mourn over. In the wake of his death, or disappearance, or whatever it was that had blotted him out, bits of his life, such as his wife, were becoming exposed by the press and the police to other bits of his life. It was like a jigsaw from which a large piece – the piece where the face should have been – was missing; like all incomplete pictures it was profoundly disturbing.

The fragments with which she was entrusted were the few personal items he had left in the caravan – those the police and that other funny Scotsman who said he was a reporter were not interested in. She had not examined them closely, for there was a special prurience about delving into the belongings of the dead, as she knew from hard experience. In the light of that experience – her discovery of incoherent little love-notes, from a woman she had never heard of, lying among the private papers of the fiancé who had died skydiving with her – she decided to take a closer look at the items she was supposed to deliver to Mrs Nicholls.

The bag was one of those olive green Army things with a heavy zip along the top. It contained a pair of American military jump boots, a few T-shirts, underwear and socks, all in need of a wash, a bunch of keys, a book about survival techniques and an illustrated guide to edible plants in the wild. She supposed that the police had taken any passports, birth certificates or other official documents. Nonetheless, it occurred to her that for a man making an unexpected departure from this life Golly had left surprisingly little to mark his progress. Tucked in the lining of the kitbag she found the letter, postmarked Bahrein and dated two years earlier. It was addressed to 'Nicholls, 22823, Bicester Prison, Oxon, UK.'

Presidential Palace,
Mahranat,
United Arab Emirates

Dear Golly,

Remember the day Muhammed Salim changed sides and joined us in Dhofar? You said he'd either get to the

137

top or get topped. He did both. He turned up here as a colonel in charge of the palace guard. Last month the President, HRH Sheikh Ashram (the one with closed-circuit TV cameras overlooking the European families' beach), turned the guard out for inspection. Salim got them to present arms, then gave the order to open fire. Two of us were on the BG (bodyguard) team that day. The other was Acker, who was with you in the malaria ward in Brunei. At a range of only twenty yards or so, the best the nig-nogs could do was wing Ashram, kill his chief slave and mallet a peacock in the royal garden.

Acker then despatched the client who fired first and all hell broke loose. We got HRH into his Land Rover and drove off toot-sweet. Order restored, but no sign of Muhammed Salim. They picked him up at the airport, dressed as a woman. That alone would have been worth a death sentence here. Next day, big public executions in the main square, a head job for Muhammed Salim as guest of honour, complete with sword. They put it on local TV between two parts of *The Desert Song*. Since then they've disbanded the old palace guard and doubled the BG contingent from UK. So now I'm on special duties behind a two-way mirror in the royal sleeping quarters. I think HRH likes an audience. Ashram has some Baluchi mercenaries as back-up and they frisk us for cameras before we go on stag. Another six months of this and we'll all be cases of wanker's doom. As Acker keeps saying, 'If Golly Nicholls was here, he'd be giving the Ruler some tips on his groping technique.'

Still, there are compensations. The money's about double what we got for serving the Queen. Then there's the hunting. Ashram's got some beautiful desert falcons – Sakers – which he uses to catch bustards. Bustards are a bit like turkeys, but less thick. Their camouflage is ace. So we put a falcon up on a recce flight and when the bustards lose their bottle and come out of hiding, another falcon's released to make the kill. If it's not bustard, it's hares. All goes into the same stew pot at the end of the day and we all sit round a fire and listen to the Arab royals big-timing.

You can forget about Martin, the guy who framed you in Belfast. The word among the lads is that he had a head job – Irish fashion – a month ago. Next day, a Green Jackets patrol lifted O'Rourke, the big Pira man from Monahan, on the Newry road. Seems they pulled him out of the car by his hair and found he was wearing a wig. He's as bald as a coot underneath and very thin-skinned about it. Anyway, it turned out that the bullet that was supposed to have done the job was the same one you fired into the McAlister car: bad case of rent-a-bullet, or mixed-up forensic samples, or something. Result: no case for O'Rourke to answer on the Martin murder. They could only do him for illegal possession of a nine-milly and throw in a few jokes about his haircut. Point is, whoever was responsible for killing McAlister, Martin has gone to the great Orange lodge in the sky, so don't get worked up. Keep your nose clean. By the time I've finished this contract, you'll be out on parole and we'll get something together.

Sorry to hear about the divorce. Bill.

Bonny folded the letter thoughtfully, replaced it in the bag and set off for the address Ivan had given her.

The woman who answered the door was slender, blonde and, in spite of a rustic Hereford accent, neither rural nor yet a characteristic victim wife-'n'-mother. The tailored dress, the careful eye make-up that gave no clue to the owner's age except that she was clearly over twenty-five, and the exquisitely manicured fingernails were all Sunday-colour-magazine stuff. Only the perfume, of which there was a little too much, was maladroit. In her jeans, plaid shirt and Navy surplus duffle-coat, Bonny felt defiantly out of place. She was not invited inside. She handed over the bag with a brief, polite explanation and left, relieved that the job had passed off painlessly. Margaret Nicholls was clearly a very self-possessed woman.

It was only when Bonny had walked down the front

path, a path clinically flanked by small rectangular white-painted stones, and had started to open the door of her car that the Nicholls woman suddenly showed some interest in her. Until then it was as if Bonny had been one of the multitude of guppies flitting back and forth in the front window aquarium, an object of vague passing interest behind heavily plated suburban insularity.

'Miss Richmond!'

Bonny paused, the open car door under her hand.

'Wait a minute.' The Nicholls woman walked down the narrow path in high heels, like a mannequin on a catwalk. 'I hope you don't mind me asking, like, but d'you know people at that parachute club place? I see you've got one of their stickers in your back windscreen.'

'Yes I do. I do some parachuting myself. That's why they asked me to bring you Golly's things.'

'I see . . . Look, there's something I'd like to ask you. Will you come in for a cup of tea – if you're not too busy, that is?'

Puzzled by the woman's abrupt change of attitude, still reluctant to get further involved, Bonny retraced her steps and followed her hostess into the house. She sat in the lounge, under the angel fish and the guppies, while Margaret Nicholls disappeared into the kitchen, taking the bag with her. She seemed to take a long time to make tea and when she returned, with biscuits and delicate china neatly displayed on a round glass tray, her eye make-up was smudged. She was paler than before and her hands shook slightly. She declined any help. Then, ignoring the tea she had poured for herself, she sat on a green sofa opposite Bonny, smoothing down first the skirt of her dress and then her long blonde hair with quick, nervous movements.

At last she said, 'Did you know Golly, then?'

'Yes. I knew him quite well.'

'You know he . . . well, he disappeared or something.'

'Yes. Everyone knows. The papers have been full of it for the last week.'

'Of course. We were divorced, see? I don't know much about it. Only what the police have said.'

'What have they said?'

'They aren't sure. That is, they're sure he's dead and his body will be found sometime. Went in the river, he did, they said, just before that terrible storm. They found his helmet and parachute under a bridge, didn't they? That's why they're sure, you see. After all this time and that big search and all, with dogs and police and soldiers and helicopters and still no sign of him . . . must've gone in the river. It's the other thing they're not sure about.' She reached one hand into her sleeve, then her handbag, and mumbled, 'Excuse me', before hurrying into the kitchen. Bonny heard her blow her nose. Then she returned and said, more softly, 'All been a bit of a shock, see. Would you like a biscuit?'

'I'm sorry,' said Bonny. 'Would you like me to go?'

'Oh no. I'm sorry.'

'We're both sorry,' said Bonny, smiling shyly. 'It's always the women who have to apologise, isn't it?'

Mrs Nicholls nodded in reply, head down, paper handkerchief neglected between her hands as the tears carved channels in her careful make-up. They resembled claw marks and she looked suddenly older. Bonny said, 'This other thing that the police aren't sure about: is that what's upsetting you?'

Mutely her companion nodded again and muttered, 'Give me a minute. I'll tell you.'

They sat in silence for what seemed a long time and then, without looking up, Margaret Nicholls said in a flat, controlled monotone. 'They think he might have done it on purpose. He'd had a lot of bad luck, see. They put him in prison over something that happened in Northern Ireland a few years ago, and it wasn't down to him at all. Nothing to do with him. Then he came out again, and things didn't work out between us and . . . well, that's why he did it. I blame myself, see.'

'I don't think you should,' said Bonny. 'I really don't think you should. Look, I did a lot of jumping with Golly. In fact, I was on the same lift with him the night he disappeared. I still can't believe it happened. I can't even believe he's dead. I mean, if he was going to do something like that he could've done it any time. It wouldn't make any sort of sense to do it on that jump.'

'Why not?' Margaret Nicholls had raised her head now, her feline, grey eyes suddenly alert.

'Well, it doesn't. This was a special occasion. It wasn't just another parachute descent. There were twelve of us, making our first big night jump together. It was special. There'd been a row in the club about another jump that Golly and two others did, which was an unofficial night jump. So this much bigger thing was a way of burying the hatchet. We'd got champagne and a disco and a party lined up afterwards. Golly wasn't out on his own. He had set up the whole thing, really, and we were all with him. If I was going to kill myself deliberately I wouldn't spoil someone else's jump like that – nor would any parachutist I know, if he could help it. Can you imagine Golly going to his grave instead of a good party with lots of pretty girls around?'

'You're not just saying that – I mean, to make me feel better? I'd rather know the truth. I'm one of those awkward people. If I got cancer, I'd want them to tell me, straight out like.'

'No way, duck. Look, people do get killed in this sport but it's usually because of their own carelessness. Golly was anything but careless. It's just possible he was very unlucky, that his main canopy malfunctioned and he couldn't cut it away and then his reserve chute blew apart. All the same, I can't understand how he could have gone into the river. We got out of the plane a long way from the Wye and we were downwind of it, too. If he'd had a double "mal", I'd have expected him to hit the ground somewhere closer to the drop zone. We should've found his body.'

'Yes, but don't you see, there was this other thing, the insurance. That's what makes the police think it was suicide. Just before it happened he took out a big life insurance and made a will and all, with a friend of ours as the person who does all the business, what they call an executor. I don't understand these things. Bill – our friend – is looking after it all.'

Again they fell silent. Then, as casually as she could, Bonny said, 'That doesn't make sense either. Insurance people don't pay out on suicides.'

'I know . . . that's what the policeman said. That's why Golly would have to make it look like an accident. And on top of it all, he got me pregnant, the bastard, just before this. He just walked in here one night and . . . and God knows how I'll explain that to my other man.'

After a pause, during which the women studied the cups in front of them, their minds elsewhere, Bonny said, 'There are times when I think we're better off without them – men, I mean.'

'You mustn't say that. It's unlucky.'

'Unlucky?'

'I couldn't live on my own, without a man.'

Margaret uttered the words with solemn conviction, like a Roman Catholic reciting the Creed.

'I once told Golly that his sort of man didn't understand that what we want is a real relationship, not just sex,' Bonny said. 'Not just bang-bang, thank you ma'am, and walk away. Men like that just use us like dustbins for their own tensions, then run away because they feel so guilty. They don't know that real sex is much more and they can't handle it. They're emotional cripples.'

'What did he say?'

'He said that's why we were never satisfied.'

'He left me two children in my dustbin,' Margaret replied fondly. 'And I'll say this for him: when he wanted me, he really wanted me, even when I didn't want myself. With him, it was the real thing.' Then, suddenly bitter, she said, 'Bloody animal, he was, at times.'

Bonny noticed that the colour had returned to her cheeks. In spite of herself, remembering his animality, as uncompromising as the elements and as dangerous, she also contracted involuntarily and was ashamed by the knowledge and the power of it, and how it diminished her separate human identity.

It was late when Bonny finally left Eden Close, having given Margaret Nicholls her address and a promise to keep in touch. She was entirely unclear whether Margaret

Nicholls still loved Golly or hated him. Probably both. Bereavement, as she knew to her cost, did funny things to people. Those who were left to clean up the mess left by a death always found a reason to blame themselves. It was just ten days since the fatal night jump, ten days and eleven nights, to be precise. Bonny liked to be precise. As she drove out of the cul-de-sac she was obliged to give way to a Range Rover. She identified the driver instantly as Golly's friend, Shakespeare. If he recognised her, he gave no sign of it. That was no surprise, either. All these Special Forces people were weird. You never really knew where you stood with them from one moment to the next.

During the months that followed, the ripples caused by Nicholls's disappearance spread wider than his immediate domestic circle. In the panelled office of Chevalier Security, Shakespeare was questioned with increasing scepticism, first by the firm's boss, Colonel John Franklin, then by Le Mesurier – Director, Special Forces – and finally by someone who was introduced as 'Mr McNeil from Five.' McNeil was short, barrel-chested, overweight and Scottish. His balding head was covered by wisps of red hair and he was sweating. Shakespeare had the feeling that he was in a permanent state of excited perspiration. He invited Shakespeare to sit, then perched himself on the polished table in Chevalier's boardroom in such a way that he could study Shakespeare in profile. To return this scrutiny, Shakespeare was obliged to turn his head uncomfortably.

'Right, laddy,' snapped McNeil. 'Turn out your pockets.'

'You what?'

'You heard.'

'Piss off.'

'Don't come it with me, Shakespeare. I can make life very uncouth for you. Conspiracy's a serious crime. It's the only law we have that says you're guilty unless you can prove otherwise. In this case, conspiring to break the Official Secrets Act could be very hard to disprove.'

'You can still piss off. As soon as Nicholls told me about this daft operation, this disappearing trick, I warned the boss here about it all. I don't think he took it very seriously.'

'You were doing that to cover your own arse, Shakespeare. You're no Boy Scout. Now then, where's Nicholls?'

'I don't know. He left no forwarding address.'

'You've been handling this bent insurance for him?'

'On his widow's behalf. He made me his executor. It's known as looking after your own. But Colonel John knew all that. I told him.'

'So why did you act as the executor? You knew this was a set-up.'

'Because Golly Nicholls asked me to . . . aye, and because I knew nothing would come of it, once the boss here was tipped off. It was all a bit of play-acting. See, there's a touch of the Walter Mitty about Golly, particularly since he did time for that killing in Belfast. So you play along, knowing that next week it'll be some other hare-brained idea he's got hold of. Golly's a good operator with the right leadership, but a bit . . . well, let's say unpredictable when he's doing his own thing without anyone to check him. I reckoned once we got him back to work, he'd settle down again.'

'So you played along with him before he disappeared?'

'Or just before he died.'

'If he's dead, as you say, laddy, where's the body?'

'You tell me. If he really did go in the river it could be anywhere by now. Probably half-eaten by fish. The Wye runs into the Bristol Channel.'

'Aye, surely. The local police have pulled two corpses out of the water since Nicholls vanished and neither of them is Nicholls. So where is he?'

'I don't know.'

'Now let's get this straight, Shakespeare, because it's very serious. My people are worried. They think your mate might be preparing to defect to a foreign power.'

'Golly defect? You must be joking. He hasn't got a secret anyone would give tuppence for unless they wanted a detailed guide to the whorehouses of the Far East, or the recipe for Army steak-and-kidney pud. Come to think of it, that's not a bad idea. We plant Golly on the Reds and they eat our compo rations and they all die of constipation in their noddy suits.'

'Forget the jokes. He did the special course, like you. And some highly classified operations afterwards with our friends across the Atlantic.'

'Aye but that was years and years ago.'

'The opposition are still interested. As for that insurance fiddle, Shakespeare, you can forget it. We will advise the Home Office to tell the coroner that he should not hold an inquest. No inquest, no death certificate, no insurance money. Nicholls is just another missing person. Think it over. When you're ready to talk to me, call the number on that card there and ask to speak to "Uncle Mac". My desk is manned twenty-four hours a day.'

The card bore only a telephone number. The first three digits Shakespeare instantly recognised as those of the Defence Secretariat exchange in London.

Shakespeare passed the next few days in limbo. Chevalier had taken him off its active strength. He was effectively suspended for an indefinite period on full pay with instructions to report to the firm's Kensington office twice a day, to remain at his London flat at other times and to be available by telephone. Chevalier's boss, Colonel John Franklin, an old Special Forces hand like himself, was apologetic.

'Sorry, Bill, but in our business we've got to toe the line and be seen toeing it, Pirbright fashion. Nothing personal, you understand. Until this Nicholls business is sorted out it could damage some rather lucrative contracts we're negotiating in Singapore and heaven knows where else . . . Oh, and can you drop your passport in to Dorothy at the front desk? Not my idea, needless to say. That chap McNeil from Five insisted on it. But don't worry. Your place here is secure. This will all blow over.'

One effect of the limitations now imposed on him was that Shakespeare's routine weekly trip to Hereford could not begin until after his second daily report to Chevalier at

1800 hours. Since he had been ordered not to leave London it was better, in any case, to go late under cover of darkness and return early. So far as he could judge he was not yet the target of heavy surveillance by the Security Services. In spite of the threats of McNeil-the-Mouth, Golly's disappearance did not merit the attention of the dozen or more men required for such a watch to be kept on him. For the same reason he did not believe that his London telephone would be tapped. Still, as he walked to his flat from Chevalier's office on the third day of his open arrest, Shakespeare took the precaution of calling Margaret from a public telephone box.

A man's voice answered. Shakespeare said, 'Sorry, wrong number', and hung up. He dialled the number again, more deliberately. Again, the same Glaswegian voice, saying, 'Hulloo, who is this please?'

'Is Margaret Nicholls there?' Bill asked.

'She's away to the shops, laddy. She'll be back in a wee while. Is that Bill Shakespeare?'

'Aye, it is.'

'This is Uncle Mac. We met at your office the other day.'

'I remember. I was having a good day till you turned up.'

'Have you had a bit of a think about what I told you? We could meet up for a beer or something, you know, somewhere discreet.'

'I've told you, you're barking up the wrong tree. Golly's dead, for all I know. I can't help you.'

'Aye, well . . . can I give Margaret any message? We're getting on just fine here. She's a fine figure of a woman, yon Mrs Nicholls. I would na'mind underwriting a wee bitty insurance for her myself.'

'No message,' Shakespeare replied, replacing the receiver.

After three days in the flat, days spent studying Glasier's *Falconry and Hawking* or, if not that, loosening up his body with a private regime of knuckle press-ups, stomach lifts and karate kata, the prospect of even another half-hour's confinement was oppressive. So having ended his telephone conversation with the Scot, Shakespeare returned to his apartment just long enough to throw small kit and basic spare clothing into a bag. He paused on the way out to tilt the telephone off its receiver. If Chevalier did ring him, the line would be out of order. More than anything else he wanted to see Margaret. Chevalier could stuff its contract if necessary.

The Range Rover was parked in its customary position below the apartment building. He carried out the usual checks beneath the vehicle. This time in the gloom he could see what appeared to be a sack lying on the concrete floor, below the vehicle's transmission system. As he sank to his knees to examine the object more carefully, it unwrapped itself. A pair of human eyes, framed by shaggy black hair, stared back at him. Another bloody wino, he thought. Or else a druggy. Since the Iranian revolution and the heroin exports that had followed, London had collected junkies like New York had cockroaches.

'Listen, mate,' Shakespeare said sternly, 'I'd get out of there if you don't want your back broken. I'm just driving off.' A soft chuckle, mixed with a cough, and the figure on the floor stretched an arm from the sleeping bag which enclosed it. 'Lend us a tenner, guvnor?' it asked.

'A tenner?'

'Ah, cummon, Shakespeare, I know you're loaded. You can afford to help an old mucker, can't you?'

'Golly! What the fuck are you doing here? Half the country's looking for you.'

Nicholls hauled himself out, his face creased in a huge smile. 'Waiting for you, Bill. Let's get going.'

'Aye, well, you'd better get in. Sling that bag in t'back. We need to have a talk.'

In spite of the complications, Shakespeare was glad to see Nicholls as well as relieved. In their soldiering days they had always been a winning team, until the day McAlister was malleted in Belfast. There was a sense of security about being together again. It was like slipping into a pair of favourite boots. They drove west, through Hammersmith and onto the M4 motorway, in traffic so dense as to make it virtually impossible for anyone to follow them. Neither of them spoke until they were past London's Heathrow Airport. The traffic, a competitive joust until that point, now settled into a smoother, calmer rhythm. In the old days, when they had taken part in anti-terrorist exercises at the airport, that peculiarity of London driving was one of the many factors they had fed into their operational timetable, as if they were answering one of those antique algebraic examination questions about two people travelling at different speeds towards the same destination.

'Where are we going, then?' Nicholls asked.

'I don't know about you, sunshine, but I'm going awol until tomorrow. Then I've got to come back to London.'

'Awol? What's that all about?'

'Absent Without Leave. A-w-o-l.'

'Yeah, I know . . . but I don't get it, Bill. I mean, you're free to come and go like anybody else.'

'I've got it in the neck, that's all. Chevalier, Group, the security lot, the "friends", the whole lot of them've got me tied up in . . . well, you could call it open arrest. No work for me, you understand, but I'm supposed to stay put in London, on call, and mark time twice daily at Chevalier's office with boots polished and medals dangling. See, ever since you vanished and I started negotiating with those insurance people, they've got it in their tiny minds that I know everything that's going on, particularly about where you are. There's a specially nasty Scottish bastard calling himself McNeil from Five, who reckons I'm Mr Big, the mastermind. Where have you been anyway?'

'Oh, here and there. Doing this-'n'-that.'

'What's that supposed to mean?'

'Well, first off I stayed at a common cold research place. Smashing, it was. Room of my own, telly, the lot. They even pay you for it. They have hot and cold running doctors, and that was handy because I'd clobbered my ribs on that night jump. I told them I'd tripped over in their bathroom and they couldn't do enough for me. Spent a month there, I did. Then the medics found I'd had hepatitis and a few other things and they decided I wasn't any use. So they threw me out. Then I went to this "squat" back in the 'Pool. Organised kiddies games and that, and nodded me head and said "yes" to all this Troops-Out-Of-Ireland rubbish. When I wasn't doing that I was shafting most of the girls in the Women's Awareness Workshop. They were always rabbiting on to me about rape, and then coming back for more of it. I even carried a banner on a protest march down to the local nick. Anyways up, it got me a Public Utilities Union ticket to go with my new driver's licence and insurance card. So far as the great computer in the sky is concerned, my name's now Jim Duncan. The real Jim Duncan's about eighty-eight years old, but I got a passport on his name with my photo in it, no trouble.'

'P'raps that's because you look like you're eighty-eight,' said Shakespeare. 'Senile decay, mate, that's what's wrong with you. A lifetime of sexual abuse. You can see it in your face.'

'So where are we at with this insurance money, Bill?'

'No hope, Golly. Lost cause. Five is leaning on the Home Office who's leaning on the coroner. Won't even be an inquest. Legally you're just a missing person.'

'Pity, that. We need a decent piggy bank, see, for the other thing. Still, there's ways and means . . .'

'What other thing?'

'The other. How to make two hundred and fifty grand apiece for two days' work. Not bad, eh, Bill? The ultimate happy contract.'

'Like your insurance caper. Pull the other one, Golly. You're in the shit already, partner, and this time I can't extract you. Best thing is to let me arrange a meet for you with Colonel John up at Chevalier and try to smooth things over.'

'No, Bill. I'm serious. Been planning this for years. It can't miss. Did you ever hear of somebody called D.B. Cooper?'

'Never.'

'Well, you should have. He's dead now, but he was a bloody genius, ahead of his time, God rest his soul.'

They turned off the M4 in gathering darkness and went north, skirting Maidenhead and on to the M40 before swinging west again towards Oxford. As the Cotswolds and Cheltenham swept past, Shakespeare listened carefully while his friend explained some of the beauties of the intricate machine he called Operation Eldorado. The talk was of aircraft and push-buttons, altitudes and air speeds, and it was pure James Bond. Finally Shakespeare turned the vehicle into a deserted lay-by alongside the lonely winding road between Ledbury and Hereford. It seemed only yesterday, though it was six years, since he had last stopped here, a designated rendezvous where he would join the Prime Minister's bodyguard to escort that august person on a visit to the regiment's rebuilt headquarters.

'Got a cigarette, Golly?'

'I thought you'd kicked the weed.'

'So I have, most of the time.'

Shakespeare lit the cigarette and drew on it reflectively. Then he asked, 'Are you serious about this? I mean, really serious?'

'Yes I am. I've even got the most tricky pieces of equipment set up.'

'Like what?'

'Like the weapons, the demolition kit and the uniforms. Picked up a lot of useful stuff in Norway. See, on that squat in Liverpool I got to hear from some visiting Norwegian anarchists about the way those Norwegian home guard armouries are just left lying around unguarded in isolated barns and things all over the country. Each armoury has enough gear for an entire infantry company, right up to TOW anti-tank missiles. Well, a lot of terrorists have been helping themselves, see? I mean, the Noggies have lost seven hundred AG automatic rifles, 7.62 milly jobs, in one year and said nothing to anyone. Then there's dynamite for booby traps, plastic, Claymore mines . . . So after the squat, I took a trip to Norway. You're not bottling out, are you, Bill? It'll need the two of us.'

'I'm not bottling in, either, mate. It sounds to me like the daftest thing since that battle below the Eagle's Nest caves at Sherishitti. Kamikaze stuff.'

'Think about it.'

'No way.'

'Just think about it. If I have to, I'll do it on my tod. Give me a critique, at least.'

'I've told you, Golly. It won't bloody work.'

'Ah, but if it did, you could get them falcons.'

'Where, Dartmoor Prison? Or do I join the Alcatraz Ornithology Society?'

'You think it over. Tell me where I've gone wrong.'

Shakespeare's answer was to switch on the ignition and swing the vehicle back onto the road, accelerating hard. As they approached Hereford it was agreed that Golly should remain in the vehicle. Shakespeare suggested, and Nicholls agreed, that it was not the best time for a domestic reunion between Margaret Nicholls and the husband she presumed dead. It had also occurred to Shakespeare that if McNeil-the-Mouth were still in the vicinity, he might just lift Golly for questioning . . . and no bad thing. That way, this whole mess could be cleared away. He and Margaret could get on with their life together as they had done before. Golly would not be pleased, but this way at least, Shakespeare reasoned, he was saving his old partner from the even greater disaster of Operation Eldorado. It was now midnight. The ring road, skirting the old city wall, was empty of vehicles and people. Traffic signals changed and changed again, but no one came or went. As they turned on to the Leominster Road, out of the city, Golly said suddenly, 'Drop us here, Bill.'

'What for?'

'Special Branch might have Eden Close staked out. If they're watching you, then sure as hell they're watching my pad. What time are you going back to London?'

'About five in t'morning.'

'You must have a woman tucked away down here, you crafty bastard. Well, pick us up here. I'll be waiting.'

Shakespeare drove slowly down the deserted road, watching his mirrors. The small, lithe figure of Golly had already crossed the road. Then, melting like a ghost into the brickwork of the high wall flanking Hereford's professional football stadium, he vanished.

Her bedroom light was still on, the only one in the close. Shakespeare switched off the engine and coasted into his usual parking space outside. As he applied the handbrake the curtain of her bedroom parted momentarily, then closed again. He did not trouble to lock his car door. It was like coming home. It was home. For the first time for days he could feel the tension generated by Golly's escapades flowing out of his body, and he realised almost with a sense of shock how tired he had become. It was like suffering from low level exposure, the sort that was insidious and hard to diagnose, but sufficient to lead to some lousy decisions, the sort you could only justify to the subsequent court martial with the excuse, 'It seemed like a good idea at the time.' Like even lending his name to Golly's insurance scheme. What he needed, if only for a brief hour or so, was the sanctuary of Margaret's body, the reassurance of her voice.

It was some time before she answered the door bell. She was wearing the yellow dress with the split skirt, the one she wore for special occasions.

'Bill! What're you doing here?'

'Come to see my best girl, haven't I, love?'

'I thought you were in London.'

She kissed him lightly, formally, and turned back into the house, leading the way to the lounge. 'Sit there, Bill. I'll be back in a minute.'

He heard her tread quickly upstairs, heard a faint buzz of voices, and she returned. Shakespeare supposed that it was the child, Cheryl, playing up as usual. Cheryl invariably insisted on being brought down to see him, however late the hour; usually the encounter would end with the child asleep in his lap, thumb in her mouth. He stretched, yawned, and unlaced his shoes. Presently Margaret returned, alone.

'D'you want anything? I mean, a cup of tea or anything?'

'Come here, Maggie. All I want, love, is inside that dress.'

'No, Bill, please!' She leaned away from him where he sat on the sofa, then slid to the floor at his feet, holding his hands, her restless fingers moving through his as if she were trying to wash them.

'What's up?' he asked.

'D'you know someone called McNeil from the Home Office? From MI5? He says he knows you.'

'Fat guy, going thin on top, sweats a lot?'

'Yes, Bill. That's the one. He came to see me today about Golly and everything.'

'Aye, I know. He answered your telephone when I rang up earlier. Evil little Scotsman.'

'He's upstairs, Bill.'

'He's what?'

'Upstairs, looking at that wedding album of ours – with Golly and you as his best man together – and all the other photos Golly left.'

Shakespeare stood and said, very quietly, 'He's off limits unless he has a search warrant. Has he got a search warrant? Have you asked him? Where's Cheryl? What's going on here?'

She scrambled after him as he moved towards the door, losing her shoes as she did so. 'Listen, Bill . . . no, stop a minute. Bill, listen! He says he'll pretend he didn't know you were down here, but you've got to go back to London straight away. He says you're in bad trouble already, you and Golly together. He says coming here makes it look as if you're up to something. Something about criminal conspiracy. Please go, Bill. Please go back.'

'You want me to go?'

She was standing in front of him, brushing the lapels of his jacket with her tiny hands, face against his chest. 'I don't know about Golly and I don't care any more. But I don't want you to do anything daft, Bill. See, I don't want to lose you as well. You can see that, can't you?'

'You want me to go, leaving him here?'

'Bill, listen. He says with you here it makes it look as if I'm involved in this thing, this conspiracy. Who's going to look after Cheryl, if . . .? Listen, Bill. I love you and I don't want to lose you. I'm going to have your child.'

'How's that again?'

'I'm pregnant, love.'

154

She looked at him through eyes huge with fear. It was an expression he had only seen before on the faces of men about to die, men he was about to kill on the jebel or in the jungle. 'It's due in seven months,' she said, speaking quietly. 'It's our child and I'm going to keep it.'

He removed her hands from his jacket and with slow, calm movements tied his shoelaces neatly in place as she watched, then walked past her to the front door; it was still open. Outside, a gentle rain was falling undisturbed by wind.

'Bye, Maggie,' he said and then added, as if it were an afterthought, 'Funny thing, that pregnancy of yours. Did I forget to tell you I got myself vasectomised years ago?'

Maggie, hands clasped to her stomach as if in pain there, head bowed and shoulders rounded, suddenly looked old, worn out and discarded. It was only when Shakespeare reached the driver's door of his Range Rover that he saw McNeil waiting for him. Shakespeare ignored his presence, swept open the door and climbed into the driver's seat. As he was about to shut the door, McNeil's hand closed round the edge of it, holding it open.

'I want a wee word with yew,' said the Scot.

'I've nowt to say to thee,' Shakespeare replied, aware that in his anger, as always, he was beginning to sound like a stage Yorkshireman. McNeil opened the door further and put his back against it.

'That's awful disappointing. I was just beginning to think you were in a mood to start taking some good advice. Mrs Nicholls has been an ornament of co-operation,' he went on, rolling the word 'ornament' in a leisurely way, as a boy might toss a ball high into the air, confident he can catch it without really trying. 'Aye, an ornament of co-operation she was. They're very fine wedding pictures. Was it she and Golly Nicholls getting married there, or was it Golly and yew? Fucking Special Forces. You make me laugh. You think you've got a licence to kill, then, laddie? Think you're some kind of hero?'

Shakespeare dropped his hands from the steering wheel onto his knees, swivelled slowly round in his seat, placed his feet on the edge of the door. His tormentor backed off a pace, but not fast enough to avoid Shakespeare's right hand, which took the front of his throat. It seized the windpipe high up under the chin, fingers one side, thumb the other, bruising sensitive nerve and tissue and burning its victim with pain. Instinctively McNeil put both hands to Shakespeare's wrist, but the terrible grip on his throat merely tightened. The textbook drill to avoid such a stranglehold, as he knew, was to step backwards. But he was trapped by the door behind him. Shakespeare had emerged from the vehicle and was standing over him now, lifting him by the throat until he was on tiptoe, emitting a gurgling noise. He faintly heard the Yorkshireman's voice murmuring confidentially into his ear, as if disclosing a secret to a friend, 'Listen, you wanker. 'I'm not threatening you, yet. Just leave off baiting me, that's all. Just lay off. Get off my back.'

When the grip was released McNeil collapsed to his knees, head spinning, heart racing, chest heaving, trying not to be sick. Shakespeare helped him to his feet, then re-entered the vehicle and closed the door, the window of which was open. McNeil leaned against it with both hands, his pale blue, hyperthyroid eyes staring hate. He moved his lips, but no sound came from them. Shakespeare knew he had gone too close to the man's voice box. Maybe McNeil would recover. Then again, he might never speak another word. Whether he did so or not Shakespeare knew also that he, like Golly, was now a fugitive.

'Get yourself to t'doctor, McNeil,' he said. 'You might have some internal bleeding.'

The Scot was holding the window frame, still staring, talking soundlessly. Shakespeare switched on the ignition, started the engine and put the vehicle into gear. Still McNeil held on. Steering with his left hand, the Yorkshireman let the clutch in and began to move off. He dislodged McNeil with a blow to the face, the heel of his hand smashing against the soft underside of his opponent's nose. Hands to face, McNeil rolled out of Shakespeare's line of vision as the Range Rover picked up speed out of

Eden Close.

He was not due to meet Nicholls for another four hours. He had only one course now. This was to turn Golly in; but not to Uncle Mac. He would take his friend back to Chevalier's office and they could sort it out. Legally, he was still only a missing person. And Golly was now the least of his worries. Women . . . how could she do it? What an actress . . . and what a cunt he was. Cursing quietly, he turned left on the road leading away from town and drove towards the airfield. People came and went stealthily there at all hours for a variety of purposes; there was no reason why his vehicle should attract particular attention. He was still in the city, about two miles from Eden Close, when a police car passed in the opposite direction, its blue light flashing. He followed its progress in his mirror, but it did not pause in its journey away from him. Another vehicle was following several hundred yards behind him; so far as he could judge, it was neither a police wagon nor anyone else pursuing him.

The events of this night and their implications had not yet touched him emotionally, and he knew it. This was crisis management, with no time to reflect on what was, or might have been, or – most painfully – what had seemed to be and was not. He did not want to think about Maggie. That was gone, finished; ancient history. Whatever wound it had inflicted would bleed later, but not now. Not now . . .

How would McNeil react? He'd want vengeance, that was for sure. Job with Chevalier; London flat; everything . . . washed up. But an immediate hue and cry, with the local fuzz laughing up their sleeves at MI5? That was unlikely. McNeil had too big a chip on his shoulder about the regiment to allow anyone to see him losing a round. Daft, but there it was. There were a lot of them about, in and out of the Army, with chips on their shoulders about the regiment.

Sleep. He needed sleep. He swung off the road and up the rough track towards the airfield. During the war it had been an RAF training base. The familiar Nissen huts, still bearing faded signs for 'Emergency Water Supply', came briefly to life in his headlights before he passed behind the buildings and on to the jumpers' camp ground. There was only one tent here tonight and no sign of life anywhere. No sign of headlights behind him, either. He set his alarm watch to wake him at four-thirty, stretched across the bench seat of the Rover and dozed off.

McNeil, on foot, reeled up the camp road several minutes later. His throat felt monstrously engorged and swollen as a turkey's. His head rang with pain at every step. His right hand, in his jacket pocket, gripped the butt· of a compact Walther PP automatic pistol, the safety catch of which he flicked mindlessly on and off with his thumb as an Arab might manipulate worry beads. He walked unsteadily round the buildings and on to the camp site. Somewhere above him an owl called in a strangled, rusty voice; from behind a bank of cloud the moon appeared to illuminate the Range Rover. He approached it cautiously, then fell on all fours, coming close enough to place an ear to the bodywork. The pain this caused his throat made him giddy, so he rested for a time before standing upright. Shakespeare's rubber-soled boots were horizontal against the windscreen and he was unconscious. In his own eyes, McNeil would be justified in killing Shakespeare now, for in his world to be able to get away with it, however implausibly, was to justify the action. But he wanted them both. He retraced his steps, clambered into his car, and waited.

This vehicle of his, a Porsche, was too flamboyant for the sensitive work on which he was usually engaged, but he continued to use it in spite of departmental warnings. For one thing, it was a trophy of McNeil's private war against subversion, a gift from an industrialist grateful to be let off the hook by an apparently bonhomous Uncle Mac. The industrialist had been unwisely optimistic in believing in McNeil's good faith and was imprisoned, obliquely as a result of McNeil's intervention in his affairs, a few months after parting with the car. The other, more practical reason why McNeil liked his Porsche was that it could pass anything else on the road. Now he and the Porsche sat toadlike, screened by bushes in a lay-by a few yards from the airfield entrance, waiting. To assuage the pain in his throat, McNeil sucked a boiled sweet. Occasionally his eyes glazed as he drifted into unconsciousness, but not for long. The pain in his wounded throat, the blood still dripping from his sore and battered nose, saw to that.

At the first streak of dawn in the eastern sky, the Range Rover sailed serenely out of the airfield, engine throbbing quietly, crushing gravel under its big wheels, like the sound of gentle surf, and turned towards the city. McNeil did not follow immediately. There was only one road his quarry could follow from here. While he waited, a full thirty seconds, all the birds of Herefordshire broke into song. The sound mocked him, reminding him he had no voice, no authority of speech. McNeil started to feel angry again. He switched on the engine and followed in Shakespeare's wake.

On the ring road, as he approached a big traffic island, Shakespeare glanced in his mirror and saw the steel grey hump of the Porsche behind him. As a routine precaution, he turned three hundred and sixty degrees round the island and drove back a few yards the way he had come. The other vehicle turned into a suburban side road. Satisfied, he swung the Range Rover in a tight, noisy U-turn, mounting the pavement as he did so, and resumed his way. Golly was waiting where he had dropped him the previous night. Bill flicked open the door for him and said, 'Morning, sunshine'; then, glancing in his mirror again, snapped, 'Get in quick. We've got trouble.'

Even before he could let the Rover into first gear, the Porsche had hurled itself along the road behind them, headlights full on, brakes screeching as it pulled across their path. Shakespeare found reverse, and started to drive around the car, but it instantly pulled out to the right also. They were approaching another traffic island. Shakespeare accelerated round it to the right, praying that there would be no vehicle coming the opposite way at this early hour. His prayers went unheeded. A slow-moving electric milk float appeared in front of him as he completed

159

his illegal turn-round the island. It swung right to avoid him and into the path of the Porsche. The Porsche struck the rear of the milk float with a ringing sound, like battle-axe against shield, spinning the float round, sending bottles of milk in an explosive barrage of glass across the road. Shakespeare held to the centre of the road, aware now that he could not hope to outstrip the Porsche, equally aware that his advantage in the Range Rover was greater weight, wheel height and, if need be, cross-country capability. For perhaps five miles out of Hereford on the road to Ross-on-Wye the Porsche harried them along a dual carriageway, passing now on the nearside, now braking immediately in front. At times McNeil's face, bloated with rage, was only inches from that of Golly Nicholls in the passenger seat.

'Ram the bastard,' said Nicholls. 'Push him off the road.'

They had come to a single carriageway and Shakespeare knew that he could not long postpone the inevitable. McNeil, he was certain, must be mad. As they climbed a long, straight hill the Porsche roared past them yet again on the offside, then edged across Shakespeare's front. This time he did not apply the brake to evade contact. Instead, he accelerated hard and swung out to the right.

The thud of his bumper as it struck the nearside of the Porsche was followed by a crack like gunshot as McNeil's tyre exploded. The vehicle snaked out of control in front of them, left and then right, into the path of a truck whose driver, after more than twelve hours at the wheel, was fending off sleep. Instinctively the truck driver swung left as the Porsche rammed into the cargo of petrol riding behind his cab. Although the Range Rover was now more than two hundred yards away, the blast as the tanker exploded hit the rear of Shakespeare's vehicle like a giant sledgehammer, pushing in glass and metal bodywork alike. Shakespeare stopped the Range Rover and the two men looked first at one another, then at the blazing wreckage outlined behind them against the distorted silhouette of their own vehicle. Even a hedge was on fire.

'I think you just failed your advanced driving test,'

Nicholls said reflectively.

'We'd better check for survivors,' Shakespeare murmured miserably.

'Survivors? From that? They'll have trouble finding enough pieces to make up a decent burial. Come to that, even a decent sandwich . . . reminds me, I could use some breakfast. Cummon. Let's go. We'll call the law from the first phone box we find.'

'Then what?'

'Then we get down to work on Operation Eldorado.'

'Aye.' Shakespeare spat on the ground. 'Eldorado, then. There's nowt else going for us, is there?'

'Nothing, Bill, except a bloody fortune and the good life.'

'Meanwhile, what about ready cash?'

'No sweat. I've got a sort of Post Office account. They're very good, really. I just walk into any Post Office and show them my I/D and they give me the money.'

'Your I/D?'

'Yes, Bill. Unmistakable, it is. A nine-milly Browning.'

# Chapter Eight

'You know, Major Tom,' said Kazanovitch, 'we have been thinking of how we should say adieu. To do so correctly, we really need a candle for each member of the orchestra and our full complement of instruments.'

Lumbering towards them on its fork-lift truck, the first of the tea-chests was approaching the rear door. By now Nicholls was becoming as wary of the conductor's leisurely, artless build-up to insult as the musicians were. He also wished that Kazanovitch had chosen some other time to discuss the small print of the handover. 'How's that, maestro?' he asked.

Tempo purred a little at this hard man's glancing recognition of his status. 'There was a composer called Haydn who lived through the golden age of music, two hundred years ago; his band was working overtime for a prince. They wanted to go home, you see. So he wrote a piece of music which ends slowly, while the players creep away, one at a time, and each one extinguishes his candle at the end of his part in the music, until finally only one violinist is left playing, with one candle burning. It is called the Farewell Symphony.'

Nicholls smiled like a relaxed schoolboy. 'Wouldn't do for us,' he said. 'Like in that poem of Miss Tremlington's, our candle burns at both ends, just like she said. Now take a seat for a few minutes, sir. Bill and me've got to watch this a bit careful, like.'

With the hostages moved forward and the curtain re-rigged behind them, the way was clear for the first chest to be manhandled into the cabin by Shakespeare. He moved quickly, aware that this would be a good moment for the Pagoda team to smash its way in through the main port exit at the front, or one of the emergency doors, just as they had done at Mogadishu. Nicholls, balaclava down,

162

studied the driver of the fork-lift truck. It was not a face he recognised but the man was a lean, hard character who would not look out of place in the regiment. He also took his time, either because he was unfamiliar with the machine he was controlling, or because he wanted to observe as much of the scene inside Juliet Bravo as he could. Somewhat ostentatiously, Nicholls swung the Armalite down from his shoulder and cocked the grenade launcher attached to it, though without pointing it directly at the fork-lift. The driver, taking the hint, swung the vehicle into a tight backward turn, and hummed away in the direction of the terminal.

The delivery of the second box also went according to plan, leaving at the rear entrance to Juliet Bravo only the narrowest passage for people of average size. Nicholls, working with his Swiss Army knife, prised the lids from both boxes and delved inside them like a hamster checking its hoard of nuts, then nodded to his partner and said, 'Take it away, Bill.'

'Their bus hasn't arrived yet,' Shakespeare objected.

'All the better. The more people there are swanning round the runway at the moment, the better. Anyway, they could use a walk and some fresh air.'

This time it was Diana Garrard who occupied a symbolic position of official and entirely fictitious normality at the foot of the steps. Led by the father of the orchestra, Basil Krivine, who was supported on one arm by Paddy Moynahan and on the other by Moira Tremlington, the musicians straggled in an untidy crocodile across the oil-stained puddles of the runway. The last three to leave were Anders, Legrange and Tempo Kazanovitch.

Anders said: 'One day, if you guys live long enough, you'll find too much adrenalin is bad medicine.'

Legrange told them: 'It's turned out better than I expected. I'm surprised no one got hurt.' His face was as pale as death; he shook his head and smiled as if at some private joke. 'Even been fun, some of the time.'

Tempo shook both their hands. 'You know, gentlemen, you should invest some of that money in something worthwhile,' he said. 'I know of an orchestra – not this one, but a real orchestra – which would make good use of your patronage. Here is my card.'

In a sealed area of the terminal, a young officer was reinforcing the final points of his briefing. 'We must wait until the hostages have been accounted for. Only if they start chopping the hostages do we go straight in. The code for that, as you have been told already, is, "Apex". Now, once that is given, a lot rests on the point man, Sergeant Collison, but remember, this isn't the Somme, or even Princes Gate. There are only two adoo in there. We'll see to it that one of them is tied up talking to the negotiator. So we don't need a lot of people storming in there. Two good marksmen only, plus the perimeter team as back-up, should keep the risk of battle accidents to a minimum. Now, marksmen: when you open fire, don't ponce about. You shoot to kill.'

The released hostages were no more than a hundred yards from the aircraft when a gunshot somewhere off to their right sent a frisson of panic through the group like a powerful charge of electricity. Some ran, others threw themselves to the ground. From his eyrie in the control tower, Wainwright demanded, 'What the hell is that about? Who's shooting?'

Alongside him, a civilian official suggested soothingly, 'Oh, that will be nothing. Nothing to be concerned about at all. It will only be one of our bird scarers. To prevent bird strikes, you know.'

The professionals on both sides held their fire, and one by one the musicians slowly rose to their feet. Then it gradually dawned on them that one figure was still flat against the ground, face and fingers pressed to the concrete as if in bed, bald patch uppermost like a large mushroom. The figure was unnaturally still. An instrument case lay beside it; nearby a flat check cap lifted gently with the wind.

'Will you not get on your feet, Bob Legrange, like the rest of us?' Moynahan shouted at him. 'Sure and if Basil Krivine can hoof it a few hundred yards, so can you.'

Still the figure did not move. Anders bent over and shook its shoulder, then put three fingers to Legrange's temple. Finally he turned the man over, onto his back.

'I just don't believe this!' he shouted. 'Bob's dead, goddammit. Dead, you hear? Not a mark on him!'

Watching the scene through binoculars, Wainwright said calmly, 'Apex, Sergent-major.'

The orchestra now split into two unequal groups. There were those who spotted the approaching bus and sensed even more keenly, after the death of Legrange, the danger they were in. They ran towards the sanctuary of the vehicle in panic, thrusting through its doorway even before it stopped near them; jostling and sobbing, sometimes cursing, all dignity destroyed. Tempo, arriving at the door when it was already crowded, elbowed his musicians aside and roared, '*Allez-y!*'

The second, smaller group remained clustered about Legrange like some modern *pietà*. Moira Tremlington knelt beside the motionless figure and murmured, 'I'm to blame for this. It's my fault. I should have made him take his pills.'

They were joined by Diana Garrard. She stood over the body of Legrange. Fingers instinctively patting her kiss-curl, she said brightly, 'Anything I can do?'

The bus stopped alongside them, the door on the driver's side swinging open like an exclamation mark. A young hatless policeman stumbled out of the vehicle. 'Quick,' he said. 'Quick for God's sake.' Behind him and behind the bus the ungainly shapes of two more fork-lift trucks bore yet more boxes towards Juliet Bravo. Diana Garrard stepped demurely into the bus but the others remained where they were.

'What about Bob Legrange?' said Moira Tremlington. 'We can't just leave him here.'

'If he's dead, mistress, you'll have to,' said the policeman. 'They're starting shooting. If we don't go now we'll all be dead.'

'Oh no,' Anders replied, rising to his feet. 'Moynahan! Get out here and help us.'

Moynahan, arms folded, chin on chest, sank further

165

into his seat near the back of the bus.

'Come on!' the young policeman said, taking hold of Legrange's feet. Anders and Moira Tremlington supported the dead man's head and shoulders. The noise of the bus's engine, which had been ticking over irregularly, now died away. Legrange was half in and half out of the bus, his feet still trailing on the ground. Abandoning them, the policeman ran round the front of his vehicle, hauled himself back into the cab and turned the ignition key. The engine fired at the third attempt and he put the vehicle into reverse.

Moira Tremlington, still holding one of her friend's arms, started to scream.

'Help! Please help me!'

At last, as they swung round in a sickening turn towards the airport buildings and gathered speed, other members of the orchestra joined her in the doorway. It was impossible to haul Legrange's body fully into the vehicle. Without someone to lift the inert legs, the weight, added to the lack of working space in the door, left a choice between dragging Legrange like a rag doll across the tarmac or ditching him completely. During a grisly journey which was to stay in Moira Tremlington's mind for ever, she noted that the dead man lost his shoes and his watch on the way.

Nicholls, leaving Shakespeare to cover the rear entrance to the aircraft, scrambled to his position on the flight deck and called up the control tower.

'What's going on?' he asked. 'Is that Wainwright?'

'Colonel Wainwright will be with you in a few moments,' a voice replied. The accent was unmistakably Camberley. Probably, Nicholls guessed, a young cavalry rupert on his first tour with 'G' Squadron. As Nicholls waited, the black internal telephone buzzed. 'It's Bill. What did the man say?'

'Nothing, yet. We're being given the run-around and I don't like it. Close the door, Bill.'

'You what? That means I'll see damn all. I want a clear field of fire back here.'

166

'Have it your own way, then!'

The first fork-lift truck halted, its load held high, and the driver dismounted. As he walked towards the aircraft, Shakespeare, flat on the floor, peered over the rim of the fuselage at him. 'What d'you think you're doing, sunshine?'

'Just checking the height. I was told to load this tea-chest.'

The man glanced up, turned and jumped back into the seat of the vehicle.

'We don't want it,' shouted Shakespeare. 'Piss off!'

The man stopped his machine and leaned out of the driving cab. 'What d'you say?' he called. At that moment an RAF Harrier jump jet swept over the scene at no more than a hundred feet, slowed, descended further, then crept like a grotesque flying beetle until it was hovering fifty yards from Juliet Bravo. The noise of its engines blotted out all further efforts at communication with the truck driver.

'Yes,' said the control tower. 'This is Colonel Wainwright. How're you doing, Golly?'

'My name's Major Tom.'

'Come off it, Nicholls. I was all set to bring Margaret up here. But I wasn't sure who she'd want to talk to, you or Bill Shakespeare.'

'What do you mean? Why should she talk to Shakespeare?'

'Oh, Golly . . . I'm sorry. Didn't you know Bill was shafting her while you were inside?'

'You bastard, Wainwright! You're trying to wind me up! You fucking liar . . . Listen, get those trucks out of here or we'll blow them up. And who killed that musician guy just now?'

'I guess the same team that killed the McAlister boy in Belfast, and the air steward, Archer. I did warn you, Golly—'

From the cockpit Nicholls felt rather than heard the sound of something exploding. Snatching up his weapon he darted back into the passenger section. Kilvert and his co-pilot were still in their places, heads down as

Shakespeare had instructed. Sitting just in front of them, in the same posture, was Naomi Lewis. There was no sign of Diana Garrard. Shakespeare was firing at something, from a position between the two tea-chests. As Nicholls squirmed into a gap to the right of him, Shakespeare said: 'Nothing much happening, Golly. Hold your fire. I just wanted to stop that fork-lift job.'

'You did that all right,' said Nicholls. The vehicle was now on fire, the box still sitting on top of the fork-lift mechanism. There was no sign of the driver. At a safe distance beyond the truck, the canopy of the Harrier was flung open. The pilot climbed out, apparently unconcerned, and ambled with his flight documents towards the control tower. Shakespeare and Nicholls continued watching as fingers of flame slowly reached up and caressed the tea-chest, which swelled in the heat. Then the varnish began to melt in great bubbles as the fire took hold of it.

When the box was finally buckling, one of the sides flew away to be followed by the figure of a man dressed in black, still holding in one hand a Heckler & Koch submachine-gun fitted with a long silencer. The masked figure crumpled as it hit the ground, rose to its knees, then collapsed again. Nicholls, eyes dancing with malicious excitement, took a slow, careful aim on the man. 'This one's for you, Wainwright,' he muttered. As he squeezed the trigger Shakespeare's boot kicked the barrel of the weapon, sending the shots uselessly into the grass beside the runway.

'Sorry, Golly. He's more use to us alive. Bargaining chip, see? You cover me. I'm going to snatch him.'

Without waiting for a reply Shakespeare slid over the rear entrance and, ignoring the stairway, dropped the ten feet or so like a happy, confident monkey. The truck was still burning. The fire had taken hold of the tyres now and these gave off a dense cloud of smoke that provided perfect cover. Shakespeare dropped to his knees and approached the man in a sinuous crawl. The weapon first . . . safety catch on and sling over his head and shoulders.

'Hold your fire, Golly,' he called. The man was almost as tall as Shakespeare himself and built like a tank. When

Shakespeare tore off the gas mask, the face beneath it was one he faintly recognised from long ago. Confident that no one – not even Nicholls – would shoot now, he bent to haul the dead weight onto his shoulder; because his captive was so heavy Shakespeare was obliged to kneel to place the body in a fireman's lift. As he stood, his legs buckled momentarily under the burden. He clambered ponderously up the steps and into the aircraft like someone immersed in an antique diving suit. Wainwright's assistant, studying the scene through binoculars, reported, 'Looks like they've got Sergeant Collison, sir.'

'Yes,' said Wainwright bleakly. 'I noticed.'

An hour later, with the robust cheerfulness of someone asserting that dinner was about to be served, Brigadier Vincent Butcher, the Special Forces supremo, announced: 'Gentlemen, all the hostages except the two aircrew and one stewardess were released at fifteen hundred hours.'

The Cobra committee was in session again. Butcher, delivering the military briefing, noted that some of the big political guns were being wheeled out. In addition to Mackie there was Sir Harold Murtchison, Chancellor of the Duchy of Lancaster and unofficial Minister for Propaganda, representing Downing Street; Lord Everest, a mandarin's mandarin, as well as Angus Howard, for the Foreign Office; Sir Charles de Tassigny, as well as Wilkins, for the Treasury; and the Home Secretary, Macdonald Pope in person, accompanied by a swarm of acolytes. Defence was represented by one junior minister. The rest were at that moment confined in what one of them described as 'the headmaster's study'.

'What has happened since is not clear,' Butcher continued. 'We are still getting reports. There has been some shooting, but not by us. One musician, a Mr Legrange, died after leaving the aircraft. We think this was accidental, a heart attack. The ransom has been loaded onto the aircraft in two tea-chests. We now have the choice of putting further lives in jeopardy by trying to storm the aircraft or permitting it to leave. You will be aware that the option of playing out this affair is now closed. The PM's instructions are to resolve this crisis today. On the military side, we think it is a dead certainty that an attack on the aircraft at this time would result in loss of life on both sides. Now if we are given orders to that effect, we will go in hard, using AFVs as back-up if necessary.'

'AFVs?' someone asked.

'Armoured fighting vehicles. Tanks, armoured cars. A small-calibre gun could blow the aircraft's tail section away and we could finish off the terrorists inside with machine-guns. That would inevitably bring about the deaths of the aircrew. Alternatively we allow the aircraft to leave. The key here is the provision of generators to start the engines. We positively help them to fly but we refuse to supply more fuel, limiting the aircraft to British air space. The terrorists are then faced with the reality we have counted upon throughout: they have the aircraft, which is a diminishing asset without civilian hostages, and they have the money, but so much money they cannot possibly move it out of the aircraft without a vehicle. In other words, they are more trapped now than ever before. The stress of the operation is beginning to wear them down and they have very few bargaining chips left. By confining them to British air space, we think we can still bring this affair to a fairly peaceful, cost-effective conclusion. However, it does mean giving them a little more rope with which to hang themselves.'

The long silence which followed Butcher's briefing was broken by a rasping smoker's cough from Harold Mackie. 'Sorry,' he said, waving his handkerchief before stuffing it back into his pocket. Wilkins, the Treasury man, pointedly rose from his seat next to Mackie and moved to a safer place.

'Seems to me,' said the Foreign Office representative, Angus Howard, 'we only know what the terrorists' intentions are if we can assess their capabilities. Have you identified them yet?'

'No,' Butcher said. 'Not one hundred per cent.'

Murtchison, his polished white shirt and polished white face and hair gleamed like some marbled statue, said: 'I think we all agree that the use of tanks in a situation like this would be quite intolerable. That sort of thing was all very well in Egypt in the fifties but it's totally unacceptable in the United Kingdom today. We haven't even resorted to that in Northern Ireland. Can't you wait for these people to nod off, as it were, and use the element of surprise?'

'That could take a long time,' Butcher replied. 'The PM wants something done now. Because the situation is currently static at Prestwick, it has developed into a sort of theatrical event from which we're having difficulty in excluding television and so forth. At the very least – given the PM's requirement – we need to move the thing somewhere else. That process in itself piles the pressure on the terrorists. I'm certain they will make a mistake. If we don't win, at least we will play for a draw.'

Pope, the Home Secretary, had been apparently busy throughout the conference reading through documents which he extracted from a red box, pausing every so often to initial one of them. He was young, younger than any of them, with a controversial career at the bar and in the academic world already behind him; his innocuous, owl-like appearance behind large spectacles belied a tough politician's instinct for an opponent's jugular. He now closed the red box and handed it to one of the acolytes.

'Brigadier, I think you should come clean with this committee. There is a widespread belief among the police at the scene that the terrorists are former members of your own unit. Can you confirm that?'

'No, sir. We will not know that until they are in custody, dead or alive. They are British, they have had military training, but whether in this country or elsewhere I am not prepared to say yet. If I may say so, Minister, speculation of the kind you are bandying about could be very damaging.'

Everest interjected, 'Let me be sure, Brigadier, I follow your plan, if such it is. We allow the aircraft to fly away with half a million pounds of taxpayer's money and then sort of fiddle about?'

'We follow it, sir. We stick with it. The RAF will have

Phantoms for close pursuit and observation. Not far behind them a late Hercules with one of my regiment's freefall parachute teams will be ready to jump into whatever airfield is chosen by the terrorists as their next port of call. That team will provide an instant *cordon sanitaire* to block any escape route. We continue to deny them fuel. What can the terrorists do then? Kill the pilots as a reprisal? If they want to preserve some freedom of movement, that isn't an option. We want them to discover that even in the air they are already in custody. There is no way they can escape. Our only problem now is to get that point across to them. We have to edge them quietly into a corner, as softly as possible, without pressing them so hard that they do something stupid.'

The committee broke up in a mood of quiet confidence, even if the outcome of Butcher's strategy was unclear. One of his greatest strengths was his knack of making the unlikely seem plausible; the impossible, mundane. In Parliament Square, the late London editions declared: 'Hijack Terrorists Kill Musician – They Will Pay, Says PM'. As they passed the news-stand together, Mackie, the Downing Street spokesman, chuckled and asked Butcher: 'Brigadier, would you really have used tanks?'

'Only little tanks,' Butcher replied. 'Say a lightweight aluminium Scorpion running on a Jaguar car engine and firing a 76 millimetre gun. Would have done the job nicely. But I don't think HMG is really ready for force on that scale yet. So what are we left with, Mr Mackie? The PM won't tolerate the present situation. It has to be unfrozen, somehow. I wasn't being entirely Jesuitical in concentrating minds on what a quick solution might mean. What we've now got might seem at first glance to be a bit wet, I grant you that, but it's all we have. A bit of movement's what we need now to cure a potentially dangerous case of constipation.'

Back in his own headquarters, Butcher listened gravely to the latest reports from his staff. 'Even worse than I thought,' he said. 'Sounds like a one hundred per cent cock-up. Extract Tim Wainwright. Put him in charge of the pursuit team, aboard the Hercules. He is a freefaller isn't he? From now on I'll handle the negotiations myself.'

When Sergeant Edward Collison started to regain consciousness the first thing of which he was aware was the spittle dribbling down his chin under a mask across his face. For a second or two he thought it was the CS gas mask. Danger! He was in danger! He was rolling clear of the burning crate and he had dropped his weapon and . . . and now his hands would not move. He opened his eyes but could see nothing. Blind! He was blind and paralysed and yet not without sensation in his limbs. Didn't they say you could suffer pain in an amputated limb, because the nerve endings remained intact after the limb was cut off? If his arms were immovable, his legs and feet were not. Nor was his trunk. He braced his feet against . . . something that had not been there before. What was more, this was not his CS mask.

'Looks like he's coming round,' a voice said. 'Nothing like a shot of oxygen to clear the lungs.'

'Aye then,' another replied. 'We'll take that mask off.'

The cool hand on his forehead was definitely not hostile. It pressed his head gently backward into a soft cushion, and a plastic cup touched his lips. He drank the water greedily.

'There's nothing to worry about,' the woman's voice whispered to him. 'You're going to be OK.'

'I can't see,' he said and coughed with the effort of speaking. 'What's more, feels as if someone's been at my throat with sandpaper.'

'You're on the aircraft,' the woman replied softly. 'Remember the aircraft? You were trying to rescue us. Now you're a prisoner, like us.'

Collison remembered well enough. He remembered kneeling in the crate, peering through a spy-hole as it jerked up and down. He remembered concluding that even if he let loose a full burst of automatic and emptied the magazine he would not have more than fifty per cent chance of hitting the bad guys. He remembered cursing

Wainwright for a scheme that had no chance, cursing his own luck for being chosen, as often before, as the monkey with the broken short straw. As usual his willingness to obey any order, however insane, being taken for granted. What he said now was, 'No. I don't remember anything. Have I gone blind?'

'It's just a bandage on your eyes,' the woman replied. 'They insisted on that.'

'I can't move my hands,' he said.

'They're tied to your chair, so you can't escape.'

'Right, Naomi, I'll take over now.'

The woman's odour, a mixture of pungent perfume and stale sweat, receded and dissipated before he could recall completely the memory it evoked of a hot afternoon somewhere in Cyprus years ago.

'What's your name, kid?' a man's voice asked him.

'Collison . . . I think. Ted Collison. Would that be right?'

'That's what it says on your dog-tag. You ought to be in t'Brain of Britain. What's your regimental number?'

'Two-two-three-six-six-one-four-three,' Collison replied. 'Never forget your I/D number.'

'Good. What's your unit?'

'Fifty-one Field Ambulance, RAMC.'

'No it isn't. Not any more it isn't. Is it? You transferred to another unit a long time ago, didn't you?'

'Did I?'

'Stop conning, Collison,' said the voice. Like that of the woman, it spoke quietly, almost in a whisper. Unlike hers, it was laced with menace. 'You were a medic attached to B Squadron a long time ago on Op Storm, though you hadn't passed selection. You transferred to Seventeen Troop when they amalgamated the regiment with the Paras and them lot. Then they badged you because of the expansion programme and they were taking anyone who could walk at the time, and they made you up to sergeant. You've just come back from Ireland and now you're doing a tour on the Pagoda team. I fucking marked you through selection, and failed you. "Nice bloke, too nice, not one of us," I put on your report. That was before amalgamation, when the regiment was worth something, so don't fuck me around.'

'You're Staff Shakespeare,' Collison said.

On the other side of the blindfold, Nicholls grinned. 'Right first time,' he said. 'Lucky for you Golly Nicholls isn't here, 'cos if he was, he might just cut your throat. Golly didn't like amateurs sniffing around his women.'

'Me and Margaret are man-and-wife,' the prisoner announced with practised formality. 'Nicholls got killed parachuting, they said. There was a steaming great row about the inquest, though. Local coroner told the Home Office to take a running jump when they tried to stop it. Good bloke that.'

'What happened about the insurance?'

Collison paused for a long time. Then he said, 'No reason not to tell you, I suppose. Margaret's getting it all. Another big fuss, there was. You were the executor and, well, they've just disqualified you. Maggie's solicitor put a notice in the paper asking you to come forward. But I didn't marry Margaret for the money. I don't want to touch it. I don't want her to touch it, either.'

'What about the kids?' Nicholls asked.

'The kids think I'm their dad.'

'Two kids, right?'

'Right.'

'One's a little girl?'

'That's Cheryl.'

'And the other?'

'A boy. Roger. Great nipper. Named him after Golly, she did, though God knows why.'

'A son, eh? Who does he look like? Who'd you say was his dad, Shakespeare or me?'

'But you are Shakespeare, aren't you?' asked Collison from behind his blindfold. 'You sound like him. If not, who are you?'

'Mind your own fucking business.'

Nicholls went aft, angry with himself for a stupid, unnecessary blunder, to where Shakespeare was still sitting, apparently watching the smouldering remains of the fork-lift. As he slid into the space beside him, Nicholls

175

noticed that his partner's eyes were closed.

'Bill,' he whispered. And again, 'Bill.' For the first time in their long years together, Shakespeare really had drifted decisively from a state of watchful stillness into sleep. It occurred to Nicholls that he could kill Shakespeare then and there . . . but to what purpose? Wainwright shouldn't have said that. If it was true, then Bill should have come clean, or Maggie should, about them carrying on while he was marking time in prison. Half the bloody neighbourhood must have known what was going on. If Wainwright knew it, that meant it had even reached the officers' mess. And he didn't know. That was what hurt. Everyone having a laugh at his expense. Now . . . well, now there was more money than either of them could carry away from this. Until Op Eldorado was safely over, they would still need each other. Afterwards as well, maybe. Maybe. Take it or leave it. When the chips were down in this world you could only depend on one person and not always then. Still, even though the partnership with Shakespeare was always provisional – just till the end of the next operation and after, well, they'd see what happened – it was standing up after a long time even if at times they hated each other. So he put a hand on his partner's shoulder and said, 'Bill, mate, I'm going to talk to Wainwright. Collison's awake and taking nourishment. Everything's under control.'

With the rear door closed, no internal lighting and an almost empty hull, the aircraft now had a cavernous quality. Soon it was dark and the cavern became colder. The aircrew, the remaining stewardess and the prisoner were wrapped in blankets. Through the darkness they caught snatches of Nicholl's latest conversation with the authorities – all, that is, except Shakespeare, sitting nearest the tail. He had now subsided into a profound sleep. Naomi Lewis, the only hostage who was not restrained, could have released the others but she dismissed the thought even as it crossed her mind. She was, she told herself, simply too tired for more crisis management. *Che sera, sera.*

In the cockpit itself, Nicholls shivered, recalling that

176

none of them had taken hot food for three days or more. The cold made him want to empty his bladder; he decided to set up a contact with Wainwright first. He called the control tower.

The cavalry rupert's voice answered. 'Colonel Wainwright is otherwise engaged. But don't worry. Someone will speak to you presently. Stand by.'

Soon there was a burst of static and an unfamiliar voice. 'Hello. Is that Major Tom?'

'Aye, speaking,' Nicholls replied. Why, he wondered, had they backed away from using his real name? 'Where's Wainwright?' he asked. 'Who are you?'

'My name is Brigadier Butcher. I don't know whether we have met at some time in the past. Possibly we have.'

'Where's Wainwright? Nicholls asked again.

'I've taken him off this job,' Butcher replied. 'That misunderstanding earlier today was not really his fault, but it should not have happened. We need to make a fresh start with these negotiations.'

'Oh, aye,' said Nicholls. 'Hold on a minute.'

He summoned Naomi Lewis. 'Get my partner in here,' he told her.

'So what's your pitch, Brigadier?'

'I'll square with you, Major. Your demands have been met. You are holding one of my men. I want him back in one piece. You can't move out of here unless I agree to supply generators to start the engines of your aircraft. You turn my man loose, and I allow you to fly out of here. How is my man, by the way? Will he require medical treatment?'

'He'll live,' Nicholls replied. 'They haven't briefed you very well, have they, Brigadier? This kite's got something called an auxiliary power unit. It's self-starting.'

Butcher paused, then said, 'I can still block the runway. I want my man back. Then you can go. Do we have a deal?'

'I'll think about it and call you back. Stand by.'

As Shakespeare's long frame loomed in the doorway, Nicholls asked him: 'Bill, d'you remember a rupert called Butcher?'

'Sure. He was with us on Jebel Akhdar back in '59. Clever, devious bastard. Leaked the route we were using to attack the jebel to the Arab mule handlers, knowing it'd get back to the adoo within a few hours. Then he changed the route. Good bloke to soldier with, though. Why're you asking?'

'He seems to be God these days. He says he's taken Wainwright off this op and he's running it himself.'

'Might be true. Wainwright might be sitting out there with a hit team at this moment. I'll tell you this, if Butcher is conning you, you won't find out until too late. "Foxy" . . . aye, that were his nickname in the old days. What's the trade?'

Nicholls outlined the deal.

'Sounds OK,' said Shakespeare thoughtfully. 'Mind you, I'm surprised they're making it that easy for us. Then again, Butcher was always a great one for loyalty. Do anything to get one of his team out of the shit, even if it didn't make military sense. Once we're in the air, we're our own masters again. I reckon we should accept. Turn Collison loose only when the engines are running and we're cleared to fly out of here.'

'If not later,' Nicholls replied. 'From about ten thousand feet. D'you know who Collison's married to?'

'No. Should I?'

'He's married Maggie. Great, in't it? I'm legally dead, she collects a small fortune on my life insurance, and he marries her.'

Shakespeare stiffened slightly. 'I wouldn't whinge about losing Maggie,' he said. 'Not worth it. All ancient history.'

'Right,' said Nicholls. His eyes lit strangely. 'I'll bet Collison's not the only one to go through her since I married her. The kids are mine, though.'

'How's that again? I thought you only had the one. Then the two of you split up.'

'Yeah, we did. But while I was based at that para club I used to turn up unexpected now and again like, catch her before she had time to get her cap in, get my end away and nip out over the back garden fence. Had to watch my step, though, didn't I? I'd heard she'd got another regular boyfriend by then. Last time I tried it on, she wasn't having any. It needed a bit of persuasion, did that. Early in the morning it were, and there she was, in the bath, soap all over her. It was like trying to shag a slippery wet fish. Anyways up, I got in the bath with her, all my gear on, grabbed her hair in one hand and one wrist with the other, and pushed her face into the bath water. She had the choice between letting it happen or drowning. She got the point eventually, same as they all do. Wrote me a stinking letter later, though. Never to darken her door again or she'd have me carpeted for rape. Reckoned I'd got her in the pudding club again, she did. She was bloody furious . . . Eh, what's up wi' you, Bill? You look sick as a parrot in an empty hen coop. I'll get on to Butcher and tell him it's a deal.'

# Chapter Nine

It was almost midnight before the pilots were fed and permitted to wash. Wearily they stumbled through their cockpit drill. With evident reluctance the captain, Kilvert, restored to his wallet photographs of two children – a boy and a girl in their early teens – which he had studied as if hypnotised by their images throughout the long hours on the ground.

A few miles away at Strathallan, the lumpish, camouflaged shape of a Hercules transport of the Joint Air Transport Establishment was also preparing to take-off with forty Special Forces parachutists on board. The two RAF Phantoms allocated to the pursuit were already airborne, as were two Victor refuelling tankers from Cambridgeshire. With his blindfold still intact, Sergeant Collison was handed over to the civilian engineer in charge of the airport's unwanted mobile generator by a balaclava-clad Shakespeare. Butcher watched as Juliet Bravo lifted off in a light south-westerly wind, under low cloud. His eyes did not blink following the winking tail-light of the aircraft as it turned to fly north. 'One mistake, that's all we need,' he murmured as it vanished into the night. 'Just one mistake.'

'OK, skipper, how's the fuel situation?' Nicholls asked cheerfully as they edged along the west coast of Scotland.

'Not good,' grunted Kilvert. 'Flying at your usual altitude, no more than two hours.'

'Didn't we tank up at Schiphol?'

'Yes, I thought we did. They must have short-changed us.'

'Is that possible? Can't you tell how much fuel you have?'

'In a normal situation, you rely on the gauges on the ground. This wasn't a normal situation. You moved me out of the cockpit at the time, remember? So no one was monitoring the fuel gauges in here. Where do you want to go?'

'Fly to Edinburgh, altitude seven thousand feet, then back here,' Nicholls told him. 'We'll give you further instructions then. In the meantime, you both stay here on the flight deck. That understood? Oh yes, and I want a met forecast for the whole of the British Isles including cloud cover and wind speed a.g.l.' Nicholls consulted his notebook. 'You'll get that from the "Volmet", as you know.'

The two partners now set up the curtain in a new position, half-way down the hull, to give themselves more working space, and placed sticking plaster over the spy-hole in the flight deck door. Confined to the area forward of the curtain, Naomi Lewis could see nothing; the jargon of broken conversation – a patois mixture of colloquial Arabic, Malay and British Army argot – obscured her comprehension of what was being said.

She heard Major Bill ask, 'Did we calibrate those AODs before we left?' Major Tom's reply was inaudible. Then Major Bill's voice again, *Tayyib*! Very *tayyib*!' Except that he chose to pronounce 'very' as *velly*'. She heard Major Tom say, 'Right, Bill, the next job's to get those crates rigged. Rope netting's in the red container . . . ' After that, silence, except for the grunts of men working physically under pressure and an occasional monosyllable, usually abusive. Once, Major Tom's voice declared loudly, 'Get in there, you cow!'

As instructed, Juliet Bravo wheeled over Edinburgh, the blackness of the Firth of Forth and Holyrood Park stark against the city lights, the dark firth decorated with a string of luminous pearls that was the Forth road bridge. Nicholls, sweeping the curtain aside, emerged to peer through a passenger window and scrutinise a pocket compass. As they made their U-turn, he spotted the tail-light dancing on one of the Phantoms. He cursed softly and walked past Naomi Lewis, onto the flight deck.

'Here, skipper. Are you talking to those Phantoms?'

'No,' replied Kilvert. 'Not necessary. You can't be

surprised, though, if they keep us in sight. The weather situation, by the way, is pretty uniform everywhere: almost stationary anti-cyclone centred over the Irish Sea, eight-tenths cloud cover at ten thousand feet and a south-westerly wind of five to ten knots on the ground.'

'Our position now?'

'Over Lanarkshire, flying west. We'll hit the coast at Rothesay in about ten minutes.'

'Good,' Nicholls said. 'You and your buddy can remove your headphones now. You won't be needing them for a while.'

'I need them all the time,' Kilvert replied. 'We're not the only aircraft flying in this area. Air Traffic need to know roughly where we are. Without the headphones and some communication, this kite's just an unguided missile.'

'Pull the other one, the one with bells on,' Nicholls grinned. 'If you haven't switched on your transponder by now you don't deserve to hold a pilot's licence. Ground radar will have us in sight all the time.'

Kilvert, hands on the steering column, eyes on the console in front of him, felt rather than saw the bleak metallic snout of a pistol barrel held to his head just behind his right ear. 'It's been a pleasure flying with you so far,' said Nicholls. 'It would be a pity if your journey came to a sudden end when it's nearly all over. I want those headphones disconnected and off your head now. And the hand mike, please.'

In the Air Traffic office at Prestwick, Butcher and a huddle of other security advisers followed the clipped, spare reports of the Phantom pilots. 'Mike Bravo . . . target bearing two-seven-five degrees at three hundred metres. Flying due west, two hundred knots, seven thousand feet a.g.1. . . .' His eyes turned from the map to the emergency scrambler telephone fitted within the first hour of the negotiations.

'This is Brigadier Butcher. Can the FCO tell us how the Irish are playing this? No, man, I mean air traffic at Dublin. We want to follow our target into their air space if necessary with a couple of Phantoms and the Jate

Hercules . . . I see. That's quite extraordinary. I don't think they have an air force as such. Wait one . . . '

He placed the telephone on the desk, lifted his head and called to the civilian controller, 'Got a copy of *Jane's Military Aircraft*? I need one in a hurry . . . '

The volume was placed in front of him as the Phantom leader reported Juliet Bravo's position over Rothesay, still flying west.

'Hullo, John? Listen, the book here suggests they have nothing which could do the job . . . a few clapped-out, second-hand Aerospatiale jet Magisters for training and eight supercharged Cessnas. I doubt very much whether they're equipped for night operations in any case. They'll have to give the RAF a free hand on this one. Look into it urgently and call me back.'

Aboard Juliet Bravo, Nicholls sat back, sweating but content that the hard labour was all but finished. He watched the lights of Glasgow pass beneath them, then moved forward to the flight deck. On the way through, he passed Naomi Lewis. She was curled up in one of the forward passenger seats. Her usually neat hair was disarranged and she was sucking her right thumb.

'Evening,' he said cheerfully. She did not reply. As he entered the flight deck, Kilvert reported, 'Rothesay just coming up.'

'Good. Now turn onto a new course – let's see – of two hundred and twenty degrees.'

'That'll take us directly over Macrihanish,' the co-pilot objected.

'So?'

'It's a prohibited military area. Top secret airfield. Not only the RAF, either. The Americans have some funny gear down there.'

Nicholls stretched out an arm and ruffled his hair playfully. 'Don't you worry your little head about that, son,' he said. 'They won't shoot. We've got a military escort already.' Then, turning to Kilvert, he added: 'One other item, skip. I want you to fly with the undercarriage down and a flap of, say, forty degrees.'

'A forty-degree wingflap?' Kilvert looked incredulous.

'That'll cut our speed to just above the stall point. It will also increase fuel consumption no end.'

'That's what I want,' Nicholls replied, grinning triumphantly. 'A forty-degree flap and a nice slow speed. I don't hold with all this rushing about.'

'Are we landing at Aldergrove, then?' Kilvert asked. 'If we are, I need to know now. We're only ten minutes away from Belfast. I'll also want my headset back.'

'No, we're not landing at Aldergrove,' Nicholls said. 'I hate Belfast.'

'In that case, Major Tom, we're busting right through the accepted safety margins so far as fuel consumption goes. It's as if we were driving a car up the motorway in first gear with the choke out. You do understand that?'

'You leave me to worry about that,' Nicholls replied. He was no longer smiling.

'No, I'm worried as well,' Kilvert persisted. 'Real worried. I'd like to think we're going to land this aircraft on a concrete runway, in one piece.'

'Did anyone ever tell you, Kilvert, that deep down you're a bit of an old woman? If we're almost out of fuel now then it's your fault for not checking the situation back at Schiphol.'

'You must be out of your mind,' Kilvert said quietly. 'If we crash, then you go with us.'

'Not necessarily. I'm a very lucky guy.'

The argument between Nicholls and Kilvert as they cruised south-west towards the Irish Republic was not the only quarrel provoked by their chosen route. Sitting on the edge of his youthful mistress's bed in Dublin's student quarter, the Irish Minister for Foreign Affairs, Malachy Fergus, was nursing a painful hangover and trying to cope with a telephone call. It was a little after two a.m. He had been on the wagon for three months. Last night he had made a roistering return to the bars which had served him, and finally thrown him out, since his own days as a student. The only difference now was that a chauffeur-driven limousine was waiting outside to pick him up.

'You can tell them to go and stuff themselves. The

British Air Force will not just march into our air space because of some bandit problem they cannot handle. I'd never live it down. I'd be the first minister since the foundation of this state to permit the return of British armed forces. Our own lads will have to deal with it.'

He turned to the slender girl curled naked on the end of the bed. She was holding, if unsteadily, a yoga posture approximating to the lotus and trying to smoke a cigarette at the same time. 'Kate, will you pass us a fag?' he asked. Then, turning back to the telephone: 'You what? Well, if our lads cannot be sure of intercepting this thing, they will have to wait until morning, surely.' He paused again, the telephone shaking a little in his hand.

'Listen to me, now. I'm no military authority, but it's surely feasible for the people at Dublin and Shannon airports – to say nothing of Cork and Dundonnell and the rest – to watch this thing on the radar. It isn't a bomber. As long as it's up there in the air, it does no one *anny* harm. Some time it will have to land somewhere.'

'Help me, Malachy,' the girl wailed.

He waved at her impatiently. 'Just alert the Gardaí and tell them they are to arrest everybody the moment the thing lands. If it flies on to somewhere else, then it ceases to be our problem. I'm going back to bed.'

With that, he banged the telephone back on its cradle, rolled sideways into the bed, farted loudly and descended into a protective, snoring slumber.

The young woman, legs crossed in front of her, hands on toes, spat out the corktip of her extinguished cigarette and murmured, 'Help me, Malachy . . the mantra. I've forgotten my bloody mantra!'

The bad news was relayed from the British embassy to the duty desk man in London with the comment, 'You'll notify Downing Street immediately, George?'

From his office in Downing Street, Mackie glanced at the clock and advised, 'It isn't something to worry about too much. The media won't be awake for hours yet. By then, I believe, this thing will be all over. We can only wait now and watch developments. I'll draft a holding statement along the lines that "HMG regrets it was denied hot pursuit of two international criminals by the policies of a friendly neighbouring state", and so on . . .' Then he, too, returned to sleep, on the sofa.

Butcher, in Scotland, was incredulous. 'The bastards are slipping through our fingers,' he said. 'They're actually getting away with it.'

RAF Aldergrove relayed the news to the captains of the two Phantoms and the Hercules. The Hercules would land at Aldergrove. The Phantoms were to continue the pursuit no further than the town of Newry, eight miles from the border with the Irish Republic. They would maintain radar contact for as long as possible by staying just inside the border.

Some objects are too small to be detected in this way. What the Phantoms' radar could not record was the ejection from Juliet Bravo of the first of the tea-chests. Satisfied that the course, speed and altitude were to his liking, Nicholls moved back to the secure zone he and Shakespeare had created at the rear of the aircraft. He studied the chest, then said: 'Seems a pity just to ditch it, when we went to all this trouble.'

'We knew all along we'd have to ditch one of them,' Shakespeare replied. He was studying his watch carefully. 'Did you say ten minutes to the Irish border? I'd say anywhere here's just about right. If the drogue works, it'll fall stable and level and only break up on impact. They find the loot and they start searching for us.'

'Rotten shame, all the same, Bill. We must be crazy, throwing away a quarter of a million quid.'

Shakespeare grinned. 'You can't take it with you, Golly. Not all of it, anyway. Come on then, let's move it.'

'Right, staff-sergeant!'

Gingerly, they pushed and pulled the chest until it was poised on one corner at the brink of the door. It was surrounded by rope netting which would snag on their boots or fingers, carrying them out with it, if they did not take care. On top of the netting, neatly folded down beneath white break-tie string, was a small drogue

186

parachute. The string was attached at its other end to a seat in the aircraft. If their calculations were correct, the string would act as a static line to break open the drogue as the box left the aircraft. Nicholls opened both doors, wincing at the noise. They looked at one another and nodded. Nicholls called the time, 'Ready . . . set . . . go!' and pushed. For a fraction of a second, like a discus thrower who is about to fall forward out of the throwing circle, it seemed as if he might overbalance, so anxious was he to follow the progress of the crate. Shakespeare, who had taken the precaution of roping himself to one of the seats, grabbed his arm. Some twenty seconds later the crate splintered at high speed in a green sheep-filled meadow. It made a small hole in the peaty earth around which tens of thousands of crisp new banknotes in half a dozen world currencies were now spread. Within an hour a gentle breeze had scattered them over several square miles.

The two men were now committed to the final, most dangerous and time-critical phase of Op Eldorado. As they moved from their secure zone into the open passenger area, Kilvert and his co-pilot were discussing the fuel level and their ultimate destination.

'Doesn't make much sense to me,' the co-pilot said, studying a manual. 'On this bearing there is no airfield that will accommodate us this side of Puerto Rico.'

Nicholls leaned over Naomi Lewis and shook her gently. 'Naomi, love. Wake up,' he said. She opened one eye as if drugged, then curled into a tighter, more defensive ball than ever. 'You've got to go to the flight deck now. You can go back to sleep there, if you want.'

'Leave me alone,' she said. 'Go away.'

Shakespeare shrugged. 'I don't think it matters,' he commented. 'Let's get on with it.'

They moved to the flight deck and peered out, over the heads of the pilots. The cloud had lifted and it was now a fine moonlit night, just as the moon tables had promised. Below them only a sprinkle of fairy lights marked the few roads and villages in the great void of central Ireland. Then Shakespeare saw what they were seeking, silently grasped Nicholls's arm and pointed. On the horizon, brilliantly lit and resembling some pagan temple, were the three white cooling towers of Roscommon power station, the steam from millions of tons of burning peat rising lazily above them. The leisurely movement of the steam confirmed that the wind was at a safe level. As Nicholls had often observed, the basic mistake made by their mentor, D. B. Cooper, was to tackle a wind far beyond the range of his rig or his experience. The FBI had never found a body, it was true, but an American guru who had simulated the operation in identical conditions had almost killed himself. The cooling towers told them something else. They signalled the wind's direction as clearly as a smoke marker.

'Give me ten left,' Nicholls told the pilot.

'How's that again?'

'I want you to change course, ten degrees left, to port,' Nicholls repeated slowly.

Obediently Kilvert swung the aircraft round onto its new bearing. Nicholls, satisfied, turned to Shakespeare and winked at him, then nodded towards the door. They walked away from the flight deck, taking care to close the door behind them. Naomi Lewis was still asleep as Nicholls bent over her, kissed her lightly on the forehead and then followed his partner through the curtain.

Neither man spoke as each unzipped a black container concealing a compact lightweight parachute rig. The rigs were pick-a-back tandems, with both main canopy and reserve in the same backpack. This had several advantages for such a risky jump. It left the jumper with a 'clean' chest, uncluttered by anything except the harness strap at breast level and an altimeter. The configuration gave the wearer uninterrupted observation below him and total manoeuvrability in freefall. Such a rig was also equipped with a superbly fast cutaway mechanism from which a parachutist in trouble could detach himself from a malfunctioning main before opening his round reserve. Barring accidents, the square, cellular Pegasus main canopy would fly easily into the wind to provide slow, soft, accurate landings in almost any conditions, on any surface from water to concrete. It was a machine which was as near foolproof as anything could be, so long as the man using it flew it correctly.

They did not hurry unduly. Fitting a parachute was a solemn ritual, always undertaken with some reverence. Arms through the harness first, humping the rig high onto the shoulders; bend over and take up the leg straps to a buckle inside each thigh; make it snug and lift the balls out of harm's way; finally engage the chest strap and tighten up. The configuration was not one Shakespeare had jumped before. He was a traditionalist in such matters who preferred a big round parachute in a bulky backpack and a burdensome chest-mounted reserve . . until now. Without such accustomed armour, he felt naked and vulnerable.

'Bill,' said Nicholls at last. 'Make sure the thing fits real tight. When you get into freefall, it'll move on your body otherwise and then you'll be groping around all over the place trying to find the throwaway to open the bloody canopy. Got that?'

Shakespeare nodded. He wished they had used traditional equipment, but he had been swayed by Nicholls's advocacy of the Pegasus as the best chance of pulling the operation off. Now, as he faced the reality of a nocturnal dive exit with totally unfamiliar gear, he was not so sure. He was only half convinced that the automatic opening device fitted to the rig – calibrated to fire at three thousand five hundred feet – would perform as it should. If it did not, he would have to deploy the canopy manually by snatching a toggle from its recess on his right hip, rather than using a traditional ripcord mounted on the chest. If he had to do that and went unstable in the process-
. . . but it was far too late for such 'ifs', and he shrugged off the tension they generated. The golden rule, as he knew, was to keep the mind on one thing at a time; that thing had to be the job in hand – not some future, hypothetical emergency, even if the future was to be counted off in seconds.

Next, they turned their attention to 'the bundle', as the remaining tea-chest was now designated, Special Forces style. Like the first box, it was already imprisoned in a rope net. It, too, had a small drogue parachute which should stabilise its position in freefall. What made it different was the addition of a complete parachute pack, also fitted with an automatic opener set to fire a traditional round canopy at three thousand feet. The weight of the tea-chest was such that it would descend faster than a human being under a single canopy, but Nicholls guessed, hopefully, it would not be sharp enough to cause damage on landing. They would need that container later. So now they hauled and pushed 'the bundle' to within a few inches of the exit.

Not for the first time, Nicholls peered through a crack in the lid to satisfy himself that it contained money. It did. He also noticed, in passing, that the paper currency had settled two or three inches. He could not guess at the reason for this but considered fleetingly whether he should ram some additional soft packaging into the crate to make it secure. In the same instant he told himself it was too late for that.

He glanced at his watch. Time was running out, fast. There was only a minute or so left before they reached their drop zone. With Shakespeare's help, Nicholls added yet more equipment to his harness: a Bergen rucksack containing spare clothes for them both, two pistols, and an entrenching tool buckled to the back of his harness just below the main parachute, its weight resting sullenly against the back of his thighs.

They had agreed that since this was Shakespeare's first jump with totally strange equipment it was better that he went in 'clean fatigue', unencumbered by the addition of a rucksack of his own. 'At least,' Nicholls had joked, 'I don't have to carry a rifle as well, this time.' The risk embodied in this extra load, as they both knew, was that the buckles could work loose, the load shift and create havoc with Nicholls's basic stability in freefall. A serious loss of face-to-earth stability at the wrong moment – and the wrong moment was during the one or two seconds the canopy was streaming out of the backpack – could be fatal if it meant that the jumper was rolling, or head down. This they knew all too well; they had attended more than one military funeral in acquiring the knowledge. Shakespeare worked away, tightening the straps. At last he slapped his partner's thigh and said, 'There you go . . . here's your helmet, goggles, gloves . . . I'll be with you in a sec.'

The new kit was wondrously light, a mere seven pounds. Taking advantage of the mobility this gave him, Shakespeare moved among the gear they were leaving behind – spare food, Armalite rifles, Collison's weapon – and thrust them away into the empty zipped containers. Then he found what he was seeking and walked forward as far as the curtain, already torn half down by the rush of air from the open rear door. He could just see the top of Naomi Lewis's sleeping head above one of the seats a few feet away. He lobbed the aircrew's two headsets down the centre aisle. These came to rest against the flight deck door, but there was no immediate sign Naomi had observed them.

From the exit, Nicholls was gesturing impatiently with his head as Shakespeare reappeared. Neither man spoke. Words wasted time, confused the mind at such moments, and they both knew it. Shakespeare donned his own helmet, dropped his goggles over his eyes, drew on his gloves, and joined his partner. Passing slowly below them was one of the cooling towers. Nicholls glanced at his own altimeter, reading just over seven thousand feet, and at Shakespeare's. They matched. Then he gave a thumbs-up sign and moved very deliberately to his position behind 'the bundle'. Shakespeare joined him on the right. This was the worst moment, the worst before the best, the time when the guts turned to iced water, and controlled aggression was the only answer.

'READY! . . . SET! . . . GO!'

They rocked back and forth over 'the bundle' and finally pushed it in unison over the brink. It disappeared instantly, the drogue hanging momentarily behind it like an exclamation mark. Nicholls dived out after it, arms spread wide for stability, lower legs curled in towards his buttocks to anchor the rucksack more firmly. Shakespeare, fearful of separation, followed his partner out so closely

191

that his nose touched the toe of Nicholls's right boot. As they cleared the exit the slipstream generated by a forward speed of 150 knots sent both men spinning like fragments of cork down a gigantic waterfall. This was not one of those jumps when the dive exit led smoothly, magically, from a head-down posture to the relaxed, birdlike position of stable freefall. Such occasions were a gentle, silken dream. This time Nicholls, even while he thought he was being torn apart, was struck by an odd, whimsical idea. 'This is like being a blue-bottle that's been flushed down the lav,' he said to himself.

It felt for both men like a long time before they achieved stability. In fact it was four seconds, during which they descended one thousand five hundred feet. Nicholls, eyeballing the three cooling towers, detected that he was in a slow, uncontrolled left-hand turn. He guessed correctly that the rucksack had shifted under the impact of the exit and he automatically corrected his position by extending the right leg and drawing the left in a little. He was now asymmetrical, but stable. He peered upward, spotted Shakespeare about fifty feet from him, looking like an enormous bat, then glanced below. There was no sign of 'the bundle'. He turned one hundred and eighty degrees, pushing the left arm down, dropping the left shoulder, leaning into the turn, then stabled out again on the new heading. 'The bundle' was immediately in front of him, no more than eighteen inches away. This was too close for comfort. Then, to his relief, 'the bundle' started moving away, gathering some strange inner momentum. Nicholls hung where he was for about two seconds, boring a hole in the sky, as he, 'the bundle' and Shakespeare hit terminal velocity of one hundred and twenty miles an hour. His altimeter, clear in the moonlight, read just over five thousand feet.

Shakespeare was exhilarated and terrified by the freedom of the new gear. It was as if he were in freefall without a parachute. The smallest change of posture, it seemed to him, produced dramatic aerodynamic effects. After the tradition of orthodox military equipment, this was like switching from a pair of standard DMS boots to featherlight running shoes. He had two tasks. The first was to lose altitude faster than Nicholls, so as to close on him. The second was to reduce the lateral space between them. Cautiously he extended his arms and legs into a delta position and humped his bottom towards the sky, to begin tracking. Like a stone released from a catapult, he instantly hurtled forward and down. As he did so, Nicholls changed direction. Then Shakespeare saw why. 'The bundle' was travelling away from them as if it, too, had gone into a fast tracking position.

Nicholls did not like the sight of two hundred and fifty thousand pounds sterling retreating from him in such a determined way. He was, on the other hand, reluctant to track after it because he would lose height more rapidly than 'the bundle', and that was unsafe. He was also unsure how well he would track with the rucksack bouncing about behind him in an increasingly unruly fashion. 'Give it a try, kid,' a voice whispered inside him. The result was a dramatic corkscrew motion which he was only just able to control without initiating a complete barrel-roll. But it did the trick. He was closing the gap between himself and his target. Just above him, Shakespeare went into a less than perfect track turn, left shoulder down slightly, head turned to the left, to stay with the party.

It was while Nicholls was still fighting for stability in his unorthodox tracking position that 'the bundle' halted its forward momentum and then, as the load inside shifted, charged in the opposite direction.

Nicholls had no chance to avoid the chest as it crashed against his right shoulder and arm. He was aware of pain, then numbness on that side of his body. The arm was out of control, and, like a bird which had just had one wing shot away, he cartwheeled out of the sky. Somewhere in his mind a sophisticated automatic pilot, Captain Survival, took over. He sensed, rather than reasoned, that his right arm would be streaming out at his side like a useless rag. He let the left arm fall into a similar posture. He was now symmetrical, face to earth and head down. From somewhere on his shoulder he heard the whirring sound of the automatic opening device unwinding and preparing to fire the canopy. Too late, he closed up his legs to avoid snagging the Pegasus as it deployed. Like a malevolent sprite, the tiny extractor 'chute and the bridle cord behind it whirled round his left boot, then tightened. The big canopy burst out from it and ballooned above him. It was a classic horseshoe malfunction, the most feared technical failure among experienced freefallers for the very good reason that there was no text-book solution to the problem . . . except the first two words of the Lord's Prayer, if there was time.

The mess behind him tightened, drawing his bent left leg backward. No hope of reaching the red cutaway tab on his right side with a hand which, for all the contact it now had with the rest of his body, did not exist. So he slipped his left thumb into the ripcord handle of the second, emergency reserve canopy and fired that. It was a forlorn hope, for the reserve, packed higher on the back than the main, in the very centre of the horseshoe, would billow forth into the rest of the main, leaving him with an elaborate bag of washing. There was nothing else left; at one thousand feet he was now experiencing ground rush.

To use his left arm in pulling the reserve handle, without a compensatory gesture with the other, meant that he inevitably lost stability and rolled to one side. This created a momentary gap in the nylon shield presented by the horseshoed main. Through this gap the reserve, a round canopy, sprang almost clear; when it deployed, it was a half-strangled parody of a real parachute. He did not dare look at the ground but watched the altimeter unwind. He was down to five hundred feet and, at terminal velocity of one hundred and thirty per second, had less that four seconds left. Then the reserve asserted itself. It gathered air and inflated properly. He felt as if he had hit a brick wall, so sudden was the deceleration.

With his left leg firmly tied up behind his back, there was no question of an orthodox landing. Nor could he reach up to the steering toggles to correct the rotation of the canopy, which was slow at first, then faster, as he swept down towards the narrow gauge railway track leading from the power station. Thousands of acres of gentle, welcoming peat surrounded him, but the Cosmic Joker hurled him onto the metal rails. He tried in the last second or so to curl up into a self-protective ball. Then one of the rails reached up and bit savagely into his spine and he lost consciousness. A few feet away 'the bundle' landed softly and safely, intact. As Shakespeare reached him Nicholls came round briefly and mumbled, 'I must be the first guy in history to get mugged by his own wallet . . .'

# Chapter Ten

Shakespeare now worked with quiet, urgent efficiency. The knife he always carried in one boot during operational jumps sliced through his partner's parachute harness, releasing him. Next he detached Nicholls's rucksack and finally dragged the unconscious body clear of the railway. He had wrapped Nicholls in his own canopies and had extracted morphine from the Bergen when the injured man drifted slowly to consciousness.

'Bill . . . ' The voice sounded remarkably normal.

'Hold it a sec, Golly. I'm going to fix you up with a jab of morphine.'

'Make it a jumbo-size dose.'

'You what? You're fucking delirious, you prat.'

'Back broken. Take the loot and scarper.'

Shakespeare bent over him. His partner's eyes were open, but not focussing properly. This he attributed to concussion.

'Wiggle your toes, Golly. Move your feet.'

'Can't, wacker. Right arm done for as well.'

'Right. I'll give you a jab and go for a doctor.'

Nicholls drifted back and forth across the no-man's-land of awareness and oblivion. 'Legally dead already, ain't I? No paperwork needed, see . . . just give us a mercy dose, Bill . . . then leg it . . . You did all right with that new gear.'

Shakespeare realised with a sense of shock that Nicholls was absolutely right. He recalled a classroom exercise for some of the young ruperts in which they were leading a theoretical op in the jungle. One serious casualty on the drop presented the commander with a choice between finishing off the injured man or blowing the security of the operation to summon medical help. What was the correct course? The answer depended on the object of the operation. If that was more important than anything else, then the casualty had to be despatched on the spot. Golly would be dead soon. All he had to do was to stay with his partner as his life ended painlessly, bury a body which no longer had an identity, bury most of the money as they had planned for retrieval at some later time, and walk away with a fortune. After what he had done to Margaret . . .

'They'll put you inside and throw away the key for this job,' Nicholls murmured, as if reading his thoughts. 'I'm sorry about Maggie, old mucker. I never did understand women, leastways none over eighteen. Tried fucking older biddies to find out, but it didn't work. Truth is, Nicholls was a failure with women. Leg it while you can, Bill. You earned it . . . '

Shakespeare calculated that Juliet Bravo would land safely somewhere, Dublin probably, quite soon. The crew would know approximately where they had got out and the hunt would be up. It was a shrewd guess, though Shakespeare could not have imagined that, as a result of Malachy Fergus's instructions, the crew would be placed under arrest, awaiting questioning, as valuable hours slipped past. His mind was on the true object of Operation Eldorado.

'Listen, Golly,' he said at last. 'Fuck the money. That wasn't what it was about. We beat everybody in sight. I'm giving you a little jab and then you're going into hospital.'

Nicholls's eyes opened again, without focussing on anything around him. He coughed quietly; blood welled out of his mouth. 'I ever tell you, Bill, how to tell the age of consent in any part of the world?'

'Aye, often,' Shakespeare replied, studying the pipette. 'According to you, you have to sit them on a European bog and if their feet touch the ground on each side, they're old enough for a bit of the other.'

'That's right,' Nicholls replied, closing his eyes again.

He had found the vein and pressed home the syringe when he heard an odd thumping sound. Chopper. Irish Army, probably. He looked up. The first tentative fingers of the morning were feeling a stealthy way over the eastern horizon. It would be hours before they spotted the two of them, Shakespeare concluded; Golly would be dead by then unless he could make a fire to summon help in time.

'I can hear a rabbit,' Nicholls said. His eyes were closed but his face crinkled into a grin. 'Would you believe it, Bill, a bloody great rabbit thumping his hind feet on the ground. You taught me that, mate. On that big survival exercise in Germany.'

'Stand easy, Golly.'

'That McAlister kid had a rabbit. He called it Jamie. That was all he wanted just before they topped him that day in Belfast. Remember, Bill? In that sewer we were, watching the house after Evans-the-Hunch vanished. Bloody twenty-four hours in a sewer, watching them with fibre-optics through the manhole cover in the middle of the road. I wanted to hit the place as soon as we saw that "Tom-Tom" bloke, the one who was supposed to be in prison, standing there with a shooter on his hip. My feet were cold. They're cold now, Bill. No feeling in them at all. You said no, we'll wait a bit. D'you remember?'

Shakespeare slipped a hand inside the top of his partner's left sock. The ankle was as cold as marble. The other leg was no different. He foraged inside the rucksack for a Gor-Tex bivvy bag and unrolled it carefully. Then he sat down alongside his partner and placed first Nicholls's feet, then his own inside the bag before drawing it up around them to the waist. That way, he hoped, he might communicate some of his own body warmth to his companion. Golly seemed to be unconscious again but then, to Shakespeare's surprise, Nicholls's left hand sought out his right hand and gripped it tightly.

'Oh, Christ, it's not my day. That's all it needed.'

Shakespeare half-turned and saw with dismay that Nicholls, eyes closed, was weeping silently. 'What's up, Golly?'

'Waterworks. Taps wide open. Peed all over myself . . . what a way to go.'

'You're certainly puddled, you daft bastard,' Shakespeare replied gently. 'But not that way.'

'McAlister.'

'McAlister what, Golly?'

'McAlister was very puddled. Big lad he was, twenty-five when they shot him; at my trial they said he had a mental age of ten. He struggled with them all the way down that little garden path in front of his house, screaming he wanted back in, he didn't want to go to Kilkeel, he wanted his Jamie. Then they despatched him. Bullet through his throat. He was making a horrible gurgling noise when I got there. Like a donkey with asthma.'

'All water under the bridge, Golly. Best forgotten, wacker.'

'Still don't know why they wanted to mallet him.'

The sound of the helicopter engine, Shakespeare noticed, was growing louder. "Cos he'd opened his mouth about what happened to Evans-the-Hunch, I suppose,' he replied, to humour his friend. 'The people we saw going into the house that night were the members of the Loyalist court martial. What surprised me was that his own mother played along with them. She were a very sharp old biddy, that Mrs McAlister.'

'Bull Martin had a centre parting and a coat with a fur-lined collar that night,' Nicholls said in a voice which seemed to come from far away. 'I remember that. Can't be that puddled, Bill, if I remember that. Spitting image of his I/D photograph. Tom-Tom-the-Hitman was wearing a cowboy jacket with a fringe, and a prison haircut that made his head look too small for his body . . . I looked the same later on. The others wore funeral suits and bowler hats, the gear they used for their Loyalist parades.'

'That's right, Golly. After you were sent down and Bull Martin was blown away by the PIRA – you know, I wrote to you at the time from Mahranat – well, after that, the regiment got the full story from a guy called John-Henry Something, when he quit the UVF and signed on as a supergrass. He was one of their judges. It was through him we got the whole story. But by then, old mucker, it didn't make any fucking difference. Evans-the-Hunch was dead and you were inside, doing time.'

'The court martial will come to order.'

The Westminster voice, soft and modulated among the

buzzing accents of the lodges, was instantly recognised by the prisoner. In spite of his bonds, he tried to stand.

'You can remove the prisoner's headgear now, Mrs McAlister.'

'Yes, Colonel Martin, sir.'

The prisoner blinked in the pale light, his tight, bubbly blond hair tousled as the hood was removed. He had a curious air of youthfulness; long after his eyes – pale, distracted, blue eyes which never made contact with those facing him – had adjusted to the light, they continued to blink.

'Your name?'

'Willie. You know who I am. You know, don't you, John-Henry? I'm Willie.'

'Tell the court martial your full name.'

'You all know who I am. I'm Silly Willie McAlister of 6 Flagstaff Road, Belfast, Northern Ireland. That's my mam, there.'

'Willie McAlister. You are charged that, between June 10 and June 17 this year, you collected funds estimated to be twenty-five pounds while falsely pretending to be authorised by the movement to do so. Do you plead guilty or not guilty?'

'I didn't mean to, sir.'

'Guilty or not guilty?'

'What's "guilty" mean, mam?'

'He's pleading guilty,' the woman said flatly.

'Guilty,' Martin repeated. 'The facts, Mr Vice?'

At the end of the table a red-faced, gnomic figure rose and grasped its lapels with butcher's hands.

'The accused called at my shop yesterday morning, so he did, and said it was a collection for the prisoners' aid. Now my assistant whose brother is in the Maze runs that fund in this neighbourhood . . . and then here's this, this whippersnapper here, trying to take up for the same thing. When we asked him how much he had taken he said he'd got twenty-five pounds already. Now we all know, with great respect to present company, that Willie isn't all there. So we do make allowances. But when he meddles in things he doesn't understand he's a menace, a real menace. Something's got to be done.'

'Mrs McAlister?' Bull Martin, the chairman, turned his ear rather than his eyes towards her.

'Well, sir, as John-Henry – I'm sorry, Mr Vice, that is – when he says Willie's a bit backward he's speaking no more than the truth. The lad's getting too much for me to handle. He's twenty-five now, and as you can see he's a big boy for his age. When he doesn't have enough to occupy his mind, he's well . . . he's like an ill-sitting hen on a nest of fleas, so he is. And I've been busy this past few days with other things, as you know, sir. Otherwise this would not have happened. He should have been mucking out Jamie the rabbit. He's been a bad boy. A very bad boy.'

'The court martial will confer.'

While the five heads came together, Willie McAlister suddenly stopped fidgeting and smiled. 'I didn't tell *them* anything, though,' he said.

'Shut up, Willie,' snapped his mother.

'Ah, but I didn't tell *them* anything,' the boy repeated.

Martin leaned forward a fraction. 'Who did you not tell, Willie?'

'The military. I didn't tell the military anything.'

They were all listening intently now. 'I didn't tell them where you put the soldier's head.'

'Which military was this, Willie?' Martin's tone was soothing, indulgent.

'Those soldiers in the armoured car the other day. They gave me a ride to their office and showed me your pictures. That was after John-Henry took the money off me.'

'Jezus-Christ-Almighty!' growled the prosecutor.

At dawn they were still questioning Willie McAlister when his mother called the members of the court martial down to breakfast in the kitchen. When they had finished the last of the fried bread, Mrs McAlister was invited to join them at the table. Her hand trembled slightly as she poured another cup of tea. Martin's eyes, luminously brown and as pious as a Labrador's, studied her with care.

'Now let me ask you something, Florence. How long

have you known me?'

'Oh, I don't know exactly, Colonel. Twelve years perhaps. Before my man – Willie's father – was murdered by the Fenians, surely. You've been a good friend, so you have.'

'How long have you known John-Henry?'

'All my life. We were at school together.'

'And the others here, all except one?'

'Yes. All good friends. Good, loyal friends.'

'So you trust us, don't you, Florence?'

'I do. I do, but I won't have any harm done to Willie. The poor wee bairn isn't responsible.'

'No harm, Florence, no harm at all, but he will have to go away for a wee while. We'll send him to Kilkeel. My brother will find him something on the farm while this blows over.'

'When?' Her face was hard now, the double chin raised aggressively, small blue eyes bulging. She looked like an embattled pigeon. 'The poor bairn has never been away from home without his mam before.'

'As soon as possible. This morning. Now. John-Henry, do you have your car?'

'I do. 'Tis parked only a block away, so it is.'

John-Henry and Tom-Tom-the-Hitman left the house by the back door, that same door through which Corporal Martin Evans, a veteran of 1st Reconnaissance Commando Regiment and a long-standing comrade of Nicholls and Shakespeare, had entered on a characteristic hunch, and vanished from the living world three months before. Evans's naked torso, branded with the word 'SPY', was found on a rubbish tip a week later, but the head was never recovered. As they left the house, John-Henry and Tom-Tom could still hear the murmur of the colonel's voice in the kitchen, reassuring Mrs McAlister that all would turn out for the best, the very best. Willie could even take his friend Jamie the rabbit. As they reached the gate at the end of the garden, Tom-Tom smiled wolfishly and muttered something.

'What was that?' John-Henry asked him.

'I said, where he's going he wouldn't be needing a

fucking rabbit.'

Although John-Henry's Cortina was as discreet as a freemason's handshake, it was clearly audible that Sunday morning to the watchers just below the road surface. Near the foot of the manhole, the two soldiers kept their eyes on the television monitor linked to the flexible lens protruding an inch or so above the surface. By the time the car arrived, Willie McAlister had agreed, tearfully, to leave home – but he would not leave, as he had arrived, inside a large box. As he explained, 'I was frightened in there, so I was.'

With his mother leading, flanked by Tom-Tom and Martin, and followed by the three other members of the court martial, he began to walk towards the vehicle. The engine was still running. In the driving seat sat John-Henry. Mrs McAlister had opened the nearside rear door when Willie, digging both heels into the pavement, legs rigid and stubborn as they had been when he was first taken to school, shouted: 'Don't take me away to Kilkeel! I'm not going there! I want back in my house! No . . leave me alone. I want Jamie! I want my Jamie . . . please, please . . .'

Along a street decorated with crisply painted Union Jacks, the respectable lace curtains moved gently as if propelled by a soft breeze, though the windows were closed. No one opened a door or lifted a telephone. The struggle continued as Mrs McAlister tried to pull Willie into the car while the others tried to push him there. They had almost inserted him into the vehicle when he twisted round out of their grasp and planted his back against the car, chin on chest, pushing them away, still shouting. In spite of their preoccupation with the boy, they all heard the thud of the manhole cover as it was turned over. A voice snarled at them, 'Security forces. Stay where you are.'

Golly Nicholls was already out of the sewer and standing in a firing position behind the car. Apart from John-Henry, who was in the driver's seat, the others saw nothing of Nicholls except the muzzle of his submachine-gun pointing at them across the bonnet; that, and a tuft of woolly black hair. Martin had started to say something – it might have been, 'Now, look here' – when the shot was fired. It blasted a window on each side of the car and everyone ducked. Bill Shakespeare, his head and shoulders just emerging from the hole, groped inside his jacket for a radio. 'Charlie One. Contact! Send QRF!'

As he crawled across the road towards the rear of the Cortina, Shakespeare's mind automatically identified the shot as that of a low-velocity weapon, probably a pistol. 'You heard the man didn't you?' he roared at the group. 'Lie down. Lie face down and don't attempt to move. I want your hands in sight and stretched out in front of you.'

Someone coughed. It was a strange sound, more like that of a tuberculose beast than a human being. Then the voice of Mrs McAlister, quiet at first but growing to a hysterical wail as she tried to revive the boy.

'My son. What've they done to you? Willie . . . oh, my poor bairn . . . The fuckin' military! They've killed him! They've murdered my son, the Fenian bastards!'

Cautiously Shakespeare rose to his knees, then his feet. As he put one foot onto the pavement the crouching figure of Tom-Tom, close against the car in a huddle of people including Mrs McAlister and Colonel Martin, turned towards him. The second shot exploded, tearing a hot path through Shakespeare's hair. In the same instant the car reversed, sending him sprawling. The Cortina stopped as Nicholls, near the front of the vehicle, swung his gun towards the windscreen and fired a single round through it, shattering the glass.

John-Henry, handbrake on and ignition off, wound down his last undamaged window and murmured blandly: 'I'm awful sorry. I was like distracted there for a minute, what with the shooting and all.' By now Nicholls was already opening the offside door and pulling him out of the vehicle by his hair with one hand while the other jammed the carbine's muzzle against the man's cheekbone.

Shakespeare, sitting in the gutter, had recovered his weapon and was pointing it at the group. 'Lie down,' he said again very calmly. 'Lie down all of you.'

The boy was on his back, blood gurgling out of a huge throat wound. His mother, still talking to him, lay half across the boy, stroking his hair, her skirt raised at the back to expose a network of varicose veins. The others lay flat as they had been instructed. There was no sign of Tom-Tom-the-Hitman.

That was all long ago, Shakespeare reflected. He felt the hand holding his slacken its grip, like that of a child lured to sleep by a reassuring, familiar story told by a trusted parent. The morphine was taking effect at last. Just as well. The helicopter, whoever it belonged to, had not found them; the sky was now full of light – though curiously the cooling tower markers remained switched on.

Then he heard it again. The engine note grew louder; with a majestic certainty which was, in all the circumstances, somewhat eerie the machine homed in on them over the low, broken horizon, circled their position once, then hovered. Shakespeare blinked in disbelief as he examined the aircraft. It was a long-range Royal Navy Sea King of the sort used for deep reconnaissance missions, rather than the homely troop-carrying Wessex. It landed about twenty yards away in a blast of sound and updrawn air, but Nicholls did not stir. One man climbed out of the machine, Armalite at the ready. Shakespeare eased himself out of the bivvy bag and stood up, hands by his side, palms facing forward in a symbol closer to truce than surrender.

'That Shakespeare?' the figure asked.

'Aye, boss. What're you doing here?'

'Navigational error,' Wainwright replied. 'Funny things can happen to a compass between here and Aldergrove. Where's Nicholls?'

Shakespeare nodded towards the inert bundle on the ground behind him. 'He's in a bad way. Broken back and probably internal injuries. Needs an urgent casevac.'

'Sergeant!'

In response to Wainwright's call, four other figures

205

dressed in blue industrial boiler-suits tumbled out of the machine. 'Stretcher. Get that casualty on board. And the crate, and anything else you see lying around here. I don't want so much as a cigarette butt left.'

Shakespeare studied their faces. Although the elements of familiarity – this one's moustache and that one's jaw – were present, he recognised only one of them. This was his erstwhile prisoner, Sergeant Collison. As for the rest, it was as if the features of his former friends had been reconstructed by an Identikit artist.

'Weapons?' Wainwright asked him.

'All in the Bergen.'

'Where?' Wainwright cupped a hand to his ear. The Sea King's engine was still turning over in readiness for departure and he had to shout above the noise.

'In the pack,' Shakespeare shouted, nodding towards it.

'And your knife, Bill, please. You always carried one in your boot on freefall ops.'

Somewhat sheepishly Shakespeare retrieved the weapon and handed it over. He noticed that, as he bent down, the barrel of Wainwright's Armalite rifle also dropped a few inches, poised immediately over his skull. He did not take this amiss. It was as if they were on the same exercise, playing – as they had done from time to time – on opposite sides; Blue Forces versus Orange, with a few shared beers and a laugh afterwards.

It was in that spirit, it seemed to Shakespeare, that they left Roscommon, just as if they were pulling out of the exercise area to go home to a good breakfast, debrief, kit-cleaning session and a good kip. They swept out fast and low, flying tactically less than a hundred feet above a sleeping countryside. He guessed that they would overfly the surly, fortified outpost of Crossmaglen where it would be raining because it always rained in XMG . . . one of the laws of nature. In fact, as he observed from the angle of the sun, they were flying due east. Now that, he told himself, was to clear the alien ground of the Irish Republic and sneak away out to sea before the Irish started to whinge.

Nicholls, still wrapped in his parachute canopy and the

bivvy bag, lay on the stretcher a few feet away. His face was the colour of chalk; the mouth hung open; the caked blood was forming a crust on his moustache. Shakespeare noticed Wainwright and his team all sat on the port side, facing him, facing the open door, while he sat alone near the door on the starboard side. No one had latched his safety belt. Wainwright's eyes, which always had an unnerving directness, bore unblinkingly into his. He turned his eyes away from them and looked at the other faces but they too had the same fixed, unblinking quality as if they were statues, or birds of prey. He was suddenly reminded, not of one of his own hunting birds but of something that had happened long ago in Africa on an operation which, officially, never took place. He was in Biafra, where rats were sold for food in village markets and the children's crinkly black hair turned red because of a malnutrition disease called *kwashiokor*. He was walking over broken glass in a modern city, Port Harcourt, in a deserted street, convinced he was being followed. If he were being followed, he had told himself, he would hear the crunch of boots like his own on the glass from the shattered shop windows. He had stopped and turned about and then saw he was being followed, on foot, by two vultures. They also stopped, their heads bobbing this way and that. He remembered the eyes most, as they sized him up for carrion; keen, intelligent, hungry and yet patient, ravenously patient.

They were over the Irish Sea now, climbing towards a cruising altitude. He supposed at any moment they would swing round on the new bearing, north-west, towards Aldergrove. But still the brittle morning sun remained at his back, illuminating Nicholls's white face. He nodded down at his partner then leaned forward towards Wainwright.

'Can I go with him to hospital?' he asked.

'No way,' Wainwright shouted back. 'You'd be wasting your time . . . tell you what, they'll probably let you go to his funeral. After all, he's officially dead and you're probably the nearest thing he's got to next of kin.'

At this the two men nearest Wainwright, one moustached like Golly, the other a smooth-faced youngster with a blond crew-cut, glanced at one another and grinned as if sharing some private joke. Then they turned their gaze back on Shakespeare, their eyes fixed like vintage car headlamps on full beam.

'How did you find us?' Shakespeare asked.

'I really shouldn't tell you that, Bill,' Wainwright said. Then his face also relaxed into a wry smile. 'Still, it makes no difference now. You use your imagination. Remember how the Yanks recovered their aircrew shot down in Vietnam? The guys wore parachutes with a tracing device fixed to the harness, right? You don't think we put just the money into those boxes, surely? Just as well, in view of the cock-up you made. Always the same when the lads leave the regiment and try to do a private enterprise job. It's the old re-entry problem, isn't it? Surprised you couldn't hack it, though.'

'We beat you all out of sight,' Shakespeare grunted. There had been something funny about the atmosphere in the aircraft until now, but suddenly he felt secure again. Such arguments were the heart and soul of a post-ex debrief. 'We just ran out of luck, that's all.'

They were still flying east. He guessed they were going straight back to London, Northolt probably. He turned in his seat a little to take in the blue sky, the slate-grey Irish Sea beneath, and to store them in his memory. It might be a long time before he saw an horizon like this again.

'You ran out of sense as well.' Wainwright's mateyness, if that was what it was, had evaporated. 'You and Nicholls there dropped all your old muckers in the cag.'

'How's that, then?' Shakespeare demanded. The helicopter began to swing in a wide arc over an empty sea, and a blast of cold air hit him through the open door.

'Knocking off Uncle Mac, that bloke from Five, was not very intelligent. Did you really have to rubber-dick him with a bomb in his car? If anything was needed to convince everyone you'd sold out to something nasty, that was it. He was a valuable guy. Carried more in his head on subversion than several computers. Politically, what you did might still be the kiss of death for the rest of us.'

'I don't know what you're on about, boss,' Shakespeare replied, but Wainwright did not seem to hear him. He merely looked sideways at Collison, nodded, and said, 'Now.'

'Here they come now, ladies and gentlemen, those intrepid freefall people!'

The vicar of St Joshua Without turned briefly from the commentator's microphone, which he always dominated on this day, and murmured to one of his churchwardens, 'Get that child off those potatoes. They haven't been judged yet.' It was ten a.m., early for a church fête to begin and hard for the participants but the vicar, Canon Peter Pickersgill, adored innovation, in contrast to his conservative Herefordshire flock. They moved, unlike the rest of Britain, with the seasons and the rhythm of time unmarked by the Industrial Revolution; for them, as in most of the tiny beautiful churches in their diocese, the parachute display was a traditional opening to the event; by tradition it followed the Sunday dinner of English roast and two veg. No one ever asked where the parachutists came from. No one needed to. The regiment, like Hereford cattle market and the River Wye, was part of the fabric of the place. On this occasion there had been doubt until the last moment whether it would happen, and if so, when. Canon Pickersgill had not asked his contact at Wingate Barracks the cause of this uncertainty. Again, it was well known that it was bad manners to ask questions of the regiment – which spoke, like an oracle, when it was minded to and not before. The culture surrounding the barracks was flattered to be trusted with such lack of knowledge about its neighbours. After all, even the men's own families, it was said, did not know where they were half the time. So Pickersgill was content to let matters take their appointed course, and he was flattered when that august personage, the brigadier, had arrived personally to deliver the good news only an hour before. Now, perched on his shooting stick just inside the roped-off display area, seventy-five yards by seventy-five, comfortable in old tweeds and country jacket, Brigadier Butcher folded his

209

arms and squinted at the sky. Standing alongside him, the regiment's veteran welfare officer and contact with the civilian community said softly, 'A Sea King, sir? Our budget must be looking up.'

They counted the blobs as they left the helicopter . . . five of them . . . no smoke canisters, no relative work. Just a straight, clean ten-second delay and then, one after the other, the canopies exploded out of the backpacks; big, round, olive-green canopies.

'Lord, they're using TAPs,' the welfare officer said, more loudly this time.

'TAPs?' asked the brigadier, an old boat-troop man who knew little about parachute technology.

'Tactical assault parachutes, sir, operational kit. They should be using those square, ram-air multicoloured jobs on a civvy display. They'll have trouble getting into a tight DZ like this with that gear . . . and what the hell are they using as jumpsuits? I'll have a word with them when they get down. This isn't good enough.'

'That won't be necessary, Michael,' Butcher said, his voice rising a little. 'I'll speak to them myself.'

'The punters will be disappointed,' the welfare officer insisted.

'Fuck the punters,' replied the brigadier.

The first of the team, with the rest stacked neatly behind him, was lined up for the centre of the arena, his canopy bucking and oscillating a little as he hit the heat rising from the tops of marquees set around the drop zone.

'Who's the leader?' asked the welfare officer.

'Tim Wainwright.'

'The word at the barracks, sir,' said the other tentatively, 'was that he made a bit of a mess at Prestwick. What's he doing jumping here?'

As Wainwright, holding a tight, neat position, head and elbows tucked well in, rolled comfortably on the crisp turf and stood up again to a patter of applause, Butcher turned and looked at his companion.

'That's bullshit, Michael, and I don't want it repeated . . . Ah, vicar, nice commentary and thank you.'

As the fifth man touched down, the brigadier, the vicar

and the welfare officer strode forward to meet Wainwright. Kneeling to field-pack the big military canopy, he
then stood up, his hands still full of rigging lines, grinning
awkwardly at the brigadier's extended hand. Before he
had a chance to shake it, Butcher had grasped both
shoulders in a welcoming squeeze.

'First rate job, Tim. Well done.'

'Allow me to endorse that,' said the vicar eagerly.
'Where would St Joshua's annual "do" be without you
fellows?'

The helicopter had also landed, and the tangled mass of
parachute gear was loaded on board. Wainwright and his
men followed it, having had no contact whatever with the
spectators.

'Hold on a second,' said Butcher. 'I'm coming with you.'

The others hauled him inboard. Grinning hugely, he
waved his shooting stick and shouted, 'Right, driver, back
to Wingate Barracks, if you please.'

The welfare officer, in civilian dress, stood to attention
as the Sea King lifted off, its updraft lifting his tie and
removing his neat felt hat. His last glimpse of Wainwright
and the brigadier was of two men holding one another in
shared merriment.

That night, Sergeant Edward Collison and his wife,
Margaret, settled together on their plastic sofa, nibbling
cream-cheese sandwiches, to watch the television news.
The end of the hijack dominated the bulletin. Behind the
showbiz froth with which the event was now decorated,
two facts glinted like polished bayonets. The money had
been recovered. There was no sign of the hijackers.

Collison, a big, gentle man, stood and switched off the
television, lit a pipe, and sank reflectively back onto the
sofa. 'Glad to have me home?' he asked.

Maggie, her eyes fixed on the blank screen, said with
quiet conviction, 'They'll be back. I know they'll be back.'

He gave her a sharp sideways glance, then hugged her
briefly, reflecting that even if she was unresponsive just
now, he had waited patiently for years before daring to
pursue his love for this woman. Telling her of his love had

been the most difficult thing. Now, here they were, bringing to life his dream, never shared with his comrades, of home, wife, family, all at peace together. The dream had started in the orphanage, stayed with him through his days as a boy soldier, his career as a medic, and was untouched by his involvement in Special Forces. It had been worth the wait. If there were times when he suspected he wasn't the greatest in bed – he had little experience of such matters, although he was now in his thirties – he was not concerned about that; he did not believe in brooding about things. He had not enjoyed this latest operation, particularly the last chapter of it, in the helicopter. It had all happened so quickly. He knew why they had chosen him. Nothing to do with Margaret, nothing at all. They knew, and he knew, that he was loyal. He might disagree with an order, but he would never challenge it, unlike some of the lads. That's why they depended on him, why Margaret could depend on him. So now he thrust it from his mind, and stood up.

'What you need, my poor old battered sweetheart, is a nice cup of tea,' he said. He heard his own voice saying the words; the domesticity of it pleased him. Then he walked out of the living room and into the kitchen, closing the door behind him.

He did not hear her say, 'You will come back, Golly. Won't you, love? You will come back to me?'

**DAVID BRIERLEY**

SKORPION'S DEATH

Cody is unique. Recruited by the SIS, trained by the CIA, and now she hunts on her own.

Her quarry is a pilot, Borries. Hired by an unknown organisation for an undercover job in Tunisia, he's gone missing and his wife wants him back.

Cody finds Borries, at an army garrison deep in the Sahara, but by then it is almost too late. By then the organisation has a name: Skorpion. And Skorpion has a secret, a secret so deadly it will torture and kill to protect it. And Skorpion has Cody in its pincers.

**Post·A·Book**

A Royal Mail service in association with the Book Marketing Council & The Booksellers Association.

Post-A-Book is a Post Office trademark.

**DANIEL EASTERMAN**

**THE LAST ASSASSIN**

Tehran 1977: as the Shah of Iran struggles to retain his fragile hold on power, seven young men are found dead. Members of an extremist Islamic sect, they will stop at nothing in their violent, Khomeini-inspired crusade against the West.

CIA field agent Peter Randall, together with a beautiful Iranian girl, soon discover that they alone can thwart the group's plans. As they embark on a dangerous mission into the Iranian interior in an attempt to prevent events from reaching their explosive conclusion, they rapidly learn the frightening extent of their opponent's power and influence . . .

**CORONET BOOKS**

**CLIVE EGLETON**

**TROIKA**

Leonid Brezhnev is dying. The way to the Presidency will soon lie clear. But who is to succeed him? Who to hold the balance of power in one of the mightiest nations on earth? These are the questions that grip Russia's all-powerful ruling body.

Georgi Kirov quickly becomes involved in the ruthless schemes of the KGB. Determined to see their man – Yuri Andropov – rise to fame, they will stop at nothing to fulfil their ambition. It is not until Kirov reaches London that the extent of their duplicity becomes clear and he vows to stage his own independent counter-attack.

**CORONET BOOKS**

**TOM HYMAN**

THE RUSSIAN WOMAN

Washington, 1982: the historic summit meeting has been a resounding success, culminating in the first ever arms reduction treaty between America and the Soviet Union. But the elation is short-lived: the presidential motorcade is ambushed, and Premier Kemenev killed. President Daniels is spared; so is Kamenev's wife, Katya.

As tensions mount and surprises multiply the Russian woman draws three men into a web of deadly passion and conflict.

– Charles Warfield – a disgraced CIA agent.

– KGB General Dmitri Semeneko – the Kremlin's masterspy.

– President Daniels – lonely, guilt-ridden, his wife the victim of an incurable mental illness.

On her actions come to depend the fate of all, but the Russian woman has a destiny of her own to pursue . . .

**CORONET BOOKS**

# HARDIMAN SCOTT

## NO EXIT

'Sokolniki Park, three o'clock.'

A coded message from an influential Russian friend sets in train a series of events over which Michael North, the BBC's man in Moscow, has little control...

Charged with delivering a top secret message of warning to the British Government, Michael is unwittingly drawn into a high-level spy drama of international proportions. For, as a helpless British Cabinet – robbed of its entire nuclear arsenal by five years of extreme left-wing rule – desperately seeks to thwart Soviet plans, Russian warships are amassing in the North Sea, and their aircraft prepare to bomb London...

**CORONET BOOKS**

**TERENCE STRONG**

CONFLICT OF LIONS

The pulsating inside account of an SAS peace mission that finds itself pitted against the insidious forces of Colonel Gadaffi.

A vicious assassination attempt is made on the President of a fragile African democracy by Libyan terrorists. The call for an advisory training team goes out to 22 Special Air Service Regiment: Whatever the cost, keep the peace.

But is it already too late? Beneath the sleepy surface of the 'friendliest nation in Africa' the dark forces of a secret enemy advance inexorably. Hampered by diplomatic ineptitude the crack SAS team struggle against the odds. Emotions and passions run high as they battle to stop the sweep of revolutionary fervour and bloodshed . . .

**CORONET BOOKS**

## ALSO AVAILABLE FROM CORONET BOOKS

*All these books are available at your local bookshop or newsagent, or can be ordered direct from the publisher. Just tick the titles you want and fill in the form below.*

Prices and availability subject to change without notice.

---

Hodder & Stoughton Paperbacks, P.O. Box 11, Falmouth, Cornwall.

Please send cheque or postal order, and allow the following for postage and packing:

U.K.—55p for one book, plus 22p for the second book, and 14p for each additional book ordered up to a £1.75 maximum.

B.F.P.O. and EIRE—55p for the first book plus 22p for the second book, and 14p per copy for the next 7 books, 8p per book thereafter.

OTHER OVERSEAS CUSTOMERS—1.00 for the first book, plus 25p per copy for each additional book.

Name ..................................................................................

Address ..............................................................................

..........................................................................................